ENSOULMENT

Ensoulment

A NOVEL

Susan Forrest Castle

Hardcover ISBN: 9781947175891
Paperback ISBN: 9781947175952
Library of Congress Control Number: 2025947838

Cover design by Susan Forrest Castle

Exterior formatting by Jacob Arms
Produced in the United States
Published by Serving House Books
Lawrence Landing Company
Raleigh, North Carolina 27609

www.servinghousebooks.com

Serving House Books is a proud member of:

Independent Book Publishers Association
 and
Community of Literary Magazines and Presses

SERVING HOUSE BOOKS

For

the GrandPeople

& Everett

ENSOULMENT

In religion and philosophy, ensoulment (from the verb "ensoul") is defined as the moment at which a human being is infused with, and thus animated by, the soul. Some believe that the soul enters the body at conception; others, such as those that believe in reincarnation, that the soul is pre-existing and enters the body at a particular stage of development––well beyond the development of the human embryo or even after death. The earliest known use of the verb "ensoul" is in the mid 1600's.

ONE

"No."

Phoebe is looking through a one-way mirror at a row of seven men lined up against a white wall marked ruler-like with black lines and numbers too faded to read, especially with eyesight as poor as hers. Behind her is another row of men, all police officers. Well, actually, there is one woman among this blue uniformed group. Unlike the rest, who stand, she sits to Phoebe's left on a molded plastic chair with a crack along the front. It squeals softly whenever the policewoman shifts her weight, as now when she leans forward, settles elbows on knees and chin between her fists. Phoebe looks over and the two lock eyes. "Not at me, darlin'," the policewoman says. She nods toward the big mirror. "At them."

Everyone is waiting for Phoebe to recognize and react, just as they were when they had her look through dozens of photos, six at a time. The seven men behind the glass, a few standing with their feet apart and hands clasped in front of their groins, cannot see Phoebe. She knows this. Even so. Even so.

She looks up as instructed but doesn't focus on the faces, doesn't even try. Her glasses, another set of gravel-blind eyes, stare out from atop her head. Ten minutes. Long enough. She lets her chin fall to her chest and her eyeglasses slide back into place, or nearly. She seats them properly on the bridge of her nose, looks down at the floor and over at the policewoman's feet. She's wearing black leather shoes with fat laces and thick soles. A wad of pink gum attached to the left sole has attracted grimy bits—a tiny stone, strands of hair, a piece of grass or something else green and living. It's a good inch or so thicker than its counterpart. Evidence. The woman must be lopsided, must need this accommodation to keep from limping, to camouflage some embarrassing infirmity. For some reason this, of all things, makes Phoebe want to cry.

She repeats herself, loud and firm, to keep the tears at bay: "No."

Phoebe had only swum 33 of her usual 52 back-and-forth's that day. Out to the enormous cloud-shaped rock, one; back to the weather-beaten cement gnome, two. She'd been doing the breaststroke—head down for the glide, then up for a breath. Taking a breath: that's when she caught sight of him, standing by the gnome at the water's edge. He was eating something bright and round. An apple? An orange? She worried she was trespassing. Thought maybe after all these years someone had finally bought the abandoned lakefront property—nothing but weeds and a cracked cement slab—she'd come to consider her own private swimming club.

As she came out of the lake, peeling off her yellow swim cap, sliding her goggles up over her brow, she spoke. "Hey, hi there—I'm so sorry. That's my car out front." She looked up to where her VW Beetle was parked and caught a hazy glimpse of an enormous wheel and slice of silver bumper nudged up against it. The rest of the truck was obscured by overgrown mimosa, Tree of Heaven, kudzu, chinaberry—the same invasive shrubs that overwhelmed all abandoned plots in Georgia.

The man said nothing.

Phoebe's eyeglasses were astride the towel she'd flung over the gnome. Without them, all she could make out was his height (tall), build (lean), age (thirty something?). He had a wide leather tool belt slung around his hips with metal handles, blades, or some such poking up from the loops and pockets. They flashed in the sun, making her squint.

She felt out of breath. Not from swimming but because she was wearing a two-piece swimsuit, dripping wet and too close to a perfect stranger. How odd that phrase is: "perfect stranger." When she tried to reach around him for her towel and glasses, he didn't budge. Made it impossible. He just stared at her, his eyes black, lost in the penumbra of shade thrown by the tan cowboy hat set low on his forehead. Not a word. So, she spoke again. "Is this your property? Is that why...?"

That's when he tossed the orange aside (unmistakable citrus smell) and grabbed her by the shoulders, not so much roughly as firmly (sweat and gasoline). His cowboy hat fell to the ground without a sound.

Days later, asked to describe her assailant, Phoebe told the detective that his hair was long and shiny black, and that his eyes were black, too.

"No one has black eyes," the detective snarled.

She should have walked out right then and there.

That same detective—his nametag reads "Silwa"—is in charge of this lineup, or at least he acts as if he is. He keeps circling the periphery of the room, predator-like, staring at the men in the line-up one moment, at his fellow officers or Phoebe the next. Silwa. He's tall and skinny-legged but with a gut that spills over his belt like fungus on a tree, forcing the lower buttons of his pale blue shirt agape just above the waist and again, higher up, where his barrel chest begins. She can see black hairs. They look greasy, gleam blue-black like feathers on a crow. Repulsed, Phoebe pulls her glasses off.

"So, what'ta we got here, Ms. Macauley?" He slaps a file folder against his leg again and again, signaling his impatience. Phoebe turns to look at him. He slices the air with the file once, twice, towards the lineup. She looks up, as directed.

It is as if the seven men on the other side of the mirrored glass—each with hair a slightly different shade, dark brown to black, each with a slightly different slope to his shoulders, each with different hands (though she cannot tell from a distance if they are the enormous rough, long-fingered hands with scratchy nails she recalls so acutely), each with a different Adam's apple and different shape to his ears—includes a fragment of every man she has ever passed on the street. Every man who has ever held a door for her. Or hit the stop button on an elevator and waited for her to breathlessly jump in. Every man who has made an obscene gesture while speeding by her on the right as she drives too slowly in the fast lane. Any and every man who has ever said, "You go ahead" when she has gotten in line at the grocery store with only three pears and a column of rice crackers. Every man who has stared too long as she walked the aisle of a city bus or sat alone at a coffee shop. Every self-centered boyfriend and generous lover. Every man, every damn man, amongst whom there may even be, no, certainly are, benevolent Everymen.

Dr. Gail, the therapist she has been seeing twice a week for going on three months now, began by asking Phoebe to tell her, in her own words, exactly what happened. In my own words? she had thought. What the hell? Whose words would I use if not my own? It didn't matter. Phoebe did not want to do that. Not again. She had already told the police everything relevant and in detail, and she knew Dr. Gail had read their report. Why in heaven's name should Phoebe go through it all again? Isn't that what telling a story is? Going all through it again? Fine if the story were a happy one. But this story? Go through it all—again?

"You read the police report, didn't you?" Phoebe had asked, softly but with an edge in her voice.

"Yes, Phoebe," Dr. Gail had answered, "but I know there must be more. More about how you felt—how you feel now about what happened that day. Feelings we should talk about."

But there wasn't more. At least nothing she could articulate. Phoebe had looked down at her hands and shaken her head. When she looked up at Dr. Gail, upright in her hideous faux-suede swivel chair, and dressed, as always, in flower-patterned yoga pants and zip-up top neither age nor profession appropriate, she felt like an underachieving student, felt she was disappointing her therapist.

Phoebe turns to look at the detectives lined up behind her, arms crossed over their chests. They look in equal parts bored and expectant. They want her to point at one of the men, call out a number, put this case to bed. But she cannot do that. Even if "the one" is there. She will have to disappoint them, too. If only she'd never gone to the police. If only she'd swum later or earlier that day. Or not at all. If only.

The young officer standing in the room with the seven suspects has them turn. The men turn. First this way, then that. They, too, look in equal parts bored and expectant.

One of the policemen coughs. Another sighs. Silwa comes up beside her. "Where's your glasses?" Phoebe grabs them from her lap and gives them a little shake so he can see.

He softens his voice. "They'd help, wouldn't they?"

The plastic chair squeaks again as the policewoman answers for her. "She didn't have 'em on that day, Craig, remember."

"Know that, Sheila. Even so." Silwa shakes his head then leans closer, his chest brushing the top of Phoebe's head and whispers in her ear. "Humor me, huh? For all our sakes."

The big white-faced, black-handed clock affixed to the wall over the viewing window is askew, so one o'clock looks like noon. Phoebe would like to drag a chair underneath it and set the time to rights. She's been in this room for nearly an hour. Tick tock tick tock. She wants to scream for the waste of time—hers and the police officers' and the suspects' and even *his*. Assuming he is there. Phoebe wonders what "the one," the guy who did it, is feeling if, indeed, he is standing there. Seeing her stare at him, is he scared? As scared as she was that afternoon? Maybe he feels cocksure that she will not risk identifying him. Cocksure she doesn't want to see his face clearly, with her glasses on, in a courtroom.

She could cry. May cry. She worries her glasses with greater and greater force until they split in two, right at the nose bridge.

Silwa shakes his head in utter frustration now. "Somebody get some tape, would you?"

Phoebe decides she will cry. Why not? There's plenty to cry about. Not about what happened—she never allows herself to go there—more over her stupidity in going to the police, and all that's been expected of her since, most especially emotions she doesn't feel, can't feel. You want a reaction? I'll give you a reaction. Easy.

Tears. She lets them come. It's easy. And once she starts they take over, take her to the brink of devolving into the sort of sobs that, having once begun, she cannot contain. The policewoman gets up out of her chair—squeak, squeal—takes a few steps and leans toward Phoebe to offer comfort. Phoebe waves her away. No one gets it. No one understands this new language she's learning. No one.

"Don't. I'm sorry. I just don't know. My glasses won't help. Please."

Phoebe doesn't bother to wipe away her tears. And she's glad for the broken glasses, glad she can't see clearly. The policewoman, who stopped a pace away, moves in closer again.

"I said no!" Phoebe stretches out her arm, palm facing up and out, a form of protection, a plea. "Just drop it," she says, then louder, for them all to hear, "Drop it. Never. I'll never—" Then, to herself, "Don't want to see. Ever."

Silwa looks up, as if to the heavens and slaps the file he's holding against his thigh with such force all the papers inside fly to the floor. He leans over, collects them, then stands, turns, and opens his mouth to speak. Before he can the policewoman walks over, another squeak, plants herself in front of him, her thick-soled shoes holding up the world, and says, fiercely, "Save it, Silwa."

Later, Phoebe will regret not having stopped long enough to thank the policewoman for standing up for her. But she can't get away fast enough. Out in the parking lot, the asphalt— sweating in the hot drizzle—gives off a faint but noxious petroleum odor. As she unlocks her car, drizzle turns to downpour. She drives straight to the lake, rain be damned. The lake. Yes. Her lake—big, blue, pocked and pulsing with relentless rain. The lake: the only living thing she can look straight in the eye, point at, and say with certainty, "Yes."

Two

There are those who attack life and those who just sit back for the ride. Try though he might to be otherwise George Paxton knew which camp he was in. He'd known it beginning Christmas Day forty-six years ago. He had just turned seven. His brother, Eddie, was eleven. The sun had barely risen. The brothers stood shoulder to shoulder at the top of the stairs waiting impatiently for their father to turn on the tree lights and shout "Ready! Set! Go!" When he did, George and his brother hurtled down the stairs and made a sharp left, sliding across the flagstone front hall in their slippers, then onward into the living room. Shirley Paxton, the boys' mother, was sitting next to their grandmother, Tutti—Polaroid in hand— and captured the moment when stout little Eddie knocked his taller, rangy little brother flat onto the carpet in his drive to get to the presents first. In fact, he ran right over George.

George lifted his head from the shaggy, avocado wall-to-wall and watched as his brother dove under the Christmas tree and extracted the strangely shaped gift Grandmother Tutti had brought him from Milwaukee. (Eddie had done reconnaissance the day before and knew exactly which presents were for him.) He tore ribbon and paper from this chosen gift and said, breathlessly, "Oh, wow, oh wow, oh wow! A trombone!" (It was the year the film adaptation of *The Music Man* had hit theaters and the song "76 Trombones" was in the air.)

Eddie picked up that miniscule instrument, put his lips up to the red mouthpiece, and began weaving through the house, knees snapping up to his chest and right arm sliding forward and back, all in perfect synchronization. It was astounding how much noise came forth from that toy slide trombone. Surely it was more noise and worse noise than three marching bands out of step could have mustered. At least it seemed that way to the rest of the family.

For the first half hour or so everyone put their fingers in their ears and laughed at Eddie. Then Shirley Paxton turned up the record player hoping Frank Sinatra's animated version of "Let it Snow!" would win the day. But even with backup singers, Sinatra proved no match for Eddie.

Thinking she was whispering, Tutti, looking grand as a queen in her quilted bathrobe, yelled at her daughter, "For God's sake, Shirley, you've got to get that boy to a doctor. I think he might be hyper..., hyper..., hyper-something. They have medications for that." Mrs. Paxton gave her mother a withering look. No one wanted to stifle Eddie's enthusiasm, least of all his parents for whom one introverted son, George, was enough.

Finally, even their patience waned. Eddie was asked to stop. By his father no less. Calmly. Kindly. Then he was threatened with no more presents. No Christmas coffee cake. Then, no allowance. And, finally, no baseball the following spring. He was eleven. He'd had plenty of years to experience the consequences of bad behavior. But he kept making as much noise as he could, smiling in between puffs in and out, his right arm never tiring from the slide, until Ed Senior grabbed the faux gold instrument and, in one deft move, snapped it in half across his knee.

There was a sharp crack. Then silence. But it didn't last. The wonder is that Eddie looked at the toy, now in two neat pieces, as it sunk into the plush carpet, shrugged his shoulders and, barely missing a beat, returned to the militaristic snapping up and down of his knees and the piston motion of his right arm, all the while puffing his cheeks and forcing air in and out through his pursed lips. Minus that toy trombone, a particularly horrid, vibrating "brrrrrr" sound ensued.

Up the stairs and down, through the kitchen, through the bedrooms and even in and out of his father's study (yes, even there), Eddie paraded until his mother shrieked, "Get! Now!" and pointed at the door to the basement rumpus room. But Eddie ran outdoors, even though he was still in his pajamas and slippers.

Everyone watched through the window. It was snowing lightly. Eddie hadn't stopped to put on his snow jacket or boots. His cheeks kept puffing out. Tiny clouds of warm moist breath sprang into the frigid air from his pursed lips. Sinatra crooned "Silent Night," but no one seemed to catch the irony.

George would never have done such a thing, would never have dreamed of making such a scene.

He thought about that toy trombone now as he walked across the backyard of his rambling Connecticut farmhouse, stopping every few yards to twist off and inhale the fresh smell of a yellow-headed weed. Good old George. Good old George. He'd made a comfortable life for himself. No, it was more than that: his discipline and hard work had fueled a privileged life, for he and his family. Yes, he referred to his home as a farmhouse. But given it sat on acres of meadow and manicured lawn, and included a barn, pool and glimpse of Long Island Sound, he couldn't, in good faith, correct those who called it an estate.

Yes. George had done well for himself. He'd excelled at school, gone to an ivy league college and then on to one of the very best law schools where he'd served as editor of the law review. From there he'd been snatched up by a top Wall Street firm and, by working day and night, made partner, much more quickly than his peers. No wonder, family, friends, business associates called him a complete success.

But he didn't really believe that. No, indeed. At fifty-three, George knew if he didn't ball up his fists and throw life a punch it might kill him. The way things were going, maybe he'd be better off dead. It was that simple. Just this past winter he'd caught every cold and flu the world had to offer and woken up more than one morning with back spasms so breathtaking he'd had to just lay on the floor and stare at the ceiling for the rest of the day. He was too afraid of the pain to move. His wife, Harriet, offered him ibuprofen and ice when it first happened then stepped over or around him the rest of the day.

He was being preyed upon for God's sake! But still, still he lay there, just taking it.

After walking out to where lawn met meadow, George turned and lapped back to the house where he stretched out in an Adirondack chair, feet up on the matching stool. He was trying to re-read a book he passionately loved in college—*Justine*, by Lawrence Durrell. He'd spotted the long-forgotten book on top of a box of things his ever-efficient wife, Harriet, had pulled from his bookcase. "I'm doing a purge," she'd said when he came into his study and found her about to close the flaps of a cardboard book box. "You haven't touched any of these for years."

When she left the room, he immediately upended the box in order to save from the local consignment store the rest of Durrell's quartet: *Clea, Mountolive, Balthazar*. Those titles, those names: he didn't even have to crack the covers, dip into the sensuous prose, to be sent reeling into a world so intoxicating—. So intoxicating that what? What? Yes, indeed, here was a fount at which even the sober George could prove over-indulgent, drink long draughts.

So, George was reading. The overwrought prose (yes, he found it so with this re-reading) was making him feel nearly drunk, so he let the book rest, open across his thighs, and closed his eyes to simply think. It was an early June Saturday, and it was fine. Cool air from overnight had left a cloud of fog over the much warmer yard, turning the way-too-long grass a dull gray. There wasn't sun enough to burn it all away.

Karen and Ben were trampling the pachysandra as they fought over the turgid hose, which bucked like a Mustang sending a forceful spray through the open windows of the car and the house. The thirsty hydrangeas got not a gulp. He could see Harriet, framed in the kitchen window, as she leafed through the mail. He'd watched her grab it from the mailbox earlier. But she stopped with a shriek after their two eldest managed to spray her, too. Out the screen door she came, then, and turned the spigot counterclockwise with such force George wondered whether anyone would ever be able to turn it on again.

Harriet chased and pretend-spanked Karen and Ben for dousing her. He took pleasure in seeing them all play. They ran a circle through the long grass once, twice, then moved as a pack indoors, taking their out-of-breath shrieks with them. That left just he and

Lila, the couple's youngest, outside. She was silently collecting caterpillars in a mayonnaise jar. But eventually Lila headed indoors, too, careful to catch the screen door before it banged shut. He looked up just then and saw her smile at him as she raised her hand in an open palm salute. George blew a kiss back and felt a stab of pain when he realized she'd vanished inside before his kiss reached her.

George tried to read again. But the words gathered themselves up, a great inhalation of black marks, into a neat cloud formation that rose off the page and flew up into the tree branches. There it broke into individual birds singing incomprehensible songs. He remembered how he'd watched sparrows outside the window last February, right after a storm. Remembered how he'd imagined himself one of them, gliding down to land and walk across the crust of ice-sealed snow with no hopes, no memories and, if the ice held, leaving no impression in their wake.

But something, some unbearable weight, had begun to press down on George. Or maybe he was the weight. Yes, he could almost imagine it—imagine his very own feet, in his very own boots—first one, then the other—the whole heft of him breaking through a skim of frozen sleet, then light snow, then the heaviest snow, all the way down, right down to the frozen earth beneath. God, wouldn't that feel good? He could even hear it: a slow, resonant crack and then no sound at all until he touched down.

George dozed off so it was nearly dusk when he roused himself to mow the lawn. Harriet had insisted it be "done—and done today." That was at breakfast. Then she'd gone on to remind him, as if he didn't remember, "Samantha and Greg are coming over for drinks and supper tomorrow. Your brother and Carole—and the Kirshner's, too, of course. They've got those same houseguests as last year. Might as well ask Sarah and Jack, too."

When George hadn't responded in a beat, he'd just taken a swallow of coffee for heaven's sake, she went on. "I have no problem getting a lawn service, you know. We've been through this..." With that he had shaken his head, "No, no—I like it. I like doing the yard work." Then he'd stood and made a grand flourish of his arm, from his knee to above his head, saying, "It shall be done!" He even leaned across the kitchen table to give his wife a kiss to seal his promise. Silvia and Ben rocked their heads back and rolled their eyes witnessing this while Lila looked down at her cereal bowl, serious, unsmiling.

By the time George began his task the fog was heavier again, a blurry cloud through which he surveyed the lane of long grass ahead and the close-cropped lane to his right, until the whole yard sported a crew-cut. But before he wheeled the mower back into the garage, before he took out the blower to clear the flagstone patio and paths, overcome in the soft dimming of the day, overcome by the soft pink cast to the light and the drowsy-making smell of the grass, he lay down in the damp clippings.

Harriet looked out from the kitchen window and hollered. "What on Earth are you doing, George?" while simultaneously forcing the double-hung window shut with a bang. It seemed to George that the glass wobbled.

George didn't get up. Instead, he spread his arms and legs open as far as they would go, as if preparing to make a snow angel. Then he began to whirr his limbs in unison, faster and faster—as fast as he could, eyes closed. And when he opened his eyes, there, high, high above him, hovering, was a dirigible. Was he dreaming? Surely such craft no longer plied the skies.

He stared. It floated. He squeezed his eyes shut again, as tight as he could, then opened them as slowly as possible. But the dirigible—and yes, it was a dirigible—was still there, floating, just visible through the laden air.

How could that beautiful, pregnant beast of a thing, be aloft? He imagined it must be cool and lovely up there, inside and alone with all the green and brown and blue earth floating below. It would be as if you were living upside down.

It was his destiny. His gut turned over and this revelation sent a shiver of joy running through him.

THREE

When George finally went into the house again it was if he carried the fog with him. "Daddy, are you going to the barn later?" Lila asked.

"Tomorrow, my little Whirligig, tomorrow."

"Can I..."

"Yes, you can join me."

Overhearing this Harriet said, "Only for a bit. She's got tryouts for the hockey team at two, you know." She waited but a beat, before saying, louder, "George?"

"Yes, yes, of course, I'll take her."

"I'm counting on it as I've got to run into the office for a while."

"I was always planning to take her, sweetie. I want to take her." Rummaging through the refrigerator George finally put his hand on a bottle of water, which he started chugging.

"You look sort of strange, Dad—green stuff on you," Karen said. She was washing lettuce and chopping vegetables with the headphones to her iPhone in her ears. Ah, the world of the sixteen-year-old! George lifted his hand to his neck, his face, and found small clumps of damp grass clippings there. He gave his head a good shake and grass flew off him in every direction. Lila giggled and pointed to the weathered wood floor where a ragged path of wet grass led from the back door right up to the place where her father now stood.

He was anxious to get to a mirror. Not to see if more clippings still clung to him. More to see if anything else from out there had stuck. Anything invisible.

"I'm off to shower. We're eating when?"

Harriet was poking at a lumpish baggie in the microwave, "No big rush. Lamb's got to defrost a bit longer."

George grabbed his cell phone and headed upstairs, punching "dirigible" into Google search as he did. He read:

"Dirigible" and "airship" are synonyms for lighter-than-air craft that are powered and steerable, as opposed to free floating like a balloon. The word "dirigible" derives from the French verb *diriger,* ("to steer"); and it was a Frenchman—inventor Henri Giffard—who built, and on 24 September 1852 flew, the first powered and steerable airship.

He stripped in the upstairs hall and dumped everything he'd worn while doing the yard work into the washer. More bits of grass fell to the floor. Evidence. The laundry room was windowless but when he stepped back out into the hall, light from the square windows, stacked like a hopscotch court, illuminated him.

George was something between ectomorph and mesomorph, in his early 50's and, thanks to long morning bike rides and a bit of luck, quite strong, quite muscular. He was anxious to get to the master bedroom bath and the large mirror there, a view he typically ignored.

He flipped on the lights and studied his face. His shock of chestnut hair stood nearly on end and his bushy eyebrows were this way and that thanks to being brushed up backwards when he'd removed his sweaty shirt. But it was the same face still—everything in its place, including the pronounced nose, the wide mouth with upturned corners. All in all, he knew he was an okay package. He remembered how fifteen years into his marriage his wife's best friend told him how Harriet had described George after their first date. "She told me she really liked you—that you seemed smart, polite, kind. She thought you were going to do well. She was right there!" George, listening, had smiled, winced, in fact, as his wife's friend continued. "She said you were rather a hunk, too, with a great face, like a Jimmy Stewart or a Tom Hanks. I think she said something like, 'He's, you know, not too, too, handsome, but handsome enough.'" George guessed that was about right. Or at least what most people saw. But it wasn't all. No, indeed.

He had looked at everything save into his own eyes. He knew it was his eyes that would give him away, so he was shy to meet them.

"Dad?" It was Ben at the top of the stairs, louder now, "Dad!"

"In here, Ben."

His son stuck his head around the bathroom door. "Mom says where are you and come start the grill."

"Five minutes or so."

He turned back to the mirror, summoned his courage, took a breath, and stared into his own two eyes. What stared back were green and deep set. More, it was as if the eyes into which he stared were not staring back but smiling back, smiling as if they were either kindly concealing something or seriously considering sharing a secret. It was not just "Good old George" in there. No, indeed. It was another George entirely—benevolent, wiser. That doppelgänger took a step back and disappeared. For now.

George got into the shower and the last of the green grass from outdoors fell from his body and circled once, twice, thrice, and then was carried away, a swirling centrifuge down the drain.

FOUR

Obsession. The rest of this story will appeal to you or not depending on how you feel about that word. If you see the word and think of philatelists, bibliophiles, oologists, numismatists, islomanists, pernalogists, epistemophilics, conchologists, virtuosi, lepidopterists, discophiles, thalassophiles, even artists of any and every stripe—a whole world of accomplished and interesting people with unusual focus and passion—well and good. If, on the other hand, you see or hear the word "obsession" and feel a bit nervous or conjure up stalkers, even murderers, or religious fanatics in robes pressing tracts into your unwelcoming hands, well, perhaps you'd best stop here. Even if I tell you George was on the verge, no, had already become, one of the former types.

For make no mistake, George was now obsessed, and his obsession meant he was in a state of becoming, becoming the man he was starting to feel stirring inside. Suddenly nothing was without meaning, without purpose. A purpose he could never have imagined years, months, weeks, days, even hours ago.

The next morning, as he sipped his coffee, he wondered if airships had electricity—whether he would have to make cold brew coffee and spread his orange marmalade on untoasted slabs of bread. Whether he would be able to read at night. Shaving, showering, using the toilet, he wondered, *How will I accomplish such tasks 'on board'?* He began to contemplate every step of the day as either a problem to be solved or a routine he would have to abandon. It set him on fire!

Of course, none of this mattered if he couldn't get his hands on, or build, an airship. Imagine even turning such an idea over in your head. As if you could just go to a showroom brimming with airships and pick out the model you like. "Cloth or full leather inside, sir?" Or get a build-your-own kit at a hobby store. By God he had a lot to do. But he was one of the hardest workers he knew. And this would not be one more tedious task such as those he was called upon to accomplish at the law firm—writing wills and DNR's, trust and estate documents. No, indeed.

Daunting? Yes. But he was smart. And he knew how to build things. Well, bikes and such. He'd already built two from scratch, assembling carbon, titanium and steel parts to create what his fellow cyclists dubbed "The Two Georges," a pair of flexible, aerodynamic bikes—one for racing, one for rough terrain—that were the envy of everyone in the cycling club to which he belonged. On those bikes, George flew. But that was on the road.

Terra firma was George's territory. The place where he felt safe. Whenever possible, he took trains rather than planes. Or drove or hopped a ferry. He didn't enjoy being in the air. But he had no choice now. Destiny whispered.

<h1 style="text-align:center">FIVE</h1>

Meanwhile, hundreds of miles south in Georgia, a petite redhead with long legs and a long braid—Phoebe by name—is driving her very old, very tired bottle-green VW Beetle down a pebble-strewn road that dead-ends at an old black mailbox on which, faded to the point of near invisibility the address "808 Heron Drive North" is crudely hand-printed in white paint. A few feet beyond is a realtor's sign, also faded, and tilted to almost a 45-degree angle: "FOR SALE • Stew Dilenschneider Homes" with a phone number and a line drawing of a two-story house.

Phoebe has been coming to this spot for two and a half years and has never seen another human being, another car. Never any sign that anyone else ever comes near the property. She first spotted the pristine curve of sand one Memorial Day weekend while out on a boat with some folks from Just Good Food, the restaurant where she's worked as a waitress for seven years now. When she got back home, she opened Google Earth and zoomed in closer and closer until she found what seemed to be the same arc of lakefront beach. Above it was a lot that looked to be a vacant, or nearly so. Oh, what a perfect little take-off point for swimming.

She jumped in the car and after many dead ends—well-kept cul-de-sacs with freshly painted mailboxes, cars in the drives and boats in boathouses—she found it: 808 Heron Drive North, the only mailbox on a weed-riddled road with no other homes. "Bingo!"

On this June day, the water will be warm. Phoebe prefers cooler water. Late September, October, even November water. And by wearing a half wetsuit, she even manages some swims into December. Then, for a few months, she endures doing laps at the over-chlorinated, often crowded indoor pool at the YMCA in town before she's back to the lake swims she so loves.

She parks, as usual, against what remains of a curb just beyond the mailbox and leans over to grab the shiny tote from Kroeger's grocery that holds her "kit:" bright yellow swim cap so boats can see her, blue goggles, big old beach towel. But, oh, no—. As she lifts the bag, she realizes that it is too light, and she knows why: *Damn! My towel. Where's my towel?* She thinks it to herself. Or maybe even speaks out loud. People who live alone sometimes talk out loud to themselves. Phoebe's one of them. She continues, "You are such an idiot, Phoebe."

Routine and discipline keep Phoebe sane, keep loneliness at bay. And swimming is an important part of that that routine. Her grandmother uses a different word, used it just this morning during their weekly phone call. "What's this obsession with swimming? You could take a day off, you know. It wouldn't kill you." But every day is what works. Routine is what works. Taking a day off might kill her, one way or another. Every day when she returns from her swim she rinses her wet bathing suit and cap and hangs them in the shower. Then she cleans her goggles with a bit of alcohol and puts them back in her bag for the next day. And she always hangs her tote at the front door, ready to throw in the car.

No wonder she is angry with herself, forgetting her towel. Better my towel than my goggles. But damn. What an idiot. Damn, damn, damn. She is muttering again and while she mutters she opens the hatch of her VW just to see if there might be a towel in there. Hopeless, she knows. It's like your wallet is stolen but you keep digging your hand into your purse or your suit jacket or back pocket thinking by some miracle it will simply turn up. Why do we do that? Why do we keep looking—hold out hope—when we know something is lost forever?

Well, in two weeks it will officially be summer. It's not as if she needs a towel to keep warm after her swim. Who cares if her car seat gets wet?

So, as she did the day she found it, Phoebe walks down the overgrown driveway, passes the cracked and crumbling cement slab—footprint of the house that once was—and wends her way down a path of oversize stones with tall grass and a few shrubs that sometimes flower on either side. Down, down, down to the lake she goes, a four-minute stroll from her car.

Right at the water's edge sits a gnome, also cement and with a few vestiges of red paint on its pointed cap. It is a repulsive thing with bits of white bird droppings on its shoulders, cheeks and lips. It marks Phoebe's point of departure and a large rock shaped like a cumulus cloud one cove over is her other marker. Back and forth between gnome and cloud she swims her slow, steady laps, rain or shine.

Phoebe is pulling off the oversized sweatshirt she wears over her bathing suit for the drive. She drops it over the gnomes' head, happy to hide its leering face from view. On top of that she balances her glasses—or tries to. They tumble onto the grass. *I'll find them after*, Phoebe thinks. She's anxious to get in the water, already pulling on her yellow cap, adjusting her goggles. Off she goes.

Depending on her schedule at the restaurant, Phoebe swims late afternoon or early morn when, as now, the lake stretches out like an ironed sheet. Perfect. With each stroke, she counts: *One, one, one, breathe,* all the way out to the rock. Then, *Two, two, two, breathe*, all the way back. Odd numbers out to the cloud, even numbers back to the gnome. And so on and so on. She keeps that metronome count and metronome breathing going until she reaches 52 back-and-forth's, which she guesses is about a mile. Sometimes she wonders what she will be like at that age—11 years from now—whether her life will have changed for the better, or for the worse. *Seventeen, seventeen, seventeen. Breathe.* Over and over. Then she turns. *Eighteen, eighteen, eighteen, breathe.*

Were you standing beside the concrete gnome you would remark on the beauty of Phoebe's stroke; how smooth and effortless it is. The lake seems to open up in front of her, take her in, and then close back up around her, no seam in sight. Under and over, under and over. Dissolving into the water she creates barely a ripple and leaves no wake.

Six

Sunday evening arrived and soon enough, so do George and Harriet's guests. Half an hour in advance, George puts a big fan out on the patio having read it disrupts the flight path of kamikaze mosquitos targeting warm-blooded hosts. But it is cool. He doesn't imagine they will be bitten to death. He slaps the cushions on the outdoor furniture to send any spiders scurrying, sets up a table to serve as a bar, and carries ice, glasses, lemons, limes, bottles of vodka, gin, whiskey, and wine, a knife and cocktail napkins out from the kitchen. And then he makes himself a drink. A real drink: Tequila and tonic with a lot of lime. It tastes great. He downs it. This way, by the time the guests arrive he will feel just fine, thank you. Yes, indeed. For once he won't have to catch up or feel as if he's sitting in the audience while everyone else is on stage, eagerly saying their lines.

Samantha and Greg are first to arrive, Samantha bursting in—as is her style—hands Harriet a huge bouquet of flowers in a cellophane funnel. George can see enormous, orange parrot tulips with serrated edges and deep purple undersides and veins, poking their heads out of the top. Breathless, handing her purse and a wrap to her husband, Samantha speaks all in one breath. "I know you're not supposed to bring your hostess flowers. They have to be dealt with, blah, blah, blah. But how could I resist these?"

"Oh, Sam...Apologize? I don't think so!" Harriet takes the flowers from Samantha with a broad smile. "George, grab that glass vase of your mother's, will you?"

He reaches up into the cabinet over the microwave and knows it when he touches it: heavy crystal with an oval base opening into an undulating collar on top. He carries it over to the sink to fill it with water as Harriet opens and shuts one kitchen drawer after another. Looking over his shoulder, George asks, "What are you after, honey?" But she is already speaking. "Ah! Found 'em."

They meet back at the counter where George puts down the vase and a pair of shears. Watching the two of them Samantha thinks, and not for the first time, how very efficient George and Harriet move about the kitchen: two trains on schedule, keeping to their tracks, avoiding collision at all costs.

What Harriet had searched for and found is an old pin cushion. Amongst the smaller pins are some longer, thicker ones, with oblong heads made of pearl. Hat pins. It is these she is pulling out and setting aside.

"What on earth are those for?" George says as he unwraps the cellophane and looks down at the tulips—their impossibly long green necks and livid heads so full of life and so very still. He catches Samantha's eye and blushes, finding their color and shape nearly obscene.

"One of my colleagues at the office shared this little trick," Harriet says. "You know how tulips always grow toward the light? They actually keep growing, even after you arrange them. It's maddening. But if you stick a pin through their necks, at an angle, right below the bloom, they won't do that. They'll just stay where you put them—stand up straight."

With that, Harriet picks up one of the tulips and drives a hatpin in and up at an angle through one of those ever so green, ever so long throats. And then she does the same with the next. And the next. She stands back when she's done and smiles. "Brilliant. Stops them from growing. I love it."

Having found it strangely painful to watch, George heads out the patio door mumbling. "I'm going to check and see if anybody's come in through the backyard."

SEVEN

The Paxton's guests have arrived: George's brother, Eddie, and his wife, Carol, Samantha and Greg Kirshner and their houseguests, the next-door neighbors, Sarah and Jack. Not to mention a passel of kids, most of them 14-and 16-year-old classmates of Ben and Karen. None of the other couples had a child late: no one else has a wee little 7-year-old Lila like George and Harriet.

After quickly singing out, "Hi, Mr. Paxton," or "Nice to see you, Mrs. Paxton," over their shoulders, the teenagers make a beeline for the huge playroom over the garage. In no time, they are watching movies and devouring the pizzas delivered earlier and kept warm in the oven. After putting their offerings on the marble counter—cheese, prepared olives, bottles of wine, a key lime pie—the adults remain clustered around the kitchen island. But before long they drift out onto the patio where outdoor couches and chairs, upholstered in a broad brown and white awning stripe, are arranged around a fire pit meant for nights much cooler than this.

Lila is sitting alone in a corner on the kitchen floor turning a wooden wine crate into a house for her caterpillars. She is making walls out of Lego pieces that lay scattered around the floor at her feet. Before joining the others outdoors, her father walks over and scrunches down on his haunches to take a look. "Lucky caterpillars, Whirligig. But how will you keep them from escaping?"

She grabs a wire cooling rack from where she left it beside her leg and lays it on top of the box. "See?"

"But the holes are too big, aren't they? They can still crawl through."

Lila shakes her head. "I am going to use two, Daddy," and she shows him how, by laying a second wire rack at an angle on top of the first, only tiny diamond shaped openings remain. "Too small for them to escape now."

"Ingenious, just ingenious."

"Is that something good?"

"Ingenious? Oh, yes, very, very good. It means you used your noggin'." He picks up a bottle cap, which Lila has filled with tiny bits of grass and leaves. "I see you made dinner for the caterpillars. How 'bout you? Pizza upstairs with the gang?"

"Ben brought me a slice."

"Did he sit with you while you ate?

"Yep. And I showed him my caterpillar house."

"Now that's what I call a nifty brother." George leans over and kisses the top of Lila's head before he stands back up.

"Yes, indeed," whispers Lila, using her father's favorite phrase.

Samantha, holding the door open for George, looks back at Lila. "She's a lot like you, isn't she? Such focus and so happy working on a project all by herself."

"Just like me, Sam? Lord, I don't know that I would wish that on anyone, let alone my daughter. But I do love seeing that she seems content to create her own little worlds."

"Content, yes. But alone."

"Maybe content to be alone, Sam."

"Well, you would know."

George rolls his eyes but when he glances back at his daughter, his playful look vanishes. Alone. Lonely. He knows the difference. Yes, indeed. He steps out of the kitchen, into the dusk, and the screen slams shut behind him.

EIGHT

George makes the rounds to check that no one is empty handed, chatting with one and all as he does. But his mind is elsewhere. He keeps imagining, even thinks he sees, the other George—the one that stared back at him in the bathroom mirror. That's him, isn't it—walking the tree line near the pool and watching his every move—always with that enigmatic smile on his face?

Samantha is biding her time, weaving her way like a bird, branch by branch, dropping in and out of conversations with the others until she can fly over to George. Having made the rounds he is lost in thought, leaning against the enormous, ancient copper beech tree near the bar he set up outdoors. Eventually Sam reaches him. "Move over," she says, and likewise leans against the tree. They are shoulder to shoulder, eyes fixed on the others on the patio.

George has never seen Samantha drink anything but a beer but tonight she, too, seems to have a real drink.

"What's that you're having, Sam?"

"Vodka and soda."

"Well, well. I didn't make that for you."

"No, I made it for myself. Surprised?"

"Nothing you do surprises me." George laughs, holds up his own glass and continues, "I'm on my second I'll have you know. Tequila, no less."

"George Paxton. You devil."

"I suddenly thought, why the hell not?"

"Why not," she says, then turns her shoulder against the tree to speak to him head on. "So. Off to Nantucket end of the month, are you?"

"Our usual summer thing."

"Well, 'our' is not really part of the program, is it?"

"Is this what you do you with all your patients, Sam?"

"What's that?"

"Keep asking the same thing over and over, year after year, until you wear them down."

"Well, one time you'll give me the real answer—explain why it's Harriet and the kids one month, you and the kids the other. You'll explain to the good Dr. Beinstock how that's such a healthy conjugal idea."

"Done that, haven't I, Sam? You know how demanding our jobs are. It's good for us each to have solo time with the kids. Best way to do that is to split things up." George pauses to down the last of his drink. "Harriet can't take off the whole summer. I could, at this point. But it's too long—I shouldn't. Wouldn't. You know me."

"Yeah, yeah, yeah. But what about you two? I know you go back and forth weekends, but..."

"And we always arrive, pack up and leave together—the whole gang..."

"Well, hell, isn't that great—such a cozy arrangement..."

By "cozy" Samantha was obviously hinting that only a couple who were—oh, that kiss of death— "good friends" would arrange things like this, something akin to separate vacations. Samantha interrupts George as he thinks about how to respond by raising her glass with a big smile, indicating she wanted a refill and, also, that she was enjoying the conversation.

He takes her glass and grabs the bottle of vodka while she goes on. "You know I don't really talk to Harriet, George. Not really. Not like we can talk. But I do care about you and so I do ask."

"Well, I am not sure what you are really asking. Anyway, what about you and Greg?

"What about us?"

"Well, you don't even have kids. Free as birds to do as you please. Even so, you never even take vacations."

"I wasn't talking about us."

"And why's that?"

"George?" It was Harriet, yelling from the patio, "Come turn on the gas. We need to get dinner going."

George yelled back, "Coming!" then, *sotto voce*, "Call of duty." He set his glass down in the grass. When he stood back up, Samantha drawled out: "Att-en-shun!" and saluted.

George wondered if Samantha could see or sense the other George way, way inside of him—the other George with whom he'd locked eyes in the mirror the night before. Maybe so. He looked over to the tree line and his other self was there. As if flesh and blood. Patient. Watching his every move. Waiting.

Samantha grabbed a cocktail napkin and waved it as if he were setting off for a sea voyage instead of the barbeque on the patio. "Until we meet again, mon cher."

NINE

Phoebe climbs out of the lake, possum blind and weasel wet. The air is so clear she can bite it. Clack, clack her tiny, white teeth snap open and closed. She drops her head back, face to the setting sun, and her red braid—a long tail—swings this way and that before coming to a full stop. The cool currents in the lake, her faster than fast swim, this clear air, are all thanks to a full moon on its way. Vroom, vroom—so energizing. By midnight, the beams will fall through the three panes of glass at the top of her front door onto the floor: a hopscotch court of light Phoebe loves to step in and out of if she stays up that late.

A boat comes in close. Phoebe swings around towards the sound and squints, not unhappy to enjoy the world as a bleeding watercolor of greens and blues before she relents and, on all fours, pats her hands this way and that to locate her glasses in the grass. She can see clearly again, even hear better. But oh, Phoebe thinks, how much sweeter the world was out of focus and muffled. Still dripping, she slides her sweatshirt off the gnome and yanks it down so it reaches nearly halfway down her thighs.

"It's a marvelous night for a moondance…with the stars up above in your eyes." She sings as she climbs up the unkempt stretch of yard and across the gravel drive to her VW, parked at the curb.

She turns the key in the ignition and her old car growls but doesn't catch. Phoebe sits a moment, hands gripping the wheel. *Please, no—not again.* She looks up to the heavens, shakes her head, and recalls another time her car stalled. It was a year ago October. She'd lingered after her lunch shift, so it was later than usual when she untied her apron, climbed into her Beetle and, damn, the old bug made a series of click, click clickety-click sounds when she tried to start it. She considered walking home rather than ask for a lift (she hates asking for help.) But four miles on a state road alone with dusk approaching? That was a bit much, even for Phoebe. And she didn't feel like dealing with Triple A after a long day. When she walked back into the restaurant, Henry—the chef—shouted from the TV-screen opening into his kitchen lair:

"Couldn't stay away?"

"Funny. No. It's my VW. Pretty sure the battery's dead."

"Happy to give you a lift," Henry said—of all the people Phoebe did not want to be indebted to—"I was going to run home to feed my dog before dinner anyway."

"I'm out the State Highway, you know," Phoebe answered. "Way out of your way." She was so hoping that someone else—Magnus, maybe—would chime in, offer her a ride. But no. Henry had been too quick on the draw and sealed the deal:

"Not a worry. Just give me a sec."

Now Phoebe gives her VW another try and it starts right up. "Praise the Lord!" she calls out as she pats the dashboard affectionately, rolls down the windows and starts for home. The breeze begins to dry her long hair, her legs, the drops of lake water still crystal lenses on her forehead and forearms. She feels good. Why the hell obsess over that night, so many moons ago? But she does.

It was—cool, nearly cold. When she got in Henry's truck, he'd put the heat on. "Be warmer in a sec."

"Good," she answered and then turned to shop talk. "Everybody at lunch loved your cassoulet, Chef."

"It was good, I think, thanks. Magnus asked to take some home. Guy's got taste," Henry replied. "And how 'bout the couple that usually only come in for breakfast? They leave you a decent tip?"

"More than decent. And Magnus, too."

"Well, of course, Magnus." Henry had answered, and sharply.

"What—you don't like Magnus?"

"Who doesn't?"

"So, no?"

"No. Meaning everyone loves him. He built a doghouse for my sheepdog, you know. It's nicer than my house. Guy's amazing."

"Oh!" Phoebe said. Then they both went silent. Phoebe focused on the rasps, like last breaths, audible through the car's air vents and realized she was holding her breath—worrying about what to do when they got to her house.

Phoebe pulls off the main highway into her long driveway, shuts off the engine, shakes her damp hair. "No way!" she says out loud, "No. Way." Which is what she kept thinking to herself that night in Henry's Land Cruiser. No way she was going to invite him to come inside: "Hey, want to come in for a glass of wine or something, Henry?" Of course, that's what he was expecting her to say. But, no. God, no.

Phoebe starts up her car again, pulls up, snug to the side of her house and rolls up the windows. It might rain. Then she just sits there, continuing to relive that night. She knew Henry had a "sneaker" for her, as her grandmother used to say. Still does. Often, she finishes serving Magnus and turns around to find Henry staring at her. Not smiling, staring, his mouth a strung bow. At such moments, frightened animals run in tight packs across her skin and into her scalp, then scatter, pausing, ears and nose to the air, alert, even after Henry's gaze softens and he lets fly a smile. Yes, Henry always makes his lean, handsome face smile. She sees the effort it takes.

Halfway down the long state road to her house that October eve Phoebe had reached for the radio dial to bring sound into the cold silence of the truck and Henry had taken hold of her by the wrist saying, "Let me." Then he'd hit one button after another, a thrusting motion with his pointer finger, bang, bang, bang, until country music came up, loud, and he smiled.

Phoebe had forced herself to laugh. "*Country? Really?*"

"Hell, yes. I left New York just for this." Henry stretched his arm in back of Phoebe to grab a cowboy hat from the seat behind her, pulled it low on his brow, and began to sing along: *"There's more here than what we're seeing, a divine conspiracy, that you, that you...la da da da da dee...could somehow fall for me."* He hummed the rest.

When they started down the sparsely populated stretch to Phoebe's house, there was a sudden wing of light to the right. It made the trees' dark fingers, stretching up out of the earth, thrum and glow. Phoebe couldn't help but exclaim, "Oh, man. I forgot. Look—full moon"

"Damn that's huge."

"Hunter's Moon."

"Why 'Hunter's?'" Henry had asked.

"Can't remember. Just know it's an especially bright one, long in the sky." Phoebe had pulled out her cell phone, turned toward the window, and tried to focus and capture it as they sped along. But they were moving too fast, way too fast. You either catch the moon early in the evening, before it floats up out of human reach, or you don't catch it at all. She'd almost put her hand on Henry's shoulder and said, "Stop!" But she couldn't bear to touch him.

Reliving that moment Phoebe shudders and stares straight ahead before rousing herself, saying aloud, "Silly girl!"

It's getting hot in her car with the windows rolled up. The sun is still visible on the horizon: all is calm, all is bright. But that night, the night Henry drove her home, it was black, save for the moon, which was so there, so very there, until, just as suddenly, they charged down the last hill to her mailbox leaving the land to rise high and the moon to fall, far below the earth. Phoebe sighed loudly, frustrated.

Henry had looked over, seen her lower her phone from her eye, and said, "Oh. Sorry." That's when he put his right arm across the back of her seat and that pack of animals ran up and down her spine, chaotic, before scattering, frantic, as his hand brushed her hair. He leaned toward her and said, softly, "Did you want me to stop or something?"

"No. Too late."

"Maybe we can catch it when we get to your house."

"No," Phoebe said, staring out her side of the car. "By then we'll be on the wrong side of the sky."

They were silent for a stretch after that. The country music still playing on the radio made the shared air inside Henry's Land Cruiser bearable—just. Only a half mile more and Phoebe pointed and spoke. "Next drive. On the left. The blue mailbox."

Henry made the turn quickly and stopped quickly, too. Phoebe had her hand on the door handle and jumped out, turned, looked back into the car and said, "Thanks, Chef" all in one fell swoop. She was about to close the door but Henry shot out his arm to keep it open.

"I'm Henry." His flat tone was a slap, and he repeated himself: "Henry."

"Sorry! Thank you, Henry." She said his name slowly, firmly.

Henry's stare didn't immediately dissolve into a smile. He drew in his chin and said, "Well, ok, then, Phoebe," before he turned the radio down and, leaning toward her asked, "How about tomorrow? I can stop in the morning and give you a lift back to the restaurant."

"No, no. I'll ride my bike. Triple A can meet me at the restaurant. But thanks. I know this was way out of your way."

Phoebe gets out of her car, grabs her swim bag and shakes her head. Her hair is nearly dry. She walks up the undulating path to her front door. Her feet are bare. The thyme she planted in between the stones is soft, even its tiny seeds, soft, and it softly releases its fragrance.

The night Henry gave her a lift Phoebe didn't look back as she walked this path, not even after she'd opened her screen door and held it ajar with her hip as she worked the key into her front door lock. She waited until she heard his truck pull back out onto the State Highway with a hail of gravel. Only then did she look across to the hills beyond and, as she is doing again now, stretch out her arms, chest height. That October night to let the hidden moon, tonight to let the tumbling sun, anoint her.

TEN

The group gathered on the Paxtons' patio are eating dinner off oversized plates set in their laps with oversized napkins underneath. Jack keeps sighing at this arrangement as his knife and fork have slid off onto the flagstone patio twice. Both times, he and Sarah shared conspiratorial smiles: they'd rather be at a proper table indoors.

Having inhaled his meal, George's brother—surprise, surprise—is holding forth. Eddie is a pharmaceutical sales rep, a job he considers a dream come true and which aligns perfectly with his intrinsic, hmm, shall we call it *joie de vivre* or, less benevolently, his refusal to ever stop pushing, ever stop talking, even when he is told, "No, thank you" or even an emphatic, blunt "No!"

At one point he was offered a promotion—a plum, in-house "Director of Sales" position. It took him half a second to turn that down. Give up his interactions with the adoring receptionists, nurses and PA's who are the gatekeepers when he brings in his drug samples? Report to a desk 9 to 5 and beyond when he can roam county-to-county in his top-of-the-line Lexus? What sort of fool would do that? Oh, and there is also the fact that days on the road means he is master of his own schedule, and no one is the wiser if some of his afternoon calls are not to an internist's office but to the condominium of his ladylove. Truth be told, his wife, Carole, is "the wiser" but accepts Eddie's dalliances on the one side, and his generous gifts to her on the other, with equanimity.

This evening, Eddie regales the group with the story of Viagra. "Developed as a heart medication," he cries out, "Can you imagine?" And then he goes on, his pitch ratcheting up an octave as he continues to explain how men enrolled in the trial studies consistently and overwhelmingly experienced a side effect they rather welcomed. He tells this part of the story while standing and acting out mens' surprise when their private parts came unexpectedly alive. He even starts to unzip his fly until the others, in unison yell out, "No, Eddie, no!"

He is only teasing. They know that. On he goes. "New studies with a new indication as a treatment for ED and…" Before he finishes this sentence Eddie drops down onto one knee, throws his arms out and yells like an MC, "Eureka! A star is born." They all laugh, mostly with relief that this tale is finally over, and exchange wincing smiles.

Viagra is a star that's made Eddie even richer than he already was, richer than his wildest dreams. (Although his dreams grow with every dollar he earns.) And as a bonus, he has all those free samples to dip into for his own use.

Eddie's wife, Carole, has heard this story a thousand times before. While her husband drones on she stands up, collects a few empty plates and glasses, and shouts, "Land the plane, Eddie, land the plane." He waves her away, failing as always to take a true measure of his audiences' interest. Eddie is congenitally tone-deaf. It is the key to his success.

Eventually, everyone helps Carole clatter the remaining plates into the kitchen before returning to the patio, wine glasses refilled, to take a breather before dessert. The kids come outside in bathing suits, towels draped over their shoulders, and head to the side yard to jump into the pool. The moon is nearly full and to George the teens seem to glow as they lope across the dark lawn together, the girls whispering, heads leaning in toward each other, the boys running ahead, laughing. He smiles and thinks how much better it is to have the teenagers with them rather than driving off in their cars God knows where.

When he turns around, George finds Samantha dragging a pair of chairs over to the big beech tree. Everyone else is relaxing around the fire pit in a ragged circle, sitting or stretched out on the chaise lounges. George is in no mood for a group chat-fest. He joins Samantha, happy again to use the tree as cover.

"So, to pick up where I left off…" Samantha sits, pulls her feet out of her sandals and draws them up under her, scooting her skirt up over her knees as she does. Starting with her preposterously thin ankles Samantha is lean all the way up to her chest where she becomes ample, an asset which no doubt exudes motherly warmth to emotionally distraught clients and conversely, the idea that she is all-woman and far from a prude to patients looking for sympathy and understanding in another direction.

"Yes?"

"My point was, is, damn it, you still have a pulse, George. I know it without even putting my fingers on your wrist."

He doesn't know how to respond. It seems rather an intimate comment, even between old friends, "a pulse" being a pseudonym for blood coursing through all sorts of human parts and in all sorts of human ways. Uncertain where Samantha is going, and rather than run in the wrong direction, he just parrots, (or does he, really?) what she's just said.

"Hell, we both have pulses, Sam. No one who knows you would think otherwise."

She takes his response to be a tentative step down the path she is eager to explore. Perhaps he had meant that, even unconsciously. It is not as if he desires Samantha, but he does desire her directness and her willingness to ferret out something that might be hidden but important. Especially now. He is grateful for someone like Samantha, someone who can imagine her clients, and so imagine him, as another person in another life.

Who provides that for her? Her husband, Greg? He wonders. So, a bit drunk (he has followed one tequila with another, and that with red wine), he folds into the chair next to her, even tugs it a bit closer before speaking. "I mean, for heaven's sake, Sam, you are just so alive. Curious. You say things. You ask things. Nobody else does that." He looks down, takes another sip of wine and she is quick to reply.

"Not everyone feels that way." Samantha shakes her head. "Or appreciates it."

George raises his eyebrows. "No?"

"Not really. You do. We are part of the same clan—even more than you and Eddie—right?" Samantha laughs. "God, what a character that guy is. Hard to believe the same blood runs through you both."

"My brother from another mother..."

"Not really?"

"No, no, of course not." Then George bungles things. He is looking up at the sky, not at Samantha when he continues. "You talk, you ask. But then again, you don't actually do anything much differently than the rest of us, Sam. Not really."

Samantha is stung by this. After all, she's a therapist and George knows it. She pushes her chin out. "'Just talking about stuff,' as you put it, is my life's work."

Maybe. But George has a hunch he's right, so he presses. "Sure. Sure. Your work is all talk. But you don't want to just be in conversation, Samantha. You want to be in life."

Samantha swings her face abruptly to the left, as if she's been slapped. Her feet shoot to the ground. She shoves them back in her sandals, stands, gives him an arch look and speaks, eye to eye. "What a crock, George. 'In life?' Seriously? And especially coming from you. Give me a refill will you, please?"

George does as he's been asked. Samantha takes her glass and heads toward the fire pit. George waits. Halfway across the grass she turns and smiles her biggest, broadest, Samantha smile. "I am not done with you, George Paxton. No, indeed."

The teens are in the pool, hidden by privet, splashing and shouting. "Marco!" "Polo!" George looks toward the tree line again. This time it is the other George he catches walking across the dark yard, bathed in the bright light of the full moon. He locks eyes with him for as long as he can stand it. Neither smiles. They are coming to terms.

ELEVEN

Phoebe's Sunday night is too quiet and not quiet enough. Even though her windows are closed, and her air conditioner noisily cycles off and on, on and off (it's 7 years old for Pete's sake) she can still hear the cicadas flexing their muscles. She would prefer true silence. Or birdsong. Anything but the incessant burr of those horrid vibrating beasts—the irritatingly imperfect white noise of their wild, random crescendos. Am I alone in this opinion, she wonders? She will be glad when a frost freezes these insects away. By then, dusk will arrive earlier. The nights will be darker, longer.

She can always make it until the dimming of the day which, mercifully, comes later and later now, at the cusp of summer. Then what? She thinks about calling her old friend, Ruth. But no. If she did, Phoebe knows she would hear Ruth's children, her hyperactive terrier, the TV—even Ruth's husband, Howard, standing at her elbow, asking, "Who is it, Ruth? Who the heck is calling at this hour?" Background sounds of talking, laughing, shouting, playing, barking. The sounds of suppertime in a real household. And Ruth would say, "Oh, Phoebe. We are completely helter-skelter here. Not a good time. Can I call you during the week—some morning when the kids are in school?"

"Of course, Ruth." Phoebe speaks an imaginary response out loud as she looks out the window and the sun blinks shut behind a cloud.

When she got home from her swim, Phoebe showered and pulled on an old pair of cut offs and a t-shirt. Then she deadheaded her flowers and swept the front stoop and the stone path leading out to her long drive. Is that when the truck went by, slowed as it passed? The annuals she planted in mid-May still have their full sparkle. That will last through August when, ugh, they will turn leggy and burnt and she will have to accept that autumn is bearing down. What then? Mums? Such depressing gold, maroon and dark purple colors. Who wants that? By mid-August the grocery store will already have pots and pots of them bleeding out into their parking lots. Gloomy still-life's with bushels of hay, scarecrows and pumpkins in the background. Seriously? No thank you. She'll replace her window box nasturtiums and sweet potato vine with cabbages when the time comes. And then with holly and evergreen branches for the holidays. Skip the mums. And bring on the frost to kill the cicadas. How dour she is tonight.

Phoebe returns to the front stoop and sits. She can smell the herbs on either side of her. Is this another truck or the same one going back the other direction she wonders? She left her glasses inside. It rumbles as it passes then hums more heavily, like the cicadas, as it slows—almost to an idle—for just for a moment. There's a logging enterprise just outside of town and on weekdays a parade of semi's—their trailers empty or laden with long logs depending on whether they are going to or fro—pass regularly. But never at this hour. And that wasn't a semi. Why on earth? She heads inside, into her air-conditioned nest.

Phoebe could have had company. Magnus invited her to join him for dinner. Her breakfast and lunch shifts over, she lingered at the restaurant, refreshing the small bouquets on the tables and chatting with Henry Gauthier, or as the staff teasingly calls him, Chef Henri. He begged Phoebe to taste the gumbo he concocted for the evening special. "Open," he'd said and raised a spoonful of thick sauce. It gave her a choking feeling to have him bring the spoon to her mouth and then into her mouth, but she played along, swallowed, and then spoke what she tasted. "Shrimp. Sausage. Celery…" Henry nodded his head "yes" once, twice. She continued. "Tomato? Bay, maybe?" Henry kept nodding. "What am I missing? Peppers or something?" Phoebe licked her lips dramatically, like a cartoon character, to make Henry laugh, trying to pretend, forcing herself to keep things light.

He did laugh and said, "Okra!"

"Ah ha! Well, *c'est fanstastique*, Henri. As always. Maybe a soupçon more pepper?"

"Brilliant, *Madame oui, non, Mademoiselle*." Henry and Phoebe quickly exhausted their high school French. He stumbled on in a patois. "Better yet, *Mon Cherie*. And *oui, oui* to more poivre. I made extra to give Magnus some to take home. One of his favorites. Give you some, too, if you like." She nodded that she did like and when she finished her shift, Henry gave her a hearty portion. (Phoebe is reheating it now and making rice to soak up all the roux.)

That was hours ago—before she'd changed into her swimsuit in the restaurant's ladies' room and gathered her things to leave for the lake. Before the bell on the restaurant door jingled and Magnus had come in, smiling at Phoebe, nodding at Henry.

Dear old Magnus. Nearly bald and built like a boxer Magnus. Since his wife died two years ago, he comes into the restaurant for breakfast most mornings and an early supper most nights as well. Always with *The Wall Street Journal*, *The New York Times*, and a book in hand— Le Carré or some other literary book.

"Where's your apron, Phoebe?" he boomed, "Not leaving, are you?"

"Yes, Magnus. Been here since seven. I am thoroughly through." Phoebe pretended to limp a few steps. "Done for, in fact. A swim and then home."

"*Uf-dah*. Come sit—join me for dinner. I'll drive you home if it's too dark after." Magnus eased himself into a booth and patted the leather banquette with his strong square hand, "Right here. Or across from me so I can look at that lovely face of yours." Magnus reached out and slid he vase full of curling ranunculus first to one side then the other. "Which side of my poor maw do you prefer?" Phoebe said, "Both" and slid the flowers all the way over to the wall to reveal the dull scar that nearly sliced Magnus forehead in half.

Before she died, Magnus and his wife, Dorothy, came into the restaurant twice a week, breakfast one day, lunch or dinner another— always sitting in Phoebe's section: table 11. Magnus had been a professor of economics at a university out in Minnesota somewhere before he and Dorothy retired to Georgia. Dorothy grew up on the lake and wanted to return. Magnus acquiesced.

Phoebe was friendly with the couple but took note that the Dahls, unlike so many who come to the restaurant hungering less for a meal than to hear others talking or to talk with others—someone else, anyone else—seemed to really enjoy one another. And they were always laughing. She recalls one time overhearing them discussing what vegetables to plant in the garden. "No more zucchini, Magnus!" Dorothy had exclaimed. "That stuff reproduces like jack rabbits." Magnus had nodded and responded, "Ach—ok! You are right, as always. Green beans, then. I'll start some seeds in the morning."

Another time, Phoebe heard them having a rousing back and forth over some political to-do that had been all over the news. Magnus was, with all good humor, making a point as he banged the bottom of the catsup bottle with his palm to get it flowing. He absent-mindedly removed the cap then hit it too hard, one too many times, and the plug of crimson sauce shot across the table like a bullet, nailing Dorothy in the chest. No one laughed harder than Dorothy, so hard tears that came to her dancing blue eyes. Magnus used his red and white checkerboard napkin to wipe them away. Days later, Dorothy was dead—a massive heart attack. The table that once shook with laughter turned to stone.

The first time Magnus came into the restaurant alone he looked at Table 11, abruptly turned, and sat in a booth, also in Phoebe's section. For the first few weeks, he would lower his newspaper only to order and ask for his check. But his good nature was such, and Phoebe's smile was such, that before long the two were chattering even as Phoebe balanced a tray of dishes in the air. Often, he lingered after finishing his meal, glancing frequently over the top of his newspaper, watching, waiting for the moment when Phoebe waved her last table goodbye. Then he would wave her over and she would come stand beside, or even half sit, on the banquette across from Magnus, knees turned out so she could hop up if new customers arrived.

One rainy morning, while serving Magnus his usual—rye bread toasted twice, ("He likes his toast toasty," Dorothy had said the first time the pair had come in), plain yogurt, marmalade—Magnus allowed Phoebe a glimpse of what losing his wife of 41 years felt like. "There's a hole in the air, Phoebe," he began, "I try to walk around it but it's too big." Phoebe put her hand on Magnus forearm, and he went on. "I think if a flock of birds were to try to fly through it, they would drop like stones, their hearts beating out of all time."

After that, Phoebe and Magnus abandoned observations on the weather and used any moments they had to share details about their pasts—monologues from Magnus on his thousand-mile moves from mountains in Norway to rural Minnesota to the large lake here, all such a contrast to Phoebe's tale of a life circling the same streets, swimming around the same lake, year after year. It took weeks for them to catch up, arrive at now, at the same place. Or nearly.

Magnus is Phoebe's favorite customer, hands down. Hell, he's her favorite man in town. Maybe in the world. There's a plan afoot to close the restaurant and have a party for him on his 70th birthday, several months away.

Retiring to Georgia had been Dorothy's dream. After losing her, everyone assumed Magnus would return to Minnesota. Or move back to Norway where he was born. He's forever showing photos of his daughter, son, their partners, and a passel of grandchildren standing in front of unimaginable mountains or unimaginable mountains of snow. He still has friends from childhood there, too. But no. Dorothy dead and gone, Magnus just gardened more, bringing the overabundance—bags of squash, tomatoes, herbs, lettuces, pumpkins—to Henry, and always putting his palm up and saying, "*Ach!*" when Henry offers a free dinner in return. And Magnus rekindled an old love: carpentry. He took on small jobs from friends, including designing a palace of a doghouse for Henry's sheepdog. Then he conjured up a project to keep himself very busy, very beloved.

Every autumn Magnus gives all the children starting at the nursery school run by his church their own set of building blocks. Squares, triangles, half circles, and rectangles large and small—all made of pine and sanded to perfect softness. How sweet is that? It takes him half a year to make enough sets to go around.

The first time he showed Phoebe a set—untied the knot on one of the suede pouches he stitches and stores them in—Phoebe "ooohed" and "ahhhed" over and over as they tumbled across the table. Then just today, as Phoebe filled his coffee cup, Magnus reached down beside him and placed on the table an oddly-shaped package neatly wrapped in burlap and tied with rough brown twine. "A gift for you," he said. "Sit a moment."

The package was so perfect and so pleasing, she just wanted to hold it, admire it, feel the rare texture.

"Go on then!" Magnus gave the package a little push. "There is something inside, you know."

Phoebe slowly untied the string and the burlap flapped open. Inside was a wooden toy. "A whirligig, right?" she asked. Magnus nodded. It was a young boy holding a fishing rod the line from which went through the base of the toy in which a round hole was drilled. A large wooden fish, painted in blue and white stripes, dangled from other end. Phoebe tugged on the fish and the fishing line jogged up and down.

"This is wonderful. You...you are amazing." Phoebe leaned across the banquet and managed to give Magnus a quick kiss on the cheek.

"One afterenoon I'll stop by with the little propeller that makes it go in the wind—and we'll find the best place to mount it. Your deck railing, maybe."

"Perfect. Then I can watch out my kitchen window."

Phoebe played with it several moments more before she stood and grabbed the coffee urn. "Keep it here for me while I work, ok?" She leaned down and gave Magnus a second kiss. His cheek was warm and full, and her cheeks burned for a moment afterward. The sweetest of men.

Why, then, had she said "No" when he asked her to join him for dinner? Stupid girl, she thinks. She picks up the whirligig and tugs on the fish, again and again, so many times the fishing pole, rising up and down seems to hum. Selfish girl, she thinks. Plain selfish. Magnus lost his beloved wife. We are two people who could share company and conversation. Even so, she answered his invitation with, "Oh, Magnus, thank you. But I can't stay for dinner, I've got—"

Aware of her ways, Magnus cut in—kindly let her off the hook before she went on. "Yes, yes. Understood. Maybe just a cup of coffee then? No. Not coffee. Not at this hour. Sit and have a glass of wine."

And Phoebe did sit. Because the thing is, she really wanted to feel completely safe for a spell. That's what Magnus gives her in spades—a sense of safety. Growing up in Norway, he'd been a cross-country skier. On the Olympic team one year, maybe several. He'd even won medals. Dorothy told everyone. She was so proud of her husband. And he'd been in the Norwegian ski infantry. There'd been medals or ribbons for that, too. Hearing these tales, Phoebe tried to imagine skis and icicles and toboggans and mittens. Snow as high as rooftops and wool underwear and reindeer. But how? She's lived in Georgia all her life, even went to college in Atlanta nearby. To her, snow—the meager coating she's seen fall and melt—is as fleeting as, well, her dreams.

When he moved to the Midwest, Magnus had kept up with his skiing. Now, in Georgia, he hikes and kayaks. In her mind's eye she sees his arms and legs like pistons, so strong and steady. Sometimes it makes her long to be closer to Magnus. Another reason she said "No" to dinner. Phoebe stops playing with the whirligig and runs her fingers along the wooden pieces, smooth as skin. Sitting on the banquette across from Magnus earlier Phoebe had thought, *He's so much older than you.* Now, sitting alone in the near dark, she thinks, *Who the hell cares?*

When she was trying to buy a house a few years ago, and was completely overwhelmed contemplating mortgage rates and such, Magnus didn't take over. Instead, he sat her down and worked with her in-between her shifts at the restaurant. "I could never choreograph a dance, Phoebe," he'd said, "That's an art. But I do understand numbers. I can teach you this stuff." And he did. Broke it all down, even told Phoebe she had a knack for it. "I think maybe dance steps are not so different from equations, Phoebe. You so easily follow everything I teach you."

But the pleasure of Magnus's company is just one of many things Phoebe denies herself. It wouldn't be right or, What would be the point? are but two of the excuses she makes. So, no dinner. But Phoebe did join Magnus for a glass of wine. And she did enjoy herself.

The restaurant hadn't been busy. The dinner crowd had yet to arrive in earnest, so Chef Henry was enjoying a breather. He left the kitchen and came over to the booth, put his hand on Magnus shoulder and said, "Our best customer," before he turned his attention to Phoebe and added, "And our very best waitress!"

"I'm a lucky man," said Magnus.

"Dinner?" Henry asked, raising his eyebrows at Phoebe as he did. Phoebe let Magnus answer.

"Miss Phoebe has agreed to have a glass of wine with me, Henry. I'm thinking two glasses of that dry Riesling. Love that one." He paused and looked at Phoebe, "Good?"

"Yes, yes, thanks, Magnus."

"You got it." Henry headed back to the kitchen, looking over his shoulder and meeting Phoebe's eye with a look she couldn't discern then or now: stern? sad? mad?

"You haven't mentioned your dancing in a long time, Phoebe," Magnus had begun, "I enjoyed those shows. Dorothy, too, when she was with us. Anything in the works?"

"Oh, I am through with that, Magnus," Phoebe answered. "An hour and forty-five-minute drive each way for practice three times a week..." Phoebe fished the pen out from the hair above her ear and rolled it back and forth on the table between them. "We never got huge audiences. So much work and for what? You were a trooper coming to our performances."

"But didn't you stay over those nights? After practice...performances. With that nice boyfriend of yours? Arthur? Or was it Alan?"

"Alex. Yes. He was nice. Is nice."

"So, which is it?"

"Oh, I still talk to him. I mean, we were together nearly a decade, and it's not as if we fought or anything. But he was...I was..." Phoebe didn't finish her sentence. Instead, she thought, *How do you explain a near miss? And why bother?*

Magnus reached across the table, squeezed Phoebe's hand and said, "All things come to she who waits." In the silence that followed, he kept his broad hand cupping hers until she slowly pulled it back into her lap.

"Is that so, Magnus?" Phoebe put both hands down on the table between them. "An old Norwegian proverb perhaps?"

"*Ach,* who knows. I'm saying it to make you feel better. But also because I think it's true. Or at least it will seem true when life falls into place, just as you want it to." Magnus lifted his wine glass and continued. "Then you will say, 'Oh, Magnus is so brilliant!'"

Phoebe clinked her glass against Magnus', said, "*Skol!,*" laughed, and went on. "Anyway, now that Alex and I have split, I don't have the wherewithal to do all that driving. I swim more now. It's fine."

"Working here is enough?"

"Oh, I miss the troupe. The camaraderie. But it's fine. I've got that here. I'm fine. Fine."

"But you orchestrated it all—choreographed the pieces. You want to keep doing that or something like it, don't you? Something creative?" Magnus slapped his palm down, color in his face. "It's not 'fine' to stop doing something you love and have a gift for."

"Maybe I can be Santa's helper, Magnus. You know, help you sand the kindergartners' blocks or something."

"Oh, I'd be happy to have your help. But that's my thing, Phoebe. You have to work on yours." He shook his large head. "'Fine.' *Ach.* Such a dull word. 'Fine' is nonsense."

"I'm thinking on it. No more choreography and dancing. But I've got some ideas. In the meantime, this really is enough. All fine." She swept her arm to take in the whole restaurant. "All of it. All of you. My family."

Magnus shook a finger at her, "There's that 'fine' again. *Ach* to that!"

Phoebe took another tiny sip of wine—she so wanted to make the glass last. "You and Dorothy were lucky. Got it right the first time. When you were young. A whole long life together. And here I am, 41, already!"

Before he could answer, Phoebe leapt into the void. "Tell me about snow, Magnus. Huge snows. You're Norwegian for goodness' sake!"

Magnus was gracious enough to bow to her turn in the conversation. He described all the different types of snow: clouds of snow, icy snow, slushy snow, flake snow, ice-crusted snow, swirling snow, melting snow, drift snow, snow smoke, snow pellets, corn snow, powder snow, ghosts in the snow. By the time he finished, their cheeks were both as rosy as if they were sitting in front of a blazing fire in a yellow clapboard house on a fjord. Barely taking a breath Magnus reeled off a string of snow words in Norwegian: *snjór, mjöll, hjarn, kafsnjór, bleytuslag, hundslappadrífa, hríð, moldbylur, snjófok, aska, ofankoma, bylur, hret, kafaldsbylur* until both he and Phoebe were laughing. He stopped to take a breath and another sip of wine. Someone came through the front door of the restaurant and with them a burst of wind entered, too: enough to lift a lock of Magnus' strawberry and silver hair and leave it curling towards his right eye. Whoosh.

"You hear that?" Magnus said dramatically. He pushed his lips out to form a little "o" and blew out a long breath. It reached Phoebe.

"It's the wind. There's a blizzard, a *snøstorm*, out there! Just wait. In a minute a sheaf of snow will slide down off the slate roof, like a duvet falling to the floor—a beautiful, soft sound."

"Whatever will we do?" Phoebe said, breathlessly, "Will the snow block the windows? The doors?"

"*Uff da!* Well, if we are *innesnødd*," Magnus continued, "trapped inside by the snow, we'll throw another log on the fire! In Norway, we practice *koselig*, just being cozy, you know. We have no choice. Long dark winters. Whole months with no sun." Magnus took a large gulp of wine and when he leaned forward, Phoebe leaned in, too, and swept the stray lock of hair back from his eye. Remembering that impulsive gesture makes Phoebe blush now. How unlike me, she thinks.

Magnus hadn't paid attention. He'd just gone on. "Maybe we'll bundle up and go for a trudge. We have a saying in Norway, 'There's no bad weather, only bad clothing.'"

Then Magnus went on to name some towns running up the coast of Norway: Florø. Bodø. Tromsø. Vardø. Spoken in a long line it made a beautiful song. He grabbed Phoebe's pen off the table as he finished, looked around for something on which to write, and settled for the square paper cocktail napkin under his wine glass. It was slightly damp so when he wrote "Tromsø'" the "o's" blurred a bit, turning them into fat snowballs. He pushed the napkin across the table to Phoebe.

"This is where I'm going to move, Phoebe." Magnus banged his pointer finger down on the napkin. "End of October or November at the latest—after the current owners move out. I want to be well settled before Christmas. My kids found the house, right in the city center on the little island called Tromsøya. It's not easy to find homes there or really anywhere in Norway these days. It's perfect. Just a walk away from my grandchildren...and the university...the lake..."

"You have a lake here." Phoebe said with uncharacteristic sharpness.

"But none of my children, Phoebe. No grandchildren, either. I think even Dorothy would approve."

"But I don't!" Phoebe blurted it out. Then she turned red, shook her head, and looked across at the kitchen to find Henry staring at her. She looked back at Magnus. "No. That's not true. Of course, being back in Norway will be wonderful for you." She pulled the cocktail napkin into her lap and began to shred it to pieces.

"Enough said, my dear. I am touched—very."

Even sipping as slowly as possible Phoebe's glass was empty and she knew if she left immediately, she'd still have time for a swim before dark. When she held up her empty glass Magnus hadn't pressed her to stay. He knew better, even knew Phoebe counted on his invitations, even if she seldom accepted.

TWELVE

No matter what time he leaves the restaurant, Henry—Chef Henri, that is—always smiles to see his mellow yellow Land Cruiser parked out back. It takes a real key, inserted into a real lock and then putting that same key into a real ignition to get the truck moving. Then move she does, albeit guzzling gas with the same exuberance that his mongrel sheepdog, Ragout, guzzles water on hot summer days. Days like today. Though he would have loved a vintage pick-up truck, bright red, thank you, Henry was damn pleased to inherit his Uncle Don's 1982 Toyota—the long-body 60 series. His Uncle only drove it around Hilton Head Island and then kept it garaged through all the years diabetes left him too hobbled with neuropathies to drive. On every visit to South Carolina, Henry took his uncle out for a spin after which they would both pat the truck on the flank and say, often in unison, "Love this baby!" On what would be their last drive together, they'd both cheered when the mileage meter ticked to "55,000." That's when Uncle Don—who had no kids of his own—had smiled his half-blind smile, clapped his hand on Henry's shoulder and promised, "Of course, she'll be yours, Henry. Sooner than later from what my doc says."

Sadly, happily, Uncle Don's death and Henry's move to the country coincided. He couldn't have afforded to garage the Land Cruiser in New York City. But here in Georgia, it's just what's needed for fetching produce from local growers, and for hauling soil, fertilizer and plants for his struggling garden. I'm no Magnus, Henry thinks as he puts the Land Cruiser into reverse: that damn old codger can grow anything, build anything. Neck craned, looking over his shoulder to back out, he sees Magnus getting into his blue Volvo wagon. Henry idles and murmurs, "Go on, old man, go on," as he watches Magnus pull away from the curb and disappear from view. Arm out his rolled-down window, Henry gives his truck a pat, and thinks, forget Magnus, nobody has a vehicle as cool as this—even if the idiots in this hillbilly town don't have the sense to know that old can be cool. He's thinking about his Land Cruiser. Not Magnus. Old. Cool. Then he does think about Magnus, bangs the heel of his hand on the steering wheel as he repeats aloud the words he overheard Magnus say to Phoebe, "All things come to she who waits." What the hell did he mean by that?

Henry backs out of the parking lot onto North Main, catching the curb as he does. His right, rear tire lets out a dull squeal and Henry thinks, "What the hell?" Five miles out he turns onto Route 23, the 12-mile stretch of road that will take him to his next turn-off. He eyes the power lines running from post to post on either side of the road and shakes his head wondering when the power company is going to trim the branches so they won't all be left in the dark for days on end when the next storm rolls across the lake.

He turns on the radio just as the announcer says, "It's eight-o-five." An hour later than Henry had planned. If dogs can be angry Ragout should be angry. But no. Like a still starry-eyed newlywed, he'll throw his delirious dog weight into Henry no matter what time he arrives home. But Henry is angry with himself. Ragout has a cedar doghouse (a Magnus masterpiece complete with peaked roof and little weathervane), a large grassy yard bordered by pachysandra on the shady side, roses on the sunny. A damn idyllic life save for the fact that Ragout spends too many hours alone, even more than usual today. Henry feels guilty about this, frets, bangs the heel of his hand on the steering wheel again, harder this time to the beat of those seven words: "All things come to she who waits." He is stung anew recalling how Phoebe brushed a lock of Magnus' hair off the Norwegian's broad and softly lined face. He wonders about the scar, how it would feel to touch.

Stupid, Henry. Stupid. Stupid. He says the word out loud. Stupid to linger and watch Phoebe and Magnus—overhear things better not overheard. See things better not seen. He fingers the hunk of lamb stowed in his pocket. Even wrapped in foil the gamey smell of it infiltrates the truck. "On my way, boy," Henry whispers, "on my way." He imagines his welcome, well knows how Ragout will nuzzle this pocket, "Soon, boy, soon." Guilt destroys the image. What if Ragout ran out of water? Henry edges too close to the side of the road and his wheels spin gravel momentarily. Guilt, guilt and more guilt. But why?

Henry slows down. Focus you damn fool. He looks left to the green, green of the unshorn grass, furry shrubs and tall timber trees—the ones the logging company hasn't cut down yet. They're going to leave the land bald by the time they get through. He's talking to himself. Dusk is a tricky time, the last of the sun is bouncing wildly on the windshield. Henry thinks back to the day he rescued Ragout from a nearby animal shelter. How he overheard one of the shelter volunteers describe Ragout's two-year history of occasional beatings, too little food, and no shelter from weather too hot and too cold. Sounds like my childhood, Henry'd thought. Even so, he refuses to measure Ragout's history of abuse against his own selfishness. He bought Ragout (Henry changed the pup's name from Sinbad) to assuage his loneliness. Without his dog, Henry would be a lost man waiting to be found. Or so his New York City buddies say. Even after three years his closest friend, Cal, still asks, "Bro'—tell me again why someone with your talent is parked in a town so tiny I can't even find it on goddamn Google maps."

The possibility of being found briefly reared its head just two weeks ago when The Atlanta Journal-Constitution—the hotshot major metro newspaper based two hours away—reviewed Just Good Food under the title, "Get in Your Car and Go for Goodness Sake" First thing Henry did was call Cal, and open with, "O ye of little faith..."

"What's up?" Cal answered, "Wait...tell me you're moving back to civilization."

"Give it a rest. No. A review. Listen." Henry put on a radio commentator voice and began, "'Warm and sunny on even the cloudiest day' and then, drum roll, it goes on: 'The menu is innovative without crossing the line into annoying, which is to say that Chef Henry Legois is clever only for taste's sake.'"

"You are the man, dude. Phone's gonna be ringing off the hook. Maybe you'll get an offer from a real city, like back here. That'd be good, right?" His friend switched to a lower pitch, "I did tell you the love of your life broke up with that gorgeous, dumb bartender?"

"Stop with that, Cal. Anyway, I like it here. Big fish and all that."

"Sure you do."

No offers from Chicago or L.A. yet, Henry thinks, but, yes, the restaurant's been busier than usual thanks to the awesome review and more out-of-town folk. Telephone pole by telephone pole, Henry recites the part of the review he's memorized: "In a six-by-six kitchen, tall, dark and handsome Chef Henry Legois turns locally-grown produce and organically sourced meats and fish into meals you might enjoy only if you were to drive out to Hartsfield-Jackson and hop a non-stop to Paris."

Pas mal. Pas mal de tout, Henry thinks to himself, which is not what Phoebe cried out when she burst into the kitchen waving the review over her head two Sundays ago: "All hail the chief. No, make that All Hail the Chef!" she'd sung out and given Henry a pat on the sleeve before taping the review to the restaurant's enormous stainless-steel freezer. Thanks to condensation, spatters of sauce, even a reminder, "Leeks/beets. Okra?" which Henry scrawled in black Sharpie when a scrap of paper wasn't handy, the newspaper review is already disintegrating. Henry frowns at the thought, passes an old couple in a rusty Honda, and makes a mental note to get a fresh copy of the review while copies are still available. Frame it safely under glass. But why bother? He knows that he, like the review, is already yesterday's news, in grave danger of becoming stale. He likes that what he cooks is consumed on the spot, or nearly so. He doesn't like paper, books, the idea of things hanging around for years, growing old and yellow. Like Magnus. But he isn't, is he, Henry? He's got more life than you.

The intersection with the state road is coming up. That's the turn off for Phoebe's place. Don't do it, Henry thinks, just go home. Ragout is waiting. Let him love you. But he turns. Can't help himself. He has to see if Magnus' car is in Phoebe's drive. Why else would he have been in such a hurry to skedaddle after his omelet? Why else would he have answered "Not tonight" when Henry had walked over and asked if he wanted his usual espresso?

As he approaches Phoebe's house, Henry slows down, then exhales with relief to see her VW is the only car in the drive. Then, oh, damn, there's Phoebe on the doorstep, her back to the street, opening the screen door to go in. Henry guns it, doesn't look back, prays she didn't catch him driving by.

THIRTEEN

Back inside, and alone, alone, alone, Phoebe is keeping busy. Busy. Busy. Busy. Empty the trash; do a load of wash. Phoebe ticks off tasks in her head. But her shoulders have begun to slump under the weight of another night alone. Stand up straighter, girl! Gird yourself. It's as if she were a piece of silk the sides of which are being pulled more and more tautly, to the point of causing an achy rupture right up though her. Does that sound too dramatic? Maybe. Maybe you've never been alone for a very long spell. Keep it together, girl, Phoebe thinks or even says out loud.

The dryer bell sounds. Something else to do. Fold. The napkin on which Magnus wrote "Tromsø," the napkin she tore to shreds and stuck in her pocket, has wreaked havoc. Tiny flakes of white—a rough dusting of snow—clings to her clean laundry and must be picked off, a tedious task. Damn. Put aside the few things that need a bit of ironing. Hmmm. Maybe I'll go ahead and do that now. Postpone dinner. Slowly fill the deep cup of night. She opens the utility closet. The flimsy bracket that holds her ironing board is loose. Before she can grab it, the board falls, awkwardly, roughly into her. Ach! Maybe I can ask Magnus to fix this damn thing—and everything else that is broken around here.

A bruise blooms on the front of Phoebe's leg. It takes on the shape of a scarab and will, she knows from experience, take on that insect's rainbow colors in a day or two: pale yellow, green, rose. Goddam, it hurts. But it is also all the vague accumulated hurts that make tears spring to Phoebe's eyes. Why even bother with ice? You can't be a redhead and not have ultra-white skin that broadcasts the brunt of any and every rough encounter. She considers all of the repercussions of being so thin-skinned. Wonders if she really is "thin-skinned," you know, in that other, metaphorical sense.

To hell with ironing. Phoebe collapses onto her couch. She hasn't turned on any lamps yet. The cicadas' cacophony dies with the light. In its place comes the clatter of crickets, the rough sound made by males hoping to mate. Phoebe reaches for the novel she's been reading, opens it at the bookmark, but cannot focus. She picks up a pen from the table next to her and draws a slanted line, from top right to bottom left, through every single "o" on the page in front of her turning them into the miniscule Norwegian "ø's." It looks as if someone has stuck shovels in a hundred little snowballs.

FOURTEEN

Thanks to his stupid but reassuring detour, Henry has to drive an extra loop to hook back up to the road to his house. His thoughts fester. A few weeks ago, he overheard Phoebe tell another waitress, "Oh, I stopped seeing Alex a couple months ago. For the best. For us both." That gave Henry agita, agita that had ebbed and flowed since and, earlier this evening slowly, painfully drew back—as if a tsunami were forming—when he caught Phoebe and Magnus toast one another over their glasses of Riesling. Henry makes the right-hand turn onto the packed dirt and stones of Pine Hollow Drive, the last stretch home, recalling as he bumps along the "*Skol*" he'd overheard Phoebe speak. What a croc. *Skol*. Out loud he says, "You are not a fucking Norwegian, Phoebe!"

No matter when he stops in, Magnus always nabs the same damn booth, in Phoebe's section, of course. Maybe he knew Phoebe would be getting off her shift when he came in early for supper. Henry served them their wine himself, smiling his broadest even as he asked himself, "Do you want to make yourself miserable, you idiot?" Back in the kitchen, eyes clouded by steam from broth boiling in a huge stainless pot, he'd shaken his head, unable to settle his feathers watching the old Norwegian with Phoebe. How cozy they look, he thought, and he went on to wonder if they were seeing one another outside of the restaurant. It's not just me, he thought, anyone coming into the restaurant would find it impossible not to note the way their eyes so comfortably hold each other's. Throwing handfuls of basmati into roiling chicken broth, he had shaken his head and said "Naw—impossible" out loud. But he kept his eye on the pair, caught Magnus reach across the table to squeeze Phoebe's shoulder, and captured like a photograph the moment when he'd cupped her hand in his. He'd thrown a metal spoon into the sink, then, and the whole restaurant had gone quiet and looked his way, even Magnus. But it was not the look he craved.

Bumping the last stretch home, Henry reviews his resume to console himself. Graduate of Academie de Cuisine in Maryland, apprenticeship with May Bromfield in Austin, hired away by The Short Giraffe in New York. He'd even been in the running for the "Oscar of the cooking world," a James Beard Foundation Award, two years ago. Hell, he thinks, I'm hardly just a cook for crike's sake! Omelet I made for Magnus earlier? Perfection.

It's no wonder his New York pals wonder why Henry suddenly packed up his knives and his toque and drove to Georgia after just a short conversation and verbal handshake with the owners of Just Good Food. He was like some young doctor who obstinately decides he wants to go to an inaccessible town in Alaska to care for patients of all ages, with a myriad of complaints, rather than stay in a well-heeled, big city practice.

The owners of Just Good Food—a local but sophisticated and well-traveled couple to be sure—were puzzled: "You've had three years at a three-star spot in Manhattan, Henry," they'd said when he arrived after a nearly non-stop drive from Manhattan to see the place. "We're thrilled at the prospect," they continued, "Be crazy not to. But take some time. Think. Do you really want to be the chef here?"

Henry well remembers how he smiled and said, "No question," quickly, firmly. Maybe he wanted to seal the deal before he changed his mind. Maybe he saw the promise of the place, with its wood floors and tables, checkered napkins, large windows, fresh flowers, spotless kitchen—saw it as an opportunity to practice his trade just as some young doctor would—in close contact with a broader range of customers, no doubt ready to lodge more complaints and, he hoped, more spontaneous praise, than even the most prestigious position in Manhattan would allow. And he needed to wipe the slate clean. Too many ill-fated relationships had left a bad taste in his mouth, most especially the last—love of his life who left him for a damn bartender. A bartender!

The restaurant is still full of promise Henry thinks as he stops at his red mailbox, jumps out, grabs the few pieces of junk mail inside, then hops back into his truck for the rocky drive down to his house. I can make magic, my own magic, with no one standing guard and with customers just feet away. I can give new ideas a try and watch folks dig in and smile, or grimace when a new spice explodes on their tongues. He considers how often customers stop at the large rectangular window that opens into the space where he cooks to give him a thumb's up. Just this noon, a regular had stopped, poked his head into the kitchen and said, "Damn it, Henry, you've done it again. Now I know the difference between fries and French fries." And last week another had said, "Don't know how you pronounce it—'pappy-ote' or whatever—but that fish in the little paper envelope was f-ing unbelievable."

Baveuse is a French cooking term meaning moist, juicy, a bit runny or undercooked. That's how Henry delivered Magnus' omelet earlier—filled with vegetables from Magnus' own garden. Phoebe had already left, her wave from the door for Magnus alone.

"Vakker!" Magnus boomed when Henry served him, "I wish Phoebe had stayed to enjoy this with me." Henry had nodded, seriously, and waited a beat, hoping Magnus would say more, maybe even, "Take a seat, Henry!" But Magnus was eating too delightedly to speak. Or so it seemed.

Henry pulls onto the matted grass that serves as parking area beside his house. The moment he opens the door Ragout rushes up to him, tail beating furiously, and begins his delirious dog dance around Henry's legs, nearly knocking him over. That performance complete, Ragout nuzzles his master's pocket, the one in which Henry has stashed the primo piece of lamb. *Tonight,* Henry misses his cue. He can't stop thinking about Magnus and Phoebe.

Ragout looks at Henry, nuzzles his pocket once more, gives up, lowers his front paws while keeping his hindquarters up and barks once, twice, even a third time—a reaction as out of character as Henry's, which is to scream at his beloved pet, "Shut the fuck up!"

<h1 style="text-align:center">FIFTEEN</h1>

George didn't waste a minute. Couldn't. As he finished securing the cargo box atop their SUV, preparing for departure to Nantucket, he told Harriet his plans, well, at least in part. No preamble: he just spat it out.

"When I fly back after the 4th, I've got a meeting scheduled with my partners."

"Meeting about...?"

George moved to the back of the car and opened the trunk. He really didn't want to face Harriet head on. "I'm telling them I'm taking a leave of absence."

"A leave? You?" Harriet stared at him, but his head was half buried in the car trunk where he pushed a box aside. "What on earth are you talking about, George?"

George stepped away from the car and faced her, but he said nothing. Not right away.

"Hel—lo—?" Harriet had stopped moving, her arms akimbo, and was staring at her husband. He turned to double-check one of the clips on the carrier. She considered hitting him, a firm but playful punch in the back. But she stopped herself. On the one hand, she didn't really believe George of all people would do such a thing, but at the same time there was something in his voice that gave her the unsettled feeling he might actually mean it. She grabbed a big canvas bag full of beach towels, tapped her husband on the shoulder and asked as she handed them over, "You are kidding, right?"

George hoisted the bag up into the carrier and then turned to look Harriet deeply in the eyes. He hoped she might look as deeply back, catch sight of something, a hint of someone new, truer. Not a flicker of recognition, so he simply said, "Completely serious, sweetie."

"What are we talking here? A few weeks? A month?"

"Longer." George slapped the side of the SUV twice. "Forever maybe."

At this, Harriet struck, jabbing her index finger into the soft hollow below his ribs. "You can't make this sort of decision alone, George." She'd used enough force it set him back on his heels for a moment. "I mean, Jesus, what in god's name are you leaving for?"

George crossed his arms over his chest and was silent. Harriet didn't wait for an answer.

"They'll keep you on full salary, won't they?" George guessed that was her uppermost concern.

"It'll depend, I guess. I'll get my share from the partnership for a good long while. And I have hundreds of billable hours stacked up. I'm just not sure what's fair. To the firm..." George let that sentence go before starting anew. "Because I don't know how long..."

"Fair to the firm? Are you fucking kidding, George? What about your family? This affects us all. Affects everything."

George reached his arms out thinking to hug his wife, but she wheeled round, shaking her head. He spoke to her back as she slid the box of beach towels forward in the pod. "You don't have to worry about money, Sweetie. You know that..."

"So, you don't know how long. I got it. So, what's your big idea, George? Let's hear it so your little hiatus from the firm makes some sense."

As Harriet said this an image came to her, an image of George and Samantha out under the beech tree during their dinner party a few weeks back. George and Samantha. George and Samantha. Talking. Talking. Talking. She dropped the stack of paperbacks she was about to put in the back of the car and rather than pick them up, she kicked at one, sending it scattering off the drive onto the lawn.

"What were you and Samantha yakking about at our party, anyway. She's like a moth to a flame with you." Harriet kicked at another book. "Hovering. Trapping you in corners. And she's always on about everyone needing to 'find their passion.' I don't know how Greg stands it. He's like a Buddha—never saying a word. Just that smile."

"He loves her." George said it flatly.

Lila's pink bike helmet tumbled off the roof of the car to the ground. "Damn!" Harriet picked it up and tried to throw it into the pod. But she wasn't tall enough. And intimations of anger and jealousy made her clumsy. Angry. "And you—you just egg Sam on by listening so intently, as if you think what she's saying is important."

"I like Samantha, honey. She's our friend. They're our friends. Anyway, it's her work. Talking. Listening. She's a therapist."

"Well, she brings it home, brings it everywhere. She's always trying to pry things apart. Leave of absence? What a crock." Harriet now tried to throw a bike pump up into the pod. It missed by a mile and fell back, glancing her on the forehead. George caught it just before it hit the driveway. "Oh, man—I'll run and get some ice for that."

"Don't bother. I'm going in. You finish here."

On the kitchen counter were a few books George had ordered: *The Zeppelin Story*, *Transatlantic Airships: An Illustrated History*, *Dr. Eckener's Dream Machine*, *America's Forgotten Airship Disaster: The Crash of the USS Shenandoah*, and the rather daunting tome, *Airship Technology*. George planned to use the hours on the ferry to continue paging through a few.

Harriet looked at the stack and away again. No curiosity. Zip. Nada. How could she ignore the cover of the topmost book which featured a photograph of an enormous beast of an airship, a gleaming, metal whale on an ocean-size field, surrounded by a crowd so large that only by looking closely could you see that they were individual people? A real photo, not an illustration on some H. G. Wells work of fiction. How could she not look? And if she had looked, how could she not have been curious enough to read the flap copy and learn that those people were on a field in Friedrichshafen, Germany, at 7:54 on the morning of October 11, 1928, waiting for the Graf Zeppelin LZ-127 to take to the sky—the first ever commercial airship passenger flight to cross the Atlantic.

When he'd gotten the book in the mail, George couldn't take his eyes off that cover. He imagined himself on that field in Germany amongst the farewell party, working his way through all those men, women and children to see the football-field long airship up close. He imagined his head falling backwards to watch as the Zeppelin took to the air. Imagined being one of hundreds, maybe it was a thousand, holding their collective breath before they began cheering, shouting, and singing the German anthem, the *Deutschlandlied*.

If he were to walk into the kitchen now, George might have picked up the topmost book, pointed to the people in the photo and said to his wife, "Look, Harriet. Look at this crowd! They were there. They witnessed the lift-off of the first lighter-than-air ship to make a transatlantic crossing. Just look at them. Listen to them singing, hollering with delight and throwing their caps into the air with joy."

Maybe he even would have said, "That's what I'm planning. To sail in an airship."

He could have told her what he already knew: that just shy of 112 hours later—on October 15, 1928—that airship had landed at Lakehurst, New Jersey with its 20 passengers and a crew of 40—all of whom, no doubt, breathed bellows-size sighs of relief having weathered not one but two lines of powerful squalls that battered the ship and necessitated life-threatening, in-air repairs.

Yes, if George had walked into the kitchen, he might have shown Harriet the books in an effort to make his dream comprehensible. He stood at the car and considered it. Even wondered if his wife would reappear shaking one of the books over her shoulder asking, "Whose book is this?" But she didn't. She was blind to those books, even though she used them as a platform when she pulled a zip-lock bag out of a drawer and stuffed it with ice. Blind even when one cube slipped out and began releasing cold drops of water, a few of which acted like miniscule magnifying glasses, highlighting select details on the photograph of the Zeppelin—a tethering line here, a propeller there. A few faces in the crowd, too—a child in a short jacket and cap holding his mother's hand. Harriet was blind to this drama. She just kept moving about the kitchen throwing snacks and drinks in the ice chest, all while pressing an ice pack to her temple which, curiously, never even bruised.

SIXTEEN

The Paxtons are on Nantucket from the first of July through Labor Day—their routine since the year before Karen was born, sixteen years ago. After they started having children, they would drive up together and one or the other of them would fly home to work for two weeks before coming to "spell" the other for the next two weeks. When they'd been at their jobs long enough, they stretched it to a month. Harriet liked July; George, August. Whoever goes home to work also flies back and forth on weekends. Usually. And, of course, they all pack up the car and drive home together. Nothing will be different this summer, at least at the outset.

The older children have jobs. Ben at the yacht club teaching at the sailing school, and Karen as an au pair for the family renting the sprawling, grey-shingled place across the street. Lila, who would have had too much time alone otherwise, is signed up for a science camp run by the Maria Mitchell Association. When Harriet and George read through the schedule of activities, they'd worried it would be a bit over Lila's head. The first day was to be spent exploring the science behind black holes. Good gracious. Black holes!

But Lila is a curious and agreeable little thing. When her parents read the brochure aloud to her, she shrugged her shoulders and said, "That's the brick building near town that also has the aquarium?" Her parents nodded and she went on, "And the dome where you can go at night to look at stars, right?"

"We took you there with your brother and sister last year."

"In my pajamas?" Lila said, "Well, I guess that's ok." Then her face turned serious. "But not all day, every day, right?" she asked, "I want to go to the beach with everybody else in the afternoons."

Her parents nodded in unison and her father said, "Just eight to twelve, Whirligig. You won't miss beach time with the gang," and he hugged her.

Since it was 4th of July week, George stayed on the island through the following Monday so he could drive Lila to her first day of camp. The two woke early, long before Ben and Karen or Harriet got up. Sitting in the kitchen, father and daughter quietly spooned mouthfuls of granola and blueberries, bathed in early sunlight and milk, as out the window heavy fog was making the yarrow and false indigo, the pasture rose and grasses that waved over the heath, wink and sparkle. They lifted their heads to see birds dart in and out of this scene, grabbing berries off the bushes below. That's where the ones they were eating now had come from. They'd picked them the day before until it was too dark to see.

The Paxton's house (they rented it for 6 summers in a row before purchasing it from the elderly owners) is in 'Sconset, on the far eastern side of the island. Often it is foggy out there an hour or two after sunrise and again late in the afternoons. Sometimes it turns sunnier each mile you drive toward town. Or vice-a-versa. This morning, the twenty-minute ride along Milestone Road is the former—foggy—like driving on a fat slab of bacon, throwing off thick, fragrant smoke.

Lila climbed onto the front seat, backpack on her lap, and immediately rolled down the window. George did the same. Then he opened the sunroof. They wanted the fog to envelop them. It made them laugh. For no reason. And when George looked over at his daughter he saw how the air had changed her. "You look wild!" And indeed she did. The wind and wet made her red hair curl and fly out from her head to such an extent that by the time she walked into the large hall where the other campers were gathering, she looked like a possessed poet, stepping inside after a long walk across the Scottish moors.

"I'll be back at noon on the dot." George gave Lila a hug as he left her, trying to quickly smooth down her hair as he did. But it was hopeless. Besides, it seemed to him that her burr of untamed curls was a perfect outgrowth of her captivating soul, one that pulled in everything around it with a unique and generous gravitational force.

SEVENTEEN

Lunch crowd gone, dinner prep done, Henry decides to run home mid-afternoon, throw a ball around with Ragout, and cut a few handfuls of basil and oregano from his garden. He needs it for a pesto he plans to use in the sauce for his evening special. Dolores and Phoebe are wiping down tables and re-setting them. He turns at the door. "Running home for an hour or so. Who's on this eve?"

Dolores looks up. "Sandy and one of her daughters."

"The A Team."

"Ha! 'A Team' my ass, Henry. You know damn well Phoebe and I run circles around everyone else here. Hell, we could probably even cook better than you do."

"Fat chance." Henry whacks the bell on the front door with force as he leaves and sings along with it. "Ring-a-ding-ding, Ladies, ring-a-ding-ding."

A few miles out on a deserted stretch of the State Highway Henry sees a solitary worker from the power company, his truck parked just off the road. He's making a lasso of thick black electrical cord that hangs down from a nearby power pole. It's pooled on the dirt in a tangle that leaps in fits and starts as the worker loops it into perfect circles using his elbow as fulcrum. The worker is tall and slim, a tan cowboy hat shading his eyes. He wears jeans and a tool belt. Henry slows to nearly a stop and his eye travels quickly down the man's torso—shoulder to chest to waist to hip—and from there down a long leg that ends in a butterscotch-colored boot, laced up the front, and discolored to pitch black a good fat inch all around the sole. Henry doesn't wait to answer the question forming in his head, *Maybe he'll know*. He pulls over quickly, sharply, scattering stones, and leaves his truck running thinking, *This'll only take a minute*.

The worker stares at Henry as he approaches, nary a hint of surprise in his eyes. "Any idea when they're going to cut these back?" Henry points up at the pines. "Or down?"

The worker yanks the circle of black cord resting between his thumb and forefinger even more taut under his elbow. Then he takes a few strides toward Henry, as a dog might, nose in, paw back. "You live nearby?"

"Close enough. I can't drive this stretch without worrying what'll happen when some storm barrels through and these pines topple."

"Not my job. Another crew takes care of that."

"So, you don't have a clue?" It is Henry's turn to move a step closer and when he does the other man transfers the fat coil of electrical wire into his opposite hand and lets it drop to his side. "Not a clue."

Henry shifts his weight onto one leg, his front leg, and his whole body follows suit. The other man slaps the circle of cord against his thigh, slowly, like a drumbeat, eyeing Henry slowly from head to toe as he does. With the fifth beat he stops and lifts the lasso of cord up, straight-armed, and brushes it the length of Henry's chest, catching Henry's chin at the end. It is the work of an instant. The two lock eyes, black and blue. Henry brings his back leg in alignment with his front, a small step that is nevertheless a leap forward, a leap into the sacred space humans trespass only with intent—that invisible circle around each of us that is, by consensus, inviolate unless we invite another in. Without a sound, the whole of his weight comes to bear.

It isn't long after that the two men come back out of the trees, not the tall pines lining the edge of the road but the blurry new growth, shoulder-height, a vulnerable soft, thick green screen that the logging company always plants after their merciless clearcutting.

Henry's truck has been running the whole time. There isn't another vehicle in sight. He opens the door to his Toyota, steps onto the running board, and calls out, "I'm the chef at Just Good Food."

The other man lifts the hat off his head, runs a hand through his matted black hair. "Maybe I'll stop by for a bite."

Henry shouts: "Do" and waits. The other man replies with a lazy wave as he leans over and picks up the electrical cord he dropped when the pair disappeared into the trees. The man is purposeful; he sets it back under his elbow and resumes making perfect circles. Yards away, the tangle of loose cord on the ground once again jerks, this way and that.

Before he sets off, Henry swings out onto the highway and turns back to and bring his truck closer to the man. His left arm is dangling out the window, palm down, cupping the outside flank of the truck which he caresses with his fingers. "Just Good Food," he says again. "You can't miss it. Wooden sign with an arm pointing."

The worker looks at Henry, his black eyes steady. "Yeah. So you said." He begins to walk away then turns and says, over his shoulder, "But this ain't my usual territory, you know."

EIGHTEEN

George flew home from Nantucket at the end of the long 4th of July weekend. He had a window seat and as the plane rose into a cloudless sky he couldn't take his eyes off the fin-shaped island floating in the blue sea below. The nearly hidden rough roads that cross the moors there, the ones only accessible by foot or four-wheel drive, were like the lines running across his own palms. Give George a map of Nantucket and he could, like a fortuneteller, trace those paths with his forefinger and tell you what lay at the end of each. He knew it that well. And knowing it that well, he loved it as he loved no other place. Leaving he always felt as if a silken thread attached to his solar plexus were being stretched more and more tautly with each mile he travelled away. First a tiny tug, then unrelenting pressure, then pain as wily as nerve pain—impossible to dull and cropping up in unexpected parts of his body and brain. He'd felt the same attachment and the same pull when he saw the dirigible.

Going to and fro the island by the slow car ferry was always George's first choice. That way, you arrived in time, in human time, the miles and the minutes closely aligned. You felt the slow push away from the dock and watched everyone in line for the next boat and the Steamship Authority workers wave goodbye. You saw the wake—a foamy "V"— take shape, its long sides growing deeper and longer as the ferry gained speed. And depending whether you were going over or returning home, watched the dockside restaurants or Coast Guard Station and Brant Point Lighthouse, and all the big summer homes on the water, become smaller and smaller. Then you settled in for the two hours plus of nothing that is everything: ocean, air, clouds; the dull roar and numbing vibration of the engines; the smell of oil from below, and of coffee and warm corn muffins and hot dogs from the snack bar above, all mixing with a whiff of Pine-Sol whenever the door to the head opened or slammed shut.

If it were stormy outside, there would be wet everywhere: huge droplets moving as slowly as spilled mercury down the big, sliding windows flanking the sides and seats of the inside decks and making the dull gray painted floors dangerously slippery. Dogs on leashes pulling children who tried to hold on tight like water-skiers.

But no matter what the conditions, and no matter how crowded the ship, George could always achieve a state of near perfect repose on the slow car ferry. Not because it was utterly quiet. No, indeed. Quite the contrary. It was noisy. But it was noise that agreed with him. A particular white noise concocted of old timers slurping coffee, mother's scolding their excited children, young couples giggling and kissing, babies crying, and always the enormous engines vibrating at a pitch that seeped into and calmed George's body like heavy water. It was noise that made the contours that distinguished George Paxton from the rest of the world disappear. How he craved that.

This year, as always, the Paxtons had taken the car ferry on their way to Nantucket. George had waited in line to park their laden SUV on board while Harriet and the kids ran up the gangway to snag seats.

"Get a booth!" George yelled, abandoned in the car.

"We know, Dad." The kids rolled their eyes in unison and Ben spoke for them all. "We've only done this like a thousand times."

"Really, George. We know the drill. Bring the cooler with the snacks, would you?" As she walked away George watched her knot the sweater she carried tightly around her neck. Just so.

But this morning, on his way back home alone, he had to fly. He had to get to work. He had called a meeting with his fellow partners. Taking a commuter flight was expedient. It was also painful. It gave him no time to adjust. To look down and see the island floating there—its singular shape—well, he just couldn't reconcile that with recent experience that included briny tastes and salty smells and thick foggy air. The experience of sandy skin and worrying about tick bites and making whistles out of sea grass and getting hammered by the big waves at Madequecham or Cisco.

At the end of one summer, way, way back when George was in college, he had postponed and postponed his departure from Nantucket until the only way to get back to the mainland in time for the start of his fall semester was to fly. Once airborne, he had looked out the window and was able to spot the house in Madaket he'd shared with eight of his buddies. He could make out the bike path he'd ridden every day to get into town where he worked as a bellhop. To not be on that path—to be going "off island" or "to the mainland" as Nantucket-folk said—was so unbearable he had broken down into quiet sobs. The young girl sitting next to him whispered to her mother, "What's wrong with him, Mom?" and her mom replied, also sotto voce, "Shhh, sweetie. Someone he knows probably just died."

She was right, in a way. Whenever he left the island, there was no way to bring back alive the person he had been there.

George remembered all this on the commuter flight from Nantucket to Westchester County. He also remembered the conviction he had had from the first summer he had taken the ferry there as a teenager—the conviction that he would not leave the island the same person he had been on the voyage over.

It had always proved true.

NINETEEN

George was at Westchester Airport by 8 and at the Starbucks in New Canaan before 9. It wasn't his favorite coffee spot, not by a long shot, but it was on his way. He wanted to grab a cup, get home, change and get to the office. He'd called for a meeting of all the partners where he planned to share, or rather declare, his intention of taking a leave of absence from the firm.

"Home again, home again." Samantha was sitting at a round table with the *New York Times* and a cup with the square tag of a tea bag dangling over the side. Was it inevitable that he would bump into someone he knew? Inevitable that person would be Samantha? Perhaps.

"Well, look who's here. Hi, Sam. Are you my welcome home committee of one?" George got into the short line at the counter and then turned back towards Samantha. "Home until Friday. May even sneak back to the island late Thursday night." George turned to tell the barista his order. "Tall black. Thanks. And one of the scones there." George tapped his finger on the display case, "Blueberry," then turned back to Samantha. "Just got back. Have to drop some things at home and then skedaddle into the office."

"Can't you sit for a second...?" Samantha smiled her biggest, broadest smile and continued, "...when I went to all this trouble to be here to welcome you?"

George was balancing his coffee and scone and it seemed simpler to put them down on Samantha's table. But he remained standing. Samantha spoke again.

"I want to ask you something."

"And that would be what?"

"Oh, for heaven's sake, George, sit, sit!

George grabbed a sugar and wooden stirrer and obeyed. "OK. I'm sitting." He smiled and shook sugar into this coffee. "Shoot."

"Lila told me about your barn. The night we all had dinner. She was sitting on the floor with her caterpillars when I brought in the dishes."

"She did, did she? And how did that come up?"

"I think I said something about her being 'handy' like her father and she told me about your 'tinkering barn.'"

"She used that word? 'Tinkering?'"

"She did."

"That's my girl."

"And all these years I assumed it was just a picturesque old ruin. A 'folly' or whatever it is the English call them. Something nice to look out at over the crest of your back 40."

"A 'folly,' yes, I like that. 'My folly.' Well, maybe that's fitting."

"Oh, for god's sake, George. Lighten up."

"It was a real ruin. But I restored it. Went all over the place—as far as New Hampshire—looking at boards people were selling after they'd knocked down old barns." George paused to take a gulp of coffee, bite of scone, before going on: "I was obsessed with finding the exact blueish gray to match the original boards, inside and out."

"Because?"

"Because I work on my bikes in there. And other stuff."

"And you like things neat and tidy. And beautiful." Sam spoke, laughed, and continued: "And here I thought it was filled with dirty lawn equipment and pesticides, pool chemicals or some such. But Lila made it sound like it's a real space, a livable place." Samantha bounced the tea bag in her cup as she continued. "She obviously thinks it's very special. Magical."

"Insulation, all new wiring—even plumbing. All the comforts of home. Ben used to like hanging out there until he hit his teens. Then all bets were off. Lila's the one who loves it most." He started to gather his things. "Listen, I've gotta' get going, Sam."

George stood, gave Samantha a squeeze on the arm. "Nice to see you. As always. Say hi to Greg. Maybe the three of us can meet for dinner one night—keep the old bachelor-for-a week company."

Samantha grabbed his wrist, nearly causing a coffee accident. "I want to visit you there one day, George."

"Nantucket?"

"No, no, not Nantucket!" Sam grimaced. "What in God's name would I want to go there for?" Samantha grimaced again and continued. "It's overrun with all my clients this time of year. No way.

You know what I want. I want to see your 'folly.'"

"My folly. Right. I feel as if your name for it is going to stick. Anyway, nothing much to see, Sam. But, sure. Yeah. You guys come by. It's light late. Maybe meet there for a glass of wine and then we can drive into town and grab some dinner."

"Not us, George, me. Me, me, me." Sam looked at him pointedly. "Anyway, it's the so-called 'nothing much' I haven't seen that I want to see."

The idea of Samantha visiting the barn, that rather isolated and very personal place with no one else around upset George's sense of equilibrium. Greatly. His folly. Yes, perhaps it was his folly. Not an artfully constructed, extravagant ornament of the sort that graced 18th century English gardens but a place for his own special madness. The place where he would begin to build his dirigible. No, George had not given up on that. If anything, the few days on Nantucket—the books he'd dipped into—had only fed his obsession.

George shook his head. He smiled, too. "You win, my dear. We'll find a time. But I'm off now."

TWENTY

Later, as George was settling into his office, logging onto his computer, he looked up and saw his doppelgänger, mere shadow, looking out the window, hands clasped behind his back, chin pointed upwards, eyes on the clouds. George looked out and up, too. When he focused back, he realized that what he'd told himself was mere shadow wasn't "mere" at all: his doppelgänger had as much substance as he did. It turned and locked eyes with George. George was quick to respond. "Yes, yes, I know. I'm on it."

Incapable of leaving anything in disarray, George was determined to finish setting up a dynasty trust for the Humphreys, a complex task given that the wealthy couple has several homes, cars, boats, art and wine collections along with five children and, at last count, 12 grandchildren. It was only by telling himself that this would be his last assignment for the firm that he was able to focus. Yes, indeed. George planned to share his decision to take a leave of absence from Glover, Epstein, Sandusky & Paxton at the partner's meeting that very afternoon. *"A leave as of July 31st. No questions, thank you. It's a private matter."* Only with this plan in mind was George able to concentrate on the legal tangle that lay in front of him.

From his days as a young attorney, George had been sought out because he was liked, easy to get along with and because his work was not only professional and effective but beautiful. Yes, beautiful. Whenever he completed a case, George would say to himself, "This is a beautiful legal instrument." If he couldn't say it his work was not done.

It wasn't hubris but a private standard that led him to use the word "beautiful." A standard set by his mentor Harold Glover, Esq., founding partner of what, at that time, was known as Glover, Epstein & Sandusky. Mr. Glover had called George in for a first review after he'd only been working at the firm for six months. George had walked across the large Oriental carpet that covered most of Mr. Glover's office floor and taken a seat. Mr. Glover did not immediately look up, but he did lift his right forefinger to acknowledge George's arrival. He was busy spreading out into a fan documents George recognized, even upside down, as the product of his own hard work. George was not nervous; he was proud of what he had accomplished so far. But he was anxious to hear what Mr. Glover had to say. He held the man in high esteem, had even studied some of his landmark cases in law school.

The mahogany desk shone, reflecting Mr. Glover's fine, high, lined forehead on one side, and George's smooth young brow on the other. When Mr. Glover did look up, he smiled at George, again lifted his right forefinger, and said one word, simply, clearly, slowly: "Beautiful." And then he'd gone on to quote Longinus: "Beautiful words are the very light of thought."

They chatted a bit longer before Mr. Glover stood, came around his desk and patted George on the back while also shaking his hand. "It's Harry, George. You call me Harry. And again, beautiful work. Just beautiful. That's what the practice of law should be. You keep it up. I know you will." Good old George, good old George. Yes, indeed. He vowed to always keep up the good work, the beautiful work.

George had come home early that day and waited for Harriet to arrive. The two had only been married for a few years and he was eager to tell his wife about his momentous meeting. George was walking in circles around their drive and ran to open the door for Harriet, beaming, when she pulled in. Harriet grabbed her purse, stuck one high-heeled foot onto the gravel and asked, "What's up?" But before he opened his mouth to share what Mr. Glover had said, his heart thumped, and his mouth closed. The simple, moving praise from Glover had given rise to a deep, precious contentment that George found he could not share, at least not with his wife. Confirmation (for Harry Glover's assessment was just that) that he had chosen a profession in which he could work "beautifully" was more than enough to keep George going. Yes, indeed.

Hiding his light under a bushel, especially his brightest lights, was George's way. He often kept things to himself. When he'd read the novel *Herzog* it was the sentence, *"And when your heart is full, keep your mouth shut also"* that most resonated most with him. Saul Bellow knew what he was talking about there. Or did he?

Seeing the dirigible had filled George to bursting. With what, you ask? Perhaps something akin to joy. And the only way to relieve the pressure was to let go, to take flight himself. He had clung so tightly to the earth. Kept the best things to himself. How tired he was of lugging those beautiful things around. He longed to give them to someone. But who? He couldn't bear to make a gift of these things which were, of course, parts of himself, and have the other person react with just a cursory, "Oh, thanks." But how long would the wrapping stay bright, the ribbon un-frayed?

In the time it took for Harriet to swing her other foot out of the car, stand, give his shoulder a little shake, and ask, "So?" George had reined in any impulse to say more than he'd had an especially good day: "Founding partner took my hand with real warmth, praised a case I'd worked on recently, and said, 'Call me Harry.'"

"'Call me Harry?' He said that? Really? Damn, you're 'in like Flynn. You'll make partner in no time." Harriet stood on tiptoe to give her husband a quick kiss. Her company ID—a stiff plastic card attached by a hook to a lanyard—was still around her neck and it turned on edge and pressed a soft spot just to the left of George's heart until she pulled away. "Make me a drink and we'll toast Mr. Glover!"

George's mind was made up. Once he finished the Humphrey case, he was done with the law. Maybe for good. Done writing legal instruments that were beautifully clear. Done helping his clients by creating agreements that were airtight. Done believing that his task was to leave no room for interpretation. Never had one of his trust or estate documents been challenged, even while other attorneys at the firm had had their work punctured, altered, subjected to requests for clarification time and time again. With each passing year, he prided himself, because not one of the legal instruments he created was ever ripped open by another lawyer or questioned in the courts.

But he could no longer bring his attention or his passion to this pursuit. He found himself turning over and over in his mind the words "revocable" and "irrevocable" —words he understood as well as anyone, but which now glowed as if lit from behind. With every appearance, as now, and with just a look, the other George forced him into a reverie that included questions about which of his personal decisions were revocable which irrevocable. Which of his feelings? Which of his likes, his dislikes, his loves, his passions?

He had to find where else beauty dwelled. He had to move beyond words. He had to take to the air and leave all this (as George thought these thoughts he unconsciously thrust out his arm and made a sweeping, 180-degree arc across the view from his corner office windows—the blue green blur of the Hudson River and Palisades.) Taking a leave of absence from work was the very least he would have to do. Having seen the dirigible in the sky, his decision was irrevocable. He said it out loud, even considered signing—with his very own signature—a beautiful airtight document, a testament to his decision.

It was not revocable. It was irrevocable.

TWENTY-ONE

"Could you stop by one day and work your magic?" Phoebe is finishing her shift, standing next to the booth where Magnus is nearly invisible save for the spray of silver- blonde curls cresting over the horizon of his *Wall Street Journal.* Hearing Phoebe's voice he lowers the newspaper, smiles up at her, and says,

"And what sort of magic might that be?"

Phoebe laughs. "I've got a list, actually. You always offer, and I don't want some random handyman, some stranger, coming in my house. No hurry. Whenever you have a minute."

"And what might your list include, my dear?"

"Bracket that's supposed to hold up my ironing board broke and the damn thing's crashed into me twice. See? Phoebe pushes her sleeve up to reveal a kaleidoscopic bruise on her forearm.

"*Ach*! Hard to miss. What else?"

"Drawer with my silverware is off the runner or something..."

"I can fix that."

"Washed all my windows last weekend and now I can't get two screens back in." Phoebe pauses for a breath. "And the toilet downstairs just runs and runs and runs."

Magnus shakes his head dramatically. "You do need help!" He takes a sip of coffee. "I've got an appointment late afternoon, but I could stop by after. Around 5 or so work?"

"Today? That'd be great, Magnus. Broken things make me crazy."

"Well, we can't have that."

"Maybe a glass of wine together—if you like. Usher in the weekend."

"*Utmerket*!" Magnus claps his hands, watches her untie her apron, "You're off?"

"Dolores took my lunch shift. So, yes, off for a bunch of errands, a swim, then home again, home again." Phoebe heads toward the back hall to hang her apron on one of the large wrought iron hooks there calling, "See you later, alligator," over her shoulder as she does.

"Alligator who?" Henry asks. But the back door has already banged shut. Phoebe is gone. Even so, he replies. "In a while, crocodile."

Phoebe stops at the grocery for some staples and a few special nibbles to have with cocktails. Her stepmother called them "num-nums." What would Magnus like? She's not sure so she chooses pâté, prosciutto wrapped around sticks of mozzarella, a block of Emmental cheese, a triangle of brie, crackers with seeds, crackers without. She picks up a little plastic tray with premade crudités. No, no. That won't do. Instead, she grabs a yellow pepper and an orange one to cut up herself. And some fat purple grapes. She's already in the check-out line but turns, says, "Sorry—forgot something," and strides back down the long aisles, slides the crackers back in their proper slots on the shelf, and grabs a crusty baguette from a basket near the deli instead. She returns the little casket of prosciutto-wrapped cheese, too, and instead chooses a tub of olives—green and black—bobbing in a tiny dark sea of herbs and oil.

If only she had taken longer. Or saved the shopping for after her swim. Or taken the groceries home first—before—even though it would have been out of the way. For days, weeks, afterwards she wonders if somehow her timing had been off. If only. If only. But she had the insulated bag with her. It wasn't a hot day. Nothing would spoil. If only. If only. Because you know what happens next. She heads to the lake where her swim is interrupted by the guy with the tool belt. The guy eating the orange.

Long after he speeds away, Phoebe lay on the grass. The word, "Sorry," hangs in the air. She waits and waits, measuring how much complete silence is enough. Finally, she lifts her head, high enough to turn and rest her right cheek on the pebble and weed-riddled grass. She stares at the lake. No thoughts fill her head. She won't allow them, swats them away the minute one tries to circle, land, bite. It's harder to pinpoint and swat away the points of pain, coming from so many directions and taking so many different forms, inside and out: burning, stinging, aching, itching, throbbing. Then she remembers and says his name out loud: "Magnus." It is the thought of him arriving at her house and worrying—even calling the police if she doesn't appear—that rouses her. She pulls her bikini bottom back up and crawls toward the gnome until she lays hands on her glasses and towel. She stands to leave, takes a step toward the road, then turns, replaces glasses with goggles and cap, and heads back down to the shore.

Water. Yes, it makes the scratches and scrapes sting. At first. But only as she wades in. Once she begins to swim and it closes over her—water—it is like an eraser, taking her back to before. Sort of. How many lengths had she swum? No idea. She starts counting anew: one, one, one across, two, two, two, back. She tries to focus but loses count. The water is so clean. She rolls onto her back and floats awhile, legs and arms outstretched. The sky above is a weather-less white, betraying nothing. She puts her feet down and can touch the lake's soft bottom. Walking toward shore, a cloud of sandy dirt disturbed by her steps gathers, rises to the surface, and bursts into a circle of tiny bubbles like exhalations around her waist. It feels as if the lake has its hands on either side of her small hips—firm, strong—and is trying to pull her back. She has no agency; her limbs are not her own.

How easy it would be to sink back. Easier than scrambling up the slope. Much. She's exhausted. The water. Why resist? What problem wouldn't it solve? But she does resist. To do otherwise would be selfish. She climbs out of the lake, stumbles up the slope and grabs hold of a root to steady herself. Magnus. Musn't worry Magnus. When she reaches the gnome, she puts on her glasses, wraps her towel around her waist and walks to her VW. As she starts the car she dials Magnus' cell. But she hits the red "End" button before it even rings.

Magnus' Volvo is parked in her drive when she arrives, off to the left, leaving her usual space free. Trusty Magnus, sitting on Phoebe's front step, toolbox at his feet. What a smile he smiles when he sees her. She attempts the same but instead spits tears, an uncontrollable eruption from mouth and eyes simultaneously. She has capsized, her boat has sunk, and here now is a lifeboat. It is only when rescue is close at hand that we fall apart. Magnus can't see her outburst from where he sits.

"You're twelve minutes late!" he yells, holding his right arm aloft and pointing at his watch. She pulls the towel she has around her up to her temples and drags it down her face. She's just come back from a swim, nothing remarkable about wet hair, wet face, right? There won't be any traces visible. Just a swim. That's all.

If only.

Magnus watches Phoebe walk up the stone path. He smells the herbs breaking under her bare feet as she moves through the air toward him. She has her glasses on, of course. Behind them, her eyes look flat, unfocused. He's never seen her right after a swim. Maybe she's always like this, distant, spent, her limbs drawn in, as if the lake has pulled a bit of life out of her, selfishly, to bolster itself.

"Sorry I'm late." Phoebe mumbles and drops down onto the stoop beside him—collapses, really—her damp towel an inelegant garment for such a beauty. He sees red scratches on her thighs.

"What's this now?" he asks. He half turns to study her face. More tiny scratches. "And a big one here." Magnus touches her forehead with tenderness. "*Liten* ones here, too." He draws his forefinger in a line down to her chin then on, softly, down her neck stopping short of a cut. He reddens to be touching her so. "And a worse one here," he nods his chin toward her forearm.

Phoebe gently pushes him back around and lets her head fall onto his shoulder. "Oh, Magnus, I took a tumble coming up the slope from the lake. That's why I'm late. No big. It's a wonder I haven't fallen before with no glasses to see properly. Damn roots or some such."

Her fingers, curled into her palms, lay in her lap. Without thinking, Magnus puts his arm around her, looks down, and sees dirt under her nails. And blood. He knows those hands. They have served him so often.

"You are not yourself." Magnus speaks in a low, very serious voice.

"Nope."

"I should leave you to yourself, perhaps?" Magnus voice goes very high pitched at the end.

Phoebe shudders and says all in one breath, "For heaven's sake no, Magnus. Stay, stay! You start—the screens in the front windows here, the laundry closet. I'll shower and you'll see."

"See what?"

"Me. Good old Phoebe." She stands and the towel slips down from her shoulders to her waist. "Anyway, you can't leave. I bought stuff for us—bread and *pâté* and olives and..." Phoebe motions her hand vaguely. Magnus sees there is blood on the towel, maybe from the cut now visible on her lower back. He doesn't touch that wound because the sight of the curve from her shoulders to her lower back, and most especially the pair of dimples at its base, leave him breathless for a moment. That is where her apron ties in back, he thinks, where the little loops of the bow flare.

Phoebe unlocks her front door, pushes the screen open, and goes in. Magnus follows but Phoebe stops him. "I forgot—groceries in the trunk." She starts up the stairs. "I'm going to shower. Can you bring that stuff in?" She doesn't wait for an answer.

Magnus goes out to the car. The insulated grocery bag is zippered and standing upright. Next to it is another tote, slumped, empty. He brings both inside and sets them on the kitchen table where there's a "To Do" list, complete with hand-drawn boxes to check off:

- ☐ Hinges on iron board holder/pantry
- ☐ Screens on lv.rm windows
- ☐ Downstrs toilet
- ☐ Top 2 kitch drawers
- ☐ Ceiling fan noise?

After putting what needs to be cool in the refrigerator, Magnus retrieves his toolbox from the front stoop and sets to work.

When she comes out of the shower and begins to dry herself off, Phoebe can hear "tap, tap, tap" then Magnus sigh, "*Ach!*" then more taps, in 4/4 time. Before she pulls on her cut-offs and a baggy white terry sweatshirt she stands and looks at herself, naked, in the big bathroom mirror. She has swum. She has showered. Vigorously. Soaping upon soaping. She even found an old bottle of Betadine and used it to expunge whatever horror she couldn't see but knew must be there. Save where there are scratches and, of course, the first bloom of bruises just above her knees, on her right cheek and the ultra-white undersides of both arms, her skin seems nearly translucent, so translucent her pale blue veins appear painted on, as if her insides are now exposed—not just the blue veins but the blood running through them—in and around her bellows lungs, her thumping heart, the mysterious workings of her brain. As if another Phoebe made of something gossamer is talking flight inside of her, batting its wings to escape.

She starts down the stairs. Her feet are bare and whitest of all, the veins crisscrossing them a Maxfield Parrish blue. They seem too vulnerable, so she goes back upstairs to grab an old pair of leather-soled slipper-socks.

Magnus' back is to her. She takes a bottle of wine out of the refrigerator and a corkscrew from the drawer he's working to fix. She has to reach around him to grab it. And it is true: when Phoebe's arm circles round him, Magnus notices that the long strands of veins running down her arm—what he would call Baltic blue—seem only a hair's-breath under her skin, lines disappearing into something unfathomable. The sight of it drags him under.

When he was a boy and on into adolescence, Magnus often went ice fishing with his father. He thinks now of the crystalline fissures that would emanate from the hole into which they would drop their fishing lines. Oh, the hours he spent, sitting in the windless cold, next to a father who rarely spoke, waiting to feel a tug, hoping to bring home a perch or zander, char or rainbow trout. Knowing how pleased his mother would be.

The ocean moves, whereas lakes, so quiescent on the surface, struck Magnus as unfathomable. Especially when frozen. When he was very young, the idea of the lake's depth was his nightmare. The black hole in the ice, created by repeated cuts with his father's awl—gushing like a geyser when they finally broke through—became, in his dreams, a black vortex into which he would be sucked. He would fall and fall and fear never to return. Many were the nights he woke screaming. Hearing him, his mother would come sit on his bed, gather him in her arms and softly sing.

> *"Vi har ei tulle med øyne blå*
> *Med silkehår og med ører små*
> *Og midt i fjeset en liten nese*
> *Så stor som så"*

When he was a grown man, his mother described how she would find him awake but not awake—his eyes open but focused not on what was in front of him—his bedroom, his own mother—but something beyond or within. *"Nattværdiers,"* she told him. Night terrors. Even now, even months away from turning 70, the thought of that fearsome dream—of an awl spinning down, down, down into the fathomless ice—is difficult to tamp down. He still can't remember the waking, only the dreaming.

"Maybe you'd like a real live cocktail instead?" Magnus is roused by Phoebe's voice. "I have vodka. In the freezer."

"Utmerket," Magnus says but he is still back in the cold, remembering now that it was after catching his first fish, a salmon, on a black February afternoon, that his dad had poured him his first taste of *Akevitt*, tapped his glass against his son's, and said, *"Skål!"*

By the time they sit, a meal-worthy tray of hors d'oeuvres between them, Magnus has checked 3 of the 5 boxes on Phoebe's "To Do" list. He raises his glass and speaks that same word, *"Skål!"* Their glasses sing out. Phoebe drinks the freezing vodka and immediately it begins to serve as anesthesia. She isn't going to sip tonight. She empties her glass like a Cossack. Falling on a root could not have created this sea change. Magnus knows this but refuses to press or even feign surprise. He grabs the vodka from the freezer to refill Phoebe's glass and when he turns to put it back, Phoebe grabs his wrist. "Just leave it here."

She will ask for another refill before long, and then simply pour refills herself. Such behavior by a girl who only ever lingered for one glass of Riesling.

When they have had their fill of vodka and olives, cheese and bread (and Phoebe more drink than food), Magnus lets her take his hand and lead him up the stairs to her bed. Neither speak. This is a first. But it will not be the last. Both of them know their days are numbered: Magnus' birthday party is only a few months away and then he is moving—oceans and oceans away. But it is not that.

Phoebe clings to him as if life depends on it. Magnus knows he is an antidote to something. What, he dare not ask. He feels no remorse, only joy. After so much talking, there is no need to talk. Even without this, before this, they could hardly have been closer. His long dormant body surprises him. They go through motions expected and unexpected, all in near silence, Phoebe with surprising urgency; Magnus carefully, gently—she has wounds.

Finally, suddenly, Phoebe drops into sleep, as if after another long cleansing swim. She is curled like a small animal, Magnus' arm circling her belly. He dare not move; he decides it best to keep watch. Laying in the dark, gazing up at the white ceiling with its texture like blown snow, he is back ice fishing with his father. He thinks less about the times he caught a fish than of the miracle of the frozen lake and of anything still living—darting here, darting there—under the foot or more of ice his father opened, first with the awl then wider, with a maul. A big open eye from which lake tears flowed.

Magnus stays awake most of the night; yes, to serve as watchman but, also, to keep his own, ancient nightmare—his childhood *Nattværdier*—at bay. But there is no night terror tonight. For the first time, he recognizes what all of those years of ice fishing, of night terrors were: patient practice for a night like this.

Just before dawn Magnus inhales so deeply the walls of Phoebe's house seem to contract and then swell as he breathes out again. Phoebe raises a tiny paw and squeezes Magnus' arm. Pure reflex. But she doesn't surface. And soon Magnus, who briefly woke, joins her, falling into a deep and dreamless sleep, his lips lax, half smiling, but not before he mouths that Norwegian lullaby, in translation now, for Phoebe:

> *This is how we all begin*
> *A single sound*
> *Evolves into a human being*
> *This is the creation of life*

Twenty-Two

Was it inevitable that Samantha would come to George's barn? That word again. Inevitable. How does the saying go? Nothing in this world is certain save for death and taxes, right? You could just as easily switch out "certain" for "inevitable."

It is true, too. The rest is people going along, nudging things in this direction or that, making decisions large and small, or sitting back and allowing things to happen. Whether you push or don't, things happen. And when they happen, they always seem inevitable, don't they?

Samantha has been pushing for greater intimacy with George for as long as he has known her. It's always seemed to him it sprang from her innate curiosity about people, and especially people who intrigued her. Even if many of those were not her clients. It's no wonder she chose to be a therapist. That was a huge difference between she and Harriet. Harriet was not curious. Not once had she asked George for details about what he planned to do after he left the firm. Whatever was in front of her was enough. Hearing, "We've got plenty of money," was enough. She had no interest in diving below the surface. She had taken George at face value all those years ago. Perhaps, God love her, that was enough for Harriet. But he should have known it would never be enough for him. He had fallen for Harriet or, if he were honest, been seduced and flattered by the idea that Harriet seemed to have chosen him, good old George, when she could have had her pick.

Back then, Harriet was one of those creatures other women envied and men were proud to have on their arm: a blonde right out of "California Dreamin'" with skin that tanned easily, a pretty face, a great figure. If that all sounds too pat it's because, at the end of the day, she was just that: too pat. Oh, you might walk across the room and think you'd like to talk to her, just as you might walk across an antique store if you spotted a beautifully shaped vase as it suddenly shone in the sun. But up close, that vase would turn out to be nothing extraordinary, dull once the sun moved off, and clearly the work of an assembly line. You would turn the vase over in your hands to confirm it. Not an antique at all. No history there. Not a vessel with stories to reveal. Just a pretty vase.

The owner of the shop, having seen you walk across to look more closely might come up behind you. "Now, that is a fine one, is it not? So pleasing to look at and, since I have used it myself, I can assure you it is watertight. Functional and beautiful."

You could run up one side of Harriet's body, her face, and down the other without finding a spot—even the palest of scars. Something, anything that might make you pause and think, "Whoa—now that is interesting," or wonder, "Hmm. What's this?" Something, anything to make you hungry to know more, to ask, "What is the story behind this...or this?"

It wasn't long into their marriage that George wished Harriet had a nose a bit crooked but still handsome—a nose with character. Or large, square hands—a bit out of proportion but suggesting that wild and wonderful objects or meals or works of art might be wrought by them. Even a whimsical cowlick or freckles. Elfish little ears. Any feature not perfect and yet perfectly charming.

Harriet was a good mother. A good wife, too, whatever that means. Anyway, he had no specific complaints. They rarely said anything unkind to one another or fought. Perhaps they both realized that fights were a risk only people who are really in love can take—couples who can repair words spoken in anger with wordless lovemaking. No such dynamic existed between them.

Harriet was a valued employee, too—head of IT at a prestigious financial institution. A huge job. Impressive. But. But. But. George considered beating himself up. Giving himself a full-blown lashing. That would be damn easy. Maybe even deserved. Why? Because it wasn't fair, one could even say cruel, not to have loved Harriet enough. But he knew better. He knew it was also true that he hadn't known what "enough" was at the time. And yes, what little vanity he had had gotten the better of him. Maybe it was the same for Harriet. He rather hoped so. Anyway, perhaps you only know "enough" when you have found "enough" or at least had intimations that "enough" is a possibility. All he believed now, what he intuited, what he hoped for, was that there was more than enough somewhere, with someone, with something. No that wasn't quite right. That sounded as if he were asking for something *from* someone when the key was really to find someone who would be rendered mute by what he had to offer. "And when your heart is full..." Truly, he wished the same for Harriet.

Anyway, that person was not Samantha. But he knew she was rooting for him and would understand if he were to, quite literally, take off. He might need her help. Perhaps that was why, at the dinner party, he had been more open to her rather insistent pursuit of his thoughts. It was as if she intuited that he was untying the many strings that kept him tethered to the George who had walked the earth up until this point. Where she had always been playful there was now something more pointed in her questions. Invite her to step across the threshold of the barn? Well, wouldn't that be like introducing her to the other George? And what might that other George do when he had Samantha to himself? He thought it was well-nigh time to find out.

Yes, George loved Samantha in a way. But not like that. Between two adults, even two adults of opposite sexes who really like one another, it is never inevitable that something happen, something beyond mere conversation. That would be too boring. No. The only inevitability was that now that he had seen the other George staring back from the other side of the mirror, watching him from the tree line, lit by the full moon, more than mere shadow in the corner of his office, and helping him to recall the soul he had always been on Nantucket, he would burst if he did not let someone else see that heretofore buried self. See what he was becoming. Burst. He was bursting. He could hardly contain himself and had taken to longer and longer bike rides just to expend the energy that seemed limitless.

At the end of July, nearly dusk, George walked across the back field to his barn for a quick look around before he flew back to Nantucket to spend the rest of the summer. After turning the key on the big padlock, he realized the other George must already be there, just inside. So instead of having to bend his knees and use his full weight to really pull on the hammered door-pull, really heave-ho to set the old iron wheels in motion, another pair of hands, identical to his own, there on the other side, lent their heft, so the enormous old door just slid open along its track. Like magic.

TWENTY-THREE

You can't make this stuff up.

When George settled back into life on Nantucket the last weekend of July he couldn't stop grinning, ear to ear. The family wouldn't pack up and return home until after Labor Day. Five solid weeks on the island. The cherry on top? His work at the firm was complete. Though his partners and his wife might be hoping otherwise, he knows he will never return. He feels a tad disingenuous—even a measure of sadness—having to hide the joy he feels from those for whom, in most cases, he also feels respect and affection.

Weekday morns he drives Lila to camp with his bike on a rack atop the SUV. After blowing her kisses goodbye, he pedals the six-and-a-half-mile route to Madaket and back. But one Friday, halfway through August, he pokes his head into the Maria Mitchell Research Center thinking there is the tiniest of possibilities he might find more of the "History of" books he's been devouring, perhaps even something about 21st century dirigibles. Sure, there is information online. He's even found an article on a Silicon Valley billionaire who commissioned his own personal airship. But he wants to turn physical pages. Research. The science of the craft. He wants to do more homework.

The library at the Center is not large, but it smells as a library should: of leather and paper pages that had slowly revealed their secrets, again and again, as curious fingers, some stained with coffee or tea, saltwater or whale oil, turned them. Sitting at a simple wooden desk to the left of the entrance was a large woman with a parrot on her shoulder. Really and truly. You can't make this stuff up. Her outfit was as colorful as the parrot's feathers: bright red cardigan over a blouse with a leaf print in greens and blues on white. He couldn't see beyond that—see whether she wore pants or a skirt and what color either might be—as the desk blocked that view. But poking out from beneath the desk was one brown, bare foot with cracked skin and yellow nails, cradled askew in a very tired, very dirty Birkenstock sandal.

"Good morning." Unlike her foot, the woman's face was soft, creamy white and unlined, rather remarkable considering she looked to be 80. And her eyes were bright and blue and her hair, the color of foam on a wave, curled like a wave into a neat bun that sat on her fat nape. The parrot repeated its welcome, twice, in a singsong. "Good Morning to You, Good Morning to You."

George couldn't help but laugh as he returned their greeting.

"Is there something we can help you with?" George loved that she said, "We." She could have been referring to the library, but he suspected she meant she and the bird. He imagined the parrot flying off the librarian's shoulder and landing in the stacks on just the volume he sought.

"Thanks, yes. I just dropped my daughter off at camp next door. Crazy... a longshot, maybe...but I wondered if you might have any books on dirigibles." He said the word slowly, distinctly. "Or some volume that might have a chapter on them."

The librarian stared at George for a second and then convulsed her shoulders as if struck by a bolt of electricity. The parrot's feathers, too, ruffled, lifted, and then settled back, smooth and green once more.

"Not our focus, to be sure. But you are in luck." The parrot squawked, "Luck," and the librarian went on. "Do you see that man over there?" She pointed. George cocked his head and looked where she was pointing. A very old, very tall, very thin man sat reading at a long table just visible behind one of the stacks. He wore a tweed jacket, even though it was rather close in the un-air-conditioned space. She went on. "He is one of the world's authorities on dirigibles. We have books here that he's written. He even gave a lecture on those ships, balloons, whatever you call them, one summer."

You can't make this stuff up. Not parrots. Not finding world authorities on arcane subjects on islands floating 30 miles out at sea. But it is all true. Cross my heart.

George asked for an introduction and the librarian put both palms on the desk, slowly raised herself to a standing position, and walked—parrot still on her shoulder—towards the reading table calling out as she did, "Mr. Niedlander? I have someone here who'd like to meet you." Her striped cotton skirt had an elastic waist, stretched to its limit, and was cocked askew on her ample hips.

The gentleman looked up then stood up, slowly. Physically, he was the librarian's opposite. He did, however, share her smooth skin and not a bun but, dazzling for his age, (he must be in his mid-80's) a thick shock of silver hair. His eyes were gray and looked both kind and piercing. He extended his hand. "Hallo there. Ernst Niedlander. And you are?

"George. George Paxton."

"And you are interested in meeting me?" He seemed perplexed that anyone would seek him out.

"I am, yes. And in talking about dirigibles which this nice lady..." George turned to the librarian and she said, "Prune." And George smiled at her and went on. "...which Prune said was your field of expertise."

"Well, you could say that."

"Remarkable to find you here, of all places, Mr. Niedlander."

"Please. Ernst. Ernst is fine." He eased back down into his chair while also putting out his hand, an invitation for George to take the chair across from him. "My legs get so damn tired these days." He sighed, looked uncomfortable or even in pain for a moment but continued. "So. You want to talk about airships."

"I do. They've quite suddenly become rather an obsession of mine."

"That's what happens. You become addicted. I did. You are a pilot, maybe? An engineer?"

"No. No. Well, yes. I did study engineering—it was my major in college. But I went on to law school. An engineer of words I guess you'd say. But no. I am very much a landlubber, have avoided both sea and sky, save for trips to and fro this place. But now I can't stop thinking about what it would be like to be up there, amongst the clouds." George felt sheepish, like a schoolboy, saying this but he couldn't help himself. "You've sailed in one, I'll guess?"

Ernst shook his head and smiled, mumbled as a question, "Sailed in one? One?" He shook his head again, still smiling. "Many."

The librarian had left them to talk but Ernst and George went silent after this short exchange. A burst of sun had thrown a patch of dazzling white squares between them on the wooden table, silhouettes of their two heads overlaid. In reaction, they both looked up and out through the six-over-six double-hung window that occupied the tall space between the floor-to-ceiling bookcases. George had to turn in his chair to do so. The panes were made of old antique glass, full of waves and tiny bubbles that made sky, sun, treetops and clouds outside appear distorted and dreamlike.

Still looking out, Ernst spoke. "Did you know that each of the little bubbles in those panes mark a moment when the glassmaker took a breath?" Ernst continued to look out and up.

"I didn't. No. So we are looking through the breath—the long exhalations or maybe inhalations—of some long-ago craftsmen?"

"Something like that.

"*Aspiro...Suspiro...Inspiro...*"

"What's that?"

"Oh, my very poor memory of Latin kicking in. To breath in...to breath out...to fill with breath...to fill with spirit, in fact. *Inspiro.*

"Well, to me those little bubbles bring to mind tiny dirigibles, floating above the land, above the waves."

"They are as fragile as glass, are they not."

"Airships? Well, a fragile idea to be sure. Especially the non-rigid ones. But whether rigid or non-rigid, you are always balancing the inescapable—gravity—with the mercurial whims of the wind. Balancing what you know—what is inevitable, what you can't escape—with that which you can't predict. Everything from the mere whisper of a breeze to a sudden squall or violent storm. You have to be meteorologist as much as pilot to pilot an airship."

Ernst shook his head. He and George turned and were facing one another again. "It's a delicate balance," Ernst smiled and continued, "Like a marriage. Or maybe a love affair."

TWENTY-FOUR

Phoebe is telling her long time "ladies' doctor," Patricia Browne, what befell her two days before. Dr. Browne is completely quiet, completely still until Phoebe finishes with, "So. Here I am."

Dr. Browne drags a chair close to the exam table on which Phoebe sits sideways, her bare legs dangling out from under the pale, yellow exam gown, "open in the back," just as the nurse instructed. Dr. Brown takes her patient's hand.

"You said Tuesday afternoon, right?"

Phoebe nods. She takes one of Phoebe's heels in her hands and turns her leg slightly this way than that "My God, Phoebe—so just days ago. Look at these poor legs...your elbows. I am so sorry." She stops for a moment, shakes her head and speaks, not a question but a statement. "It's an outrage. You've been to the police."

Phoebe shakes her head no.

"But you must, you..."

"I know, I know. I will. Right after here perhaps. I just wanted to see you first."

"You've showered since then I assume? How about what you had on? I don't really know all that's involved with this. I... this is a first for me. Evidence and such. Maybe a moot point after the time passing, I guess. I can only provide medical care. Advice..."

"No clothes anyway. I'd been swimming, like I told you." Phoebe pauses. "And I went back in the lake after. To swim more." Phoebe sees the doctor shake her head. "I had to. To clean it away."

"Understood. Well, let's take a look at you. I'll have Janet take some blood after."

Dr. Browne leaves Phoebe alone to dress after the exam. Putting on her clothes Phoebe remembers the morning after—the morning after it happened and also (she can hardly believe it herself—also the morning after Magnus first spent the night.) When Magnus got up, he had pulled the covers up over her back and kissed her neck. She didn't move. She listened as he dressed and let himself out, all so quietly. Carefully. When she rose, half an hour later, pushing herself up palms and elbows flat and turned to look over her shoulder, she smiled to see the bedclothes in such a happy tangle. But she also saw ragged little drops and razor thin streaks of blood, hieroglyphics she couldn't decipher on the white sheets. What was written there? It was blood from her scratches and wounds, but also brought to mind the proof of purity, of becoming a woman or being bound to a man. Something from the olden times. Her blood rose in love and in anger to see it, or emotions akin to love and anger. Blood like a river, she thinks, so out of human control.

Phoebe is dressed and sitting on the other side of her doctor's desk. Dr. Browne, head down, is writing a prescription which she pushes across to Phoebe.

"For?"

"Emergency contraceptive. You would have gotten it—been offered it—if you'd gone to the police right away and they'd taken you for an exam then and there. I think it's the law. To give you the choice. At any rate, you can fill this the minute you leave. I know they stock it at the CVS around the corner." Dr. Brown takes her glasses off and looks kindly at her patient before she goes on. "We're still within the window. But the sooner the better…"

Phoebe cuts her off. "No. I don't want that. What's done is done."

"You don't understand. This is to prevent *implantation*. Nothing's happened yet. Well, what I mean to say is it's not an early abortion pill. Nothing like that." The doctor trails off, shakes her head and then continues. "Given your age, the odds aren't anywhere near as great, Phoebe, but if you wait, and if you were to become pregnant then…"

Phoebe cuts her off again. "Then I will have a baby."

TWENTY-FIVE

George and Ernst sat together in the Maria Mitchell Research Center for another half hour or so. George shared his dream with Ernst. How he was determined to build an airship and make a journey. A journey of some length. With lots of stops along the way but with lots of time aloft—above the earth—as well. If it was pure folly, Ernst didn't give any indication that he thought so. He just listened, nodded, and told George he might be able to help steer him toward some helpful books, and to folks currently working in the field. "There's a whole new resurgence of interest; a whole new class of ships." He pointed to a shelf nearby and gave George two call numbers. George got up and grabbed them. One of the two, "Lighter than Air," was by Ernst Niedlander.

George sat back down and began paging through the books. Soon after, Ernst rose, grabbed ahold of a cane hooked over the library table, and began to gather up his things. "I've got to head home now, George. Naptime. Why don't you come by later—cocktail hour, perhaps—and we can chat more. I know my wife would love that. She's a fan of these ships of the sky, too. You will love meeting her. Johanna is pure joy. Bring your wife—." Ernst lifted his hand off the table toward George. "I'm assuming you, too, are married?"

"Yes, yes, Ernst, that sounds great. Thank you. But, no. I mean, yes, I do have a wife—Harriet. But she's got us booked for some tennis round robin, wine and cheese thing at the Casino starting at 4 or so. Don't know if I said—our house is out in 'Sconset.

"Nice out there."

"So, tonight's out. But Harriet flies back to the mainland crack of dawn Monday. Would a night during the week work? And maybe I could bring my wee one, Lila, the one who's here at camp?"

Ernst nodded and George went on. "Her siblings are older—always racing off to meet up with friends when they're off work. I hate to leave her alone."

"She's welcome. My wife will love that. We have a cocktail every night. 6pm sharp. So, you tell me. Tuesday? Wednesday?"

"Tuesday at 6. Done. I'm anxious to learn what you can share, Ernst." He gathered into a small stack the books Ernst had suggested, and went on. "As much as I can. Fast as I can." Balancing those books with one hand on his hip, he went on. "Who could have imagined? Meeting you here."

"The winds worked in our favor." Ernst stood and began his slow, stiff walk to the door and George walked alongside him.

"Tuesday, then." Ernst leaned on his cane with one hand and extended the other. "The first of many, George."

"Yes, indeed." George shook Ernst's hand, "So kind, Ernst. Really."

When Ernst got to the library door he turned. "We're on West Chester. One of the old places. Let me write down the number and our phone there. Haven't got a cell if you can believe it." He turned back so he could lean against Prune's desk as support then drew a little leather note pad and a Montblanc pen out of his inside jacket pocket. He wrote then handed the paper to George. "My old red Wagoneer will be in the drive, but I'll have Johanna pull way in so there's room, probably just enough, so you can park off the cobblestones."

George read the paper. "Oh, you're right in town then—near the intersection with Centre. Right? We've got friends who rented a cottage there several years running back in the 90's."

"Might have been ours. Don't rent now. Keep it free for the kids, the grandchildren. We've got a widow's walk. Your daughter might like to climb up there. Bird's eye view on a fine day." They were outside the library now each bound in a different direction. "Sometimes," said Ernst, "when it's really clear, I feel as if I can see more than the eye can see."

Ernst hadn't said "further." He'd said, "more than"—see more than the eye can see. For the rest of the day, George couldn't shake that sentence from his mind.

After lunch, George and Harriet took Lila to the beach, joining other families they knew well. Madequecham. By mid-afternoon a fog began to take shape—a wet, gray fog, like a lumpish, lazy dog, laying on its side, blocking the view to the east. George was in and out of the waves with the kids and now sat right at the water line, facing east, out to sea. As usual he had assumed the role of lifeguard while the other adults sat in a ragged line a

ways off, up on dryer sand, reading the Times or gossiping. From time to time he waded into the waves and some of the children would paddle over and grab onto his arms or torso, and he would lift them into the air, their legs kicking furiously, until they begged to be dropped into the water.

Was it a trick of the fog that made it look as if his doppelgänger were standing a few yards further out, between he and the horizon? Who else would be staring at him like that? Smiling like that. It made him think of how much time he had spent standing in the waves, the only adult in a sea of shrieking children.

Even after the children had moved back to their towels and their toys, he continued to sit on the sand as the tide came in, losing all track of time. Every other wave brought the high tide line closer. The ocean water lapped his feet, began to splash against his thighs. Even so, he was startled when Harriet came up behind him, laid her hands on his shoulders, leant down close to his ear and whispered. "We've got to pack up and go so we've got time to change for tennis."

He turned and gave her a peck on the cheek. But he kept his eyes on the horizon, on the lookout, straining to see more than the eye can see.

TWENTY-SIX

Phoebe is standing in her bathroom holding a test strip. Red bars appear in both the left and right windows. Bingo. She's not surprised. She's been feeling a sea change—something hovering between and around her heart and solar plexus, too mazy to parse. Even so, she repeats the test again. And again. May as well use them up. She'll never need them again. The results are all positive.

She goes back to see Dr. Browne and the nurse asks for a urine sample before she leaves her in an exam room. "Doctor'll be in shortly." Phoebe is sitting on the paper covered exam table when there's a light tap at the door, "Yep, here."

Instead of fully entering the exam room, Dr. Browne hovers at the door. "Urine test is positive. You are pregnant, Phoebe." She comes into the room far enough to close the door, but she still grips the knob behind her as she continues. "You told me before your mind's made up, Phoebe." Is she going to leave it at that, Phoebe wonders? But no, she turns and continues. "I don't deliver babies anymore so I'm going to refer you to a colleague—Dr. Zelevinsky. Good guy. More importantly, a good doctor. You can sign release forms out at the desk." Phoebe nods, slides off the exam table, and walks toward Dr. Browne as she continues. "We'll transfer all your medical records—the tests we've done. Examination notes and such. I'll let you share what happened yourself." Phoebe nods again and can't help but ask, "Are you angry at me?" It catches Dr. Browne by surprise. She lets go of the doorknob and turns.

"Do I sound angry? No. I just…Just please, Phoebe, find someone—a counselor, psychologist. You are going to need that."

"Will."

"You need some names?"

"No, I'll find somebody."

"Promise me?" Dr. Browne reaches out and takes Phoebe's hand.

"Promise."

Phoebe squeezes the doctor's hand, then lets it go so the doctor can leave. That's clearly what she wants.

Dr. Zelevinsky. A mouthful. When she shows up for her appointment weeks later both the sour receptionist at the check-in desk and the nurse say, emphatically, "'Dr. Z' is fine. That's what we—what everyone calls him."

Dr. Z is all business. After introducing himself and shaking Phoebe's hand, "Congratulations," he performs an ultrasound. "Given your age, I like to get a baseline early—make sure everything looks hunky-dory and get a firmer idea of your due date." The doctor steers the ultrasound wand over her tummy. "Sound good?" Phoebe just smiles. Images begin to appear on the little screen to her right and Phoebe immediately turns away. But she can't turn away from the beat of another heart.

"Hear that? Robust. And everything looks good, too. Of course, we aren't going to know anything about sex yet. Not for another month or so. But everything seems just as it should." Dr. Z removes the wand from Phoebe's abdomen and hands it to the nurse.

"All normal is all I want to know," Phoebe says.

The doctor looks surprised. No doubt all of his other patients want to see everything, know everything. She gives him an explanation that's not even close. "I'm old fashioned—want to be surprised."

Once she's dressed and sitting across from Dr. Z in his office, Phoebe—unsure what details Dr. Browne were in her medical records, shares the circumstances of her pregnancy. She doesn't want to be caught off guard by questions about "the father."

When she finishes the barest outline of her story Dr. Z sits quite still, his face a smooth mask, his lips pressed together in a tight smile. Phoebe can tell he's disturbed. And why not? His long, thin fingers open and shut once, twice, and he drops his pen to the floor.

The doctor grabs another pen from a little drawer in the desk and taps it several times before he speaks. "Dr. Browne didn't mention this."

"Left it up to me."

"That was right."

"Yes."

"I…how are you coping with that? With what happened, I mean. You've had some counseling—are talking to someone to help you work through all this…" The doctor sort of sweeps his arm vaguely in the vicinity of Phoebe's stomach. "I hope?"

Phoebe smiles and nods, "Yes." It seems that he, like Dr. Browne, would prefer to focus on the medical aspects of Phoebe's pregnancy. She wants to put him at ease and tells him, "Weekly sessions with a psychologist." She looks into her lap, "A woman Dr. Browne recommended." Then she looks him in the eyes, "Anyway, I'm looking forward, focusing on what is to come."

"Oh!" He pauses. "But you reported it. The police…?"

"Yes. They did a lineup of suspects and everything. But nothing."

"OK. We got results from the blood tests Dr. Browne ordered. You're lucky." He looks serious. "There's nothing to worry about there either. There could have been, of course. Given the circumstances."

He keeps talking but Phoebe drifts up out her body, out of the office, and back to the lake and floats, head back, looking up not at a weather-less sky but at blue made bluer by huge clouds. Nothing like the white nothing overhead on that day. Weather-less skies are behind her.

Dr. Z stands. So Phoebe does, too. There's a pink and blue striped bag, like a birthday party favor, on the corner of his desk and he hands it to her. Just then, the phone rings. "One sec." He speaks answers into the receiver. "Yes." Pause. "By next week." Pause. "I'll have the nurse take a look at that."

While he chats Phoebe peeks in the bag and sees an array of brochures, pulls one out: cheerful photos and copy about eating right and exercise, "Find a Lamaze Class Near You!" And so on and so on and so on.

Dr. Z hangs up the phone, stands, and shakes her hand. She feels as if she needs to cheer him up a bit so she says, with more gusto than she feels, "Thanks, Dr. Z! See you in a month."

The moment she gets home, Phoebe pitches the brochures in the trash. It isn't a gesture meant to dismiss Dr. Z. It's just that she has no unanswered questions. She has no worries about the birth.

But Dr. Z does not easily put this new patient out of his mind. No, indeed. Even after seeing one patient after another, all through the afternoon, he continues to think about Phoebe and only Phoebe. At one point, after finishing with another mother-to-be, his nurse turns to him. "Can't help but wonder about that woman who was raped."

"Exactly." Dr. Z even takes the idea of Phoebe home with him that night. Wrestles with it. Decides that Phoebe is in a bubble that will burst, probably right after she gives birth. And then what? A post-partum depression from hell is what he predicts. He makes a note on Phoebe's chart when he gets to the office the next morning, shaking his head, two deep parallel tracks between his eyes making his face go dark and despairing. Maybe he'll call Phoebe's general practitioner. He knows him. Or the psychologist, if that's ok with Phoebe. Good idea. Yes. Perhaps Phoebe has some history, maybe a history of depression. He wants to be ready, to anticipate. First-time mother. Over 40. Rape victim. And didn't she say she's a waitress? No parents or family nearby? Good God. How will she cope? How *is* she coping, for God's sake? Dr. Z shakes his head and frowns once more.

<h1 style="text-align:center">Twenty-Seven</h1>

George calls the Niedlander's early Tuesday morning to confirm their cocktail date and a woman answers, "Hallo?" Vague accent and beautiful lilt.

"Mrs. Niedlander?"

"Yes, that's me."

"George Paxton here. I don't know if your husband—if Ernst—spoke of meeting me…"

"Indeed, he did, George. You and your daughter are coming over later?" Her voice sings up a few notes at the end of the sentence.

"That's why I phoned. Just to make sure it's still a good day for you."

"Oh, yes, Ernst is so looking forward. And me, too. At 6, then. And I'm Johanna."

When George and Lila arrive at the Niedlander's Ernst opens the door before they even have a chance to ring the bell, which rather disappoints Lila. The doorbell is a tiny copper whale, weathered and green, and George knows she wants to ring it to see what will happen. Ernst sees her staring at it. "Go ahead. Give it a good press!" She does and the sound of a foghorn resonates from deep in the house. Lila breaks into a giggle and without asking rings it again. And then once more. The low sonorous tolls overlap one another.

Her father reaches up to pull her finger away. "OK—that's enough."

Ernst is still holding the door open. "Oh, she's fine, she's fine. I like to hear it, too. Go ahead, dear. Press it one more time!" Lila does and then she and George step across the fat granite threshold, worn smooth and slightly concave from lord knows how many souls stepping onto it over the centuries. They are in the foyer. A tall woman with bright gray hair, held back with tortoise shell combs, is walking toward them, backlit by the late day sunlight. She is tall, thin, and not beautiful but what George would call handsome, regal, with high cheekbones and dark brown eyes. "Welcome, welcome. We're so glad you've come."

Ernst smiles and makes introductions. "Johanna, this is Mr. Paxton—"

George interrupts him. "George, for goodness' sake, George."

"And his daughter…" Ernst stops and looks down at Lila. "You'll have to excuse me, young lady. Your father told me your name when we met at the library, but my ancient brain is not what it used to be."

Lila puts out her hand to shake his as she looks up at Johanna. "I'm Lila."

"You and I are going up top, Lila. To the Widow's Walk!" Johanna takes Lila's hand and off they go. Lila doesn't even look back. George watches her, happy she's so at ease with a stranger or, more, for her animal instinct. She knows herself to be in good hands.

Ernst starts down the hall then turns to the right, through a wide opening flanked by packet doors that are half pushed back. George follows. Along with Sailors Valentines, some well-worn nautical flags, an antique harpoon and family photos, the hallway is decorated with photos of airships—all black-and-white. Some of the airships are floating in the sky, some skirting just above waves, and a few others tethered to tall masts in large fields. And then there is one in pieces on the ground, smoke and fire filling the sky. Not the Hindenburg. But a crash. A horrible crash.

"What's your pleasure, George?" Ernst is standing by a high, dark table, it's top a tray with brass hinges, dipping tongs into a silver ice bucket and dropping them into a cocktail shaker when George enters the snug den. Ernst's cane is leaning against a nearby chair. "I'm having my Sunday special."

"And that would be?"

"The same as my Monday through Saturday special," says Ernst. "A martini. A real martini. Gin." He lifts his chin and says with an exaggeratedly severe tone, "Doctor's orders."

"How can I say no?"

"And an olive?"

"Or two. Yes!"

Drinks in hand the two men sit down across from one another in a pair of old, cracked leather club chairs. Ernst begins. "I started to tell you in the library—," He stops for a sip of his drink then continues, "—about the war. I worked for the government—was recruited, I guess you'd say. I'd had experience with lighter-than-air craft from way back when I was a young man in Germany."

"I thought Germany. And Johanna?"

"Born in Slovakia, well, the Czech Republic now. We were both happy to immigrate here."

"And you helped build, or pilot, airships?"

"Yes to both. So, I was valuable. I don't know how much you know but at one point the Navy had nearly 200 lighter-than-air craft in service for the war effort. The Second World War."

"I've been reading about that." George nods his head. "The Allen book and yours, too, of course."

"Well, Hugh's book covers early history. But it's a good history. You read that. Mine just focuses on the years leading up to and including World War II."

"When the Navy used airships."

"Yes, yes. Non-rigid ships—blimps you'd call them." Ernst played with the olive in his drink but didn't eat it. "Navy'd had bad luck with rigid ships. Lost the Akron in '33 and the Macon in '35. So, they developed the K-types. Not fast but they could stay aloft for upwards of 60 hours. Remarkable craft. Used for reconnaissance mostly. You know, spotting subs and mines. But also dropping supplies, searching for survivors, doing air and sea search-and-rescue, mine spotting, antisubmarine cover and such." Finally, Ernst ate his olive.

"It's remarkable. I mean, I don't think most people know about this, do they?"

"They don't. No. They know the Hindenburg if anything. But that's it." Ernst leans forward, trying to pull the nearby ottoman toward him with his cane. George jumps up and pushes it closer so Ernst can lift and settle his legs on top. It's an effort. "Thanks, George. Anyway, yes, the Hindenburg—passenger ship—crashed in 1937. But well before that—starting in the thirties—Navy'd been working with Goodyear. Goodyear made the envelope—what people call the blimp—and the Navy built the control car that rode beneath. Eventually, Goodyear took over all the production." Ernst paused. "Grab me that jar of olives, will you George?" George did, held it so Ernst could fish one out and then did the same as Ernst went on. "Anyway, less than a decade after the Hindenburg crash we had L-ships and then the much larger K-class. Ships that were built just for the war. German knowhow. Goodyear made them."

"And you were a pilot?"

"I was. Me—the whole crew—would be in the gondola down under. About 10 of us. Not very comfortable. But important work. We had radar, sonar buoys, depth charges…"

"And weapons?"

"Oh, yes, depth bombs and a Browning machine gun up front. But that wasn't really the point. It was really the scouting and the escorting, mine spotting and mine sweeping. That was key." Ernst stops. "You help yourself to a refill if you need it, George." George nods but doesn't move so Ernst goes on. "Planes only have enough fuel to last a few hours. But airships? Well, they may not be fast. But we could stay aloft for over 24 hours. The enemy didn't down even one of the nearly 90,000 ships we escorted." Ernst smiled. "Not a one."

George looks over Ernst's left shoulder. Hanging there in a black frame is the front page of a newspaper with two photos side by side. One of a huge airship intact and in the air and the second that same craft in pieces on the ground. He pointed and Ernst didn't even have to turn around. He just started to talk.

"You're looking at the Shenandoah, George. 'Daughter of the Stars.' She was a rigid ship—an alloy of copper and aluminum. Built around 1922 or 23. She was filled with helium, of course. Not hydrogen like the Hindenburg. It wasn't a fire but weather that brought her down."

"Get you another?" George asks seeing Ernst is turning the olive round in his glass.

"One a day. You help yourself."

George stands, not for a refill but to look more closely at the photos while Ernst narrates.

"Shenandoah was the first airship ever to moor to a ship at sea. Navy used her for scouting missions. She flew 56 times then broke into pieces thanks to a violent squall over Ohio. Summer of 1925. A promotional tour if you can believe it. Such a waste. Such a pity."

George moves in closer and Ernst continues, "Captain of that ship warned the Navy—he knew enough to be wary, very wary, of those Midwestern summer storms. But the Navy was more intent on publicity—getting the Shenandoah to some damn airshow. 14 killed and the other 29 rode bits of her to earth.”

“You've warned me about the weather before.”

“Yes, yes. All the technology in the world is no match for that.”

They went on talking for another half hour when, holding a little spyglass, Lila burst in the room. “Daddy!”

“What in tarnation is that, little one?”

“It's a spyglass. We went up on the Widow's Walk. We could see the harbor and we watched the ferry come in. I could even see someone get off with their dog. They looked so tiny.” Lila climbed into her father's lap and showed him the little portable telescope.

“Now isn't that dandy. Could you see our house?”

Lila rolled her eyes. “Of course not. That's way too far.”

“It is far,” George looks at his watch, “Which is why we'd better hop.” He stands, smiles at his hosts. “Ernst, Johanna, next time you can be our guests out in 'Sconset. Next week maybe?”

Ernst grabs the cane next to his chair and taps it on the wood floor twice. “We are a bit hobbled, George, so we hope you will come back here again.” Johanna is nodding agreement. “That means you, too, Lila.” George sees what an effort it takes for Ernst to get to his feet and the signs of pain that cross his features.

“Oh—the cookies!” Johanna turns to Lila and says, “Come with me.” They head to the kitchen as Ernst and George make their way to the door. Slowly. George already feels rather like a son to this man. They lean in toward one another and when they reach the screen door Ernst puts his free hand on George's shoulder.

“History is one thing, George. We can look at yellowed newspaper clippings or talk about wars till the cows come home. But you need to know about what's happening now. And that's a lot.”

“Yes, I want to know—“

“Nowadays there are ships made of super light metals and high-performance fabrics with all sorts of high-tech instrumentation. Not that it's any help if you hit a real storm. But at least you have advance warning and better maneuverability.”

There is a wooden bench by the front door and Ernst eases himself down onto it, his cane in front of him, one hand on top of the other on its carved top: a mermaid. He breathes in and out with some effort before speaking again.

"Johanna's nephew—Dieter's his name—has an operation out west. There are others in Europe—throughout the world, really. The point is, you need to talk to someone who's building ships now. And Dieter is the best. He's making airships that—what do the kids say? Blow my mind? Yes, they blow my mind. Huge craft that can carry a dozen SUV's or tanks and land anywhere. You name it. But Dieter's made some small models too, to test some of his ideas."

"I'd love that introduction, Ernst." Not wanting to stand over him George sits next to Ernst on the bench. That's better. Eye-to-eye. Ernst continues.

"Dieter's figured out a way to take-off and land an airship just like a helicopter. No masts. No ground crews. Just up and down by balancing helium and oxygen. Like a fish going up to the surface and then diving down. All the gases are stored in holds—balanced—in the belly of the beast."

"So, I could land at a small airport or even in a field or some RV site."

"Well, that's the sort of versatility you're going to need if you really intend to follow through with this...this..." Ernst pauses. George can see that he doesn't want to deflate George's hopes. Sees Ernst already regards him nearly as a son. In turn, George feels protective of this elderly father figure. He fills in the pause. "Folly? Is that the word you are searching for?"

Ernst is silent for a long moment, his face serious. Then he turns towards George. "Not folly. No. A stretch to be sure. You told me you were a lawyer. I imagine you have all the answers for your clients."

George shakes his head and opens his mouth to tell Ernst he would never make such a claim. But he knows he doesn't need to. He keeps his mouth shut. He wants to allow this wise old man to say his piece.

"You can't envision where this notion of yours will take you, George. Is that folly? Maybe. You'll do your homework and spend enough hours so you'll be a competent pilot. You'll need to get your CPL with IR for airships."

"My...?"

"Commercial pilots license and instrument rating for airships."

"Ah. Copy that."

"You're prudent enough not to take crazy chances—fly when there are storm cells anywhere in the vicinity. They'll teach you all that." Johanna and Lila's voices, laughs really, are audible down the hall. Both men turn toward the sounds and smile. Then Ernst continues.

"I remember when Johanna was pregnant with our first child. She would cover her ears when other women would start telling her about their labors. 'All the gory details' as Johanna said. She was like the three monkeys. How's it go? 'See no evil; speak no evil; hear no evil.' Maybe that doesn't really fit." Ernst stops and rubs his knee then pats George's before continuing, "The point is, Johanna wanted to be prepared, yes, but she wanted to hold onto her excitement, too. And it seemed that knowing too much beforehand might destroy that. Anyway." Ernst grabs his cane and eases himself back up to a standing position before finishing his thought. "The only folly I see, George— and I wouldn't even use that word—is going through life not encountering something beyond your ken."

"Oh, God, yes. This obsession or dream or whatever you call it is definitely beyond my ken, as you call it."

"And God help us if we never reach for that, George."

Johanna and Lila join them at the door. Johanna holds a plateful of cookies in one hand—star shaped with sprinkles of chocolate—and holds Lila's hand in the other. Both are smiling. The two are obviously fast friends. Ernst speaks to Johanna. "*Mein Schatz*, will you write out Dieter's information for George? You know, the home number or cell or whatever it is we use. And his email, too. Not the company one. You know."

Johanna gives Lila the cookies to hold and goes back to the kitchen for paper and pen.

George watches Ernst follow his wife with his eyes. "*Mein Schatz*— my wonderful Johanna—was definitely beyond my ken all those years ago. Me, a poor university student. But I set my sights, my hopes, my everything on her. People thought I was reaching too high. But here I am, here we are, 65 years together."

Johanna comes back and hands George the note she's written.

"We'll call Dieter as soon as you leave and tell him you'll be calling. Brilliant boy. And also, so nice a boy—well, a man." She laughs. "He's my nephew, you see. You two will get along."

Lila hugs Johanna around the waist. George and Ernst shake hands, but George also gives Ernst a squeeze on the arm. How thin it is! It gives him a pang to think of this man's long life drawing to a close.

Ernst holds the screen door open but stays inside as George and Lila step out onto the doorstep. Lila begins a half skip toward the car, turning to blow a kiss when she gets there. George hovers on the doorstep for Ernst to say goodbye, but he says more than goodbye:

"I saw my first airship when I was a boy in Leipzig, George. It was August. 1929. Dr. Eckener was taking the LZ-127, the *Graf Zeppelin*, on her first round-the-world passenger flight. I stood outside with my parents and brother. All of us, eyes on the sky. We marveled. All of Germany marveled. But for me it was more than marvelous. It turned my insides, my world, upside down."

George was lost in thought as they drove home until Lila roused him. "Dad, you know all the pictures of Maria Mitchell, the ones in the room we use at camp? They show her holding a spyglass."

"That's actually a telescope, sweetie. She was the first woman astronomer and became quite famous because she discovered a comet."

"That is so, so cool, Dad. She saw something our eyes can't see, right?"

"Yes, indeed, Whirligig, she saw more. More than the eye can see."

TWENTY-EIGHT

Phoebe came out of the lake nearly blind that day, her goggles cloudy with condensation. She pushed them up on top of her head but that was no better and her glasses were out of reach. Without them, she couldn't make out much save for the tool belt, the cowboy hat, the black hair, the eyes like black holes. "Why would a new owner or a real estate agent be wearing a tool belt?" That thought collided with everything that happened so fast and so slowly. It was not revocable. Not the memory, not any of it.

When Phoebe refused to once again recount the details of the attack her therapist, Dr. Gail, (yes, Phoebe had finally acquiesced to the advice of her doctors) took another approach. She told Phoebe they were going to try a technique to desensitize Phoebe using rapid eye movement. Really? Well, why not. Phoebe was happy to be asked to do something rather than talk, talk, talk. But it turned out that once she'd done what Dr. Gail asked—focus on the traumatic memory while the doctor waved her finger in front of Phoebe's face, back and forth and back and forth for what seemed like much longer than the 30 seconds she'd told Phoebe to expect—Dr. Gail was back at it, quizzing her, this time on what the exercise had been like for her.

Phoebe couldn't find the words. In fact, having Dr. Gail wave her finger so madly and so close to Phoebe's face was unnerving. Another attack. She didn't want to do it again at her next session. Or the next. Even though Dr. Gail insisted it was repetition that would allow Phoebe to "graduate" to the moment when she would be able to focus on a positive thought while also holding the still so vivid memory of that fateful swim and its aftermath in her mind.

Dr. Gail prodded, with growing intensity each session, for Phoebe to "tap into her fear, her anger." She assumed those were the emotions uppermost in Phoebe's mind and no doubt believed expressing them would somehow serve as partial antidote to what happened. Maybe not expunge it from Phoebe's memory but heal something. "Heal" is the word Dr. Gail always uses.

But over time, by pressing on that one spot and ignoring all others, Dr. Gail has only succeeded in making Phoebe feel angry—very, very angry—at Dr. Gail. It all came to a head this morning—just hours ago—when Dr. Gail allowed her large German Shepherd into the room where they sit and talk. Dr. Gail meets her patients in a little studio a short distance from her house. Phoebe adores most dogs but is always wary when she shuts her car door and sees Felix out in the yard. She has never liked the predatory look of German Shepherds: their long noses and pointy ears and most especially the way their hindquarters are at such an exaggerated, sloping, downward angle. They have always seemed menacing to her. A breed of guard dog that has always put her on her guard.

She tries to get down the path of irregular flagstone squares without Felix coming near. But he always does come near, pressing his long nose against her thigh, darting at her ankles aggressively. Only when she gets into the studio and shuts the door does the knot in her stomach relax.

But when Dr. Gail joined Phoebe in her studio office, Felix slunk in behind her and kept circling the room, sniffing at everything in his path, including the edge of Phoebe's skirt.

"You don't mind having Felix here while we talk, do you? He'll just curl up."

"I guess that's fine," Phoebe lied and the knot in her stomach returned and twisted, this way and that. And Felix did not curl up. No, indeed. He continued to slink around the room and refused to settle even when Dr. Gail said, "Down, Felix, lay down." Then she'd looked at Phoebe and said, "He's such a lamb. But if he doesn't settle, I'll put him back in the house. Just say the word."

Why should I have to "say the word," Phoebe wonders. *I'm the patient! I'm paying to be here!* Then Dr. Gail started the session. "You told me Tuesday that the doctor confirmed that you're about nine weeks along, Phoebe."

"Had an ultrasound, yes."

"There's still a window. Options. Even here in Georgia. You have an option. You were raped." Phoebe winced at the word, but Dr. Gail didn't notice. "We need to talk about that option, and soon, of course."

It was at just this moment that Felix got up and trotted towards Phoebe. Her hand sprang up, unconsciously, to ward off, ward off— what she did not know. Then she reached for her water bottle. Her throat was so dry. It was the wrong move, apparently, because Felix drove his head forward and bit her on the foot. He actually bit her! Hard. She was wearing sandals. She screamed "Ouch—," and tears sprung to her eyes, not so much from pain but from anger and surprise. "He bit me, he really bit me—." A blue bruise was already blooming above her arch with a tiny serrated red tear with specks of blood at its center.

Dr. Gail sprang up and opened the door saying over her shoulder, "He's never done anything like this." And then she addressed her dog. "What a silly, bad boy you are, Felix. You come with me now." She patted Felix' neck as she left the studio. "I'll be right back." Phoebe watched with horror thinking, *Can she actually be rewarding him with those affectionate pats?*

By the time she returned Phoebe was sitting on the very edge of the couch, on the verge of just walking out. In fact, she was silently chastising herself for not doing so the moment Dr. Gail left with her awful dog. *I should have just walked out. For good. She was more concerned about Felix than about me.* She had taken off her sandal.

Dr. Gail looked at the wound. "Oh, look at that! He really got you, didn't he?" She seemed almost fascinated by (could she even feel proud of?) the mark her dog had made.

"Should I get some ice for you to put on that?"

"Yes, you should. Please."

Dr. Gail went out and when she returned with the ice Phoebe was experiencing so many emotions at once and so strongly that for once she picked the one that was uppermost and blurted out with some force. "I don't come here to be hurt!"

Dr. Gail seemed surprised. "Of course you don't." But she had missed the point. The wound did hurt but it served more as a small opening through which something inside of Phoebe could escape. And it escaped with force as things do—water, blood, steam, semen, oil—when the escape point is smallest. She repeated herself. Twice. Three times. And with more and more urgency. With passion. With anger. "I don't come here to be hurt!" "I don't come here to be hurt!" "I don't come here to be hurt!"

But it was only Phoebe who realized that this was also what she would like to have screamed at the guy who did it, there at the lake where she takes her swims. "I don't come here to be hurt—!"

Phoebe will never return to her therapist. Even though Dr. Gail leaves near daily messages, increasingly puzzled over why Phoebe "suddenly quit" therapy when "we were making such progress...not done." We? Dr. Gail will never know that Phoebe has worked it all out by herself and has even started swimming again.

Yes. Right back here. At the lake. Right now. She is filling what would have been her 4pm Thursday slot with Dr. Gail with a swim. She finishes her 51st lap, takes a short break and a long breath at the rock, turns, takes another deep breath and begins another lap. *Fifty-two, fifty-two, fifty-two, and breathe, breathe.* Her big old sweatshirt covers the gnome's face. It warms in the sun. Her glasses are at his feet.

She is considering swimming more than a mile today. She feels particularly, wonderfully buoyant. Another deep breath, and she sets off anew. *Fifty-three, fifty-three, fifty-three, breathe.*

She flips over onto her back, tummy to the sun, and does the back stroke now, wondering as she does when she will first feel her baby move. A tiny swimmer swimming inside a swimmer. Won't that be something?

TWENTY-NINE

Their last weekend on Nantucket, George and Harriet arrived back at the cottage at the same time on the Saturday afternoon, George from a bike ride, Harriet from a tennis match. George opened the door and Harriet walked past him, sat on the rattan bench just inside, let her head fall back to rest against the wall. "Won all my matches." George smiled and took the seat beside her. "You are something, sweetie." Harriet bent over and began to remove her shoes and socks. George couldn't help but notice how beautiful her legs were—muscular, but not too; tan, but not too. He almost wanted to lay a hand on her thigh, just inches from his own, if only to remember how cool and firm it always felt. It wasn't an impulse of desire save for the desire to recall desire, and that he could do without touching his wife, beautiful though she was. They'd made it the whole summer without touching. And months, years, without what he would call love making of any ilk. No reason to start now. That habit—which is what sex in their marriage so quickly became— was long forgotten.

Ever since he told Harriet he was taking a leave from the firm, he'd waited for her to press him for details. She never had. Oh, she asked about the financial arrangements, "You confirmed it? That you'll still get your share of profits?" And when George assured her, once again, that she need not worry about money, she seemed satisfied. But he wanted her to know; wanted to share his excitement, his obsession. He briefly wondered if it might have served as a way back to some vague excitement between the two of them. But of course not. So, sitting side by side, he began the speech he'd wanted to give for weeks. "You haven't asked but I am going to tell Eddie as soon as we're back and, obviously, I want you to know first..."

"Know?"

George couldn't help but sigh and say as a series of questions.

"Exactly how and on what I intend to spend my time going forward? My project?" George's voice rose at the end of each question and rose to its highest pitch as he finished. "The reason I left the firm?"

Harriet, still hovering over her feet, aligned her shoes neatly together before sitting upright and spoke in a voice that betrayed not a shred of interest. "The sarcasm is so not you, George."

"Well, I'm sorry. But damn it, Harriet, I thought you would have asked by now."

"Okay, so tell me."

More out of duty now than anything, George began. And as he did, he got up and briefly disappeared around the corner into the front room to grab a few of the books and magazines he'd collected while doing his research. When he sat again, he showed Harriet photos as he continued to describe his plans. She said nothing. She just looked. Thinking it would be more compelling than dry old texts, he put a *New Yorker* magazine from only a few years back into her lap and flipped to an article, tagged with a yellow stickie note. "See this guy?" George tapped his finger on a rather mad scientist looking fellow—grey bangs and grey-blond hair to his shoulders, black octangle shaped glasses. "Lighter-than-air craft are his addiction, too." He moved the magazine over to Harriet's lap. "He's built half a dozen. I'm not the only crazy one."

"Too?" Harriet shook her head. Her mouth an ugly coil. She flipped to the second page of the article where there was a rather cartoonish illustration of an airship, not an intricate engineer's drawing. "Your addiction *too*?" Harriet scoffed. "Seems incredibly..." she paused with a head shake. "Silly." She closed the magazine. It blocked her thighs from view. "Completely silly. Infantile. But, whatever. If it makes you happy."

"Whatever?"

"What do you want me say. The whole thing—this whole ridiculous idea—it's got nothing to do with me."

"'Ridiculous.'" George spoke the word flatly.

"Well, yes, they are ridiculous. I mean look—," Harriet tried to push the magazine from her lap over to her husband's, but it fell to the floor, the pages rolling uncomfortably as she did. She left it there. "Impossible to imagine how they ever get off the ground."

On his last visit with the Niedlanders, George had asked Ernst and Johanna if he could bring his wife for cocktails before they left town, hoping that meeting the elderly pair would soften his wife's opinion of—he couldn't avoid using the words others had used—his flight of fancy, obsession, folly. It was impossible not to feel lucky to spend time in their well-loved antique home, impossible not to be impressed by Ernst, a real hero, and Johanna, with her quiet grace. Surely that would help validate George's dream.

George extended that invitation now. Of course, Johanna and Ernst had said, "Yes, yes" in unison as they wanted to meet, were curious to meet, George's wife, Lila's mother. But he barely got the words of invitation out before Harriet stood and answered. "I've no interest in meeting those friends of yours."

"But they've met Lila. More than once. She loves her visits there. Seems to love them. I think you would, too."

"No. Sorry. It's the last of my vacation and there's a Labor Day tournament. I'm in the finals."

"That's great, Harriet, but we still could…"

"I said 'no,' George. And I mean it. Tennis. Tennis is my thing." And with that she gathered up her tennis shoes, one in each hand, and stepped back out onto the front stoop, barefoot, where she banged the soles together, over and over. Still sitting, George watched as a fine spray of gray green clay from the tennis courts clouded the air between them.

Thirty

Phoebe is locking her front door before heading off to work when her cell phone vibrates in her hand. She tucks it between her shoulder and ear as she tests the doorknob with a turn and a tug. "Yes?"

"Mrs. Macauley?

"Miss. It's Miss. But, yes, that's me."

"Miss. Right. Well, Towne Cleaners here. Just a courtesy call. We got somethin' of yours." Phoebe hears a rustle of plastic and paper. "A dress. Short. Black. Anyway, been sittin' here for ages and we've got a policy..."

Phoebe cuts in. "Oh, sorry. Truth be told, I'd forgotten about it. I can stop and pick it up now, on my way to work."

"That'd be good. Otherwise, as I said, we got a policy—donate anything left too long."

"Understood. Be there in ten."

There are few garments in Phoebe's closet that require dry cleaning. The black silk dress is an anomaly, something she bought to wear to her dance company's last performance and kept on for dinner afterwards with Alex. Phoebe recalls it was supposed to be a special night and she supposes it was. Not the engagement they both believed was the presumed or expected next step in their relationship but, instead, the night they agreed to call it quits and "Just be friends." Was that only six months ago? One thing is for sure: Alex never wanted children, marriage or no marriage.

Phoebe opens the door to the cleaner's and a buzzer sounds from somewhere in the back of the place. She waits at the stainless-steel counter and soon sees a woman walking slowly towards her, pushing plastic covered garments away from her face, first with one plump hand then the other, as if she is moving through a dense tropical forest. She is round-faced and round-bodied, with a Mother Goose face, pink and surrounded by tight henna-hued curls.

She stares at Phoebe and when she reaches the counter asks, "Have I seen you before?" It's the same twang Phoebe heard over the phone.

"I've only been in here once or twice. Maybe at Just Good Food? I'm a waitress there."

"Aw, no. Husband and I, we're not restaurant folk. Cookin's my thing." The woman pats her tummy, and it's a large one, barely camouflaged under the flowered, tent- shaped top she's wearing over hot pink capri pants. "I'm guessing you're the Mrs. Macauley I phoned? Got your garment right here." She turns and tears the yellow tag off the sliver of plastic-covered black fabric hanging beside her.

"It's Miss," Phoebe says and then with anger, "Not Mrs. Miss. Miss Macauley." The anger works on Phoebe's face like a black cloud. Her smile disappears and the woman sees it.

"Oh, lord, I've upset you." The woman shakes her curls and looks as if up to heaven. "Forgive me, darlin'. My husband's always saying, 'Flo, for heaven's sake think before you speak.' You said 'Miss' on the phone." She pauses and then adds, "Don't you mind me, of all people. Why would a pretty thing like you be goin' and getting' married anyways."

Phoebe puts both palms flat on the counter between them, head down, to steady herself. She tries to focus on all the pale, overlapping fingerprints that cloud the stainless steel—some so fresh she can see the whorls that distinguish all the souls that have left them behind. Flo's eyebrows point upwards and nearly meet: arrows of concern. Phoebe's head is still hanging down between her arms, as if she is dizzy.

"What have I gone and done?" Flo says. "Miss? Miss Macauley? You all right?"

Phoebe is taking long slow breaths trying to steady herself but thanks to that question, and more, the woman's simple kindness, tears spring to her eyes. Seeing them, the woman immediately comes around the counter saying, "Now, now, now," and lays a palm, flat on Phoebe's supine back.

Phoebe accepts the contact, so Flo starts rubbing Phoebe's back in small circles and goes on talking, shaking her gray curls as she does. "Flo knows how things can be. Flo knows." She makes a figure 8 on Phoebe's back. "Maybe you want to talk about it?" Phoebe can't cry and talk. She shakes her head, then stands up, turns and faces Flo, taking a deep breath and holding back tears. "Of course, you can't talk. Talk to old Flo of all people. You just go on as you're doin'. Just go on and let go." Phoebe nods and cries with abandon.

"Come here baby, come here." Flo swings Phoebe's braid of red hair over Phoebe's shoulder, circles her arms around her as if she were her own child, and draws her in tight. As she cries on, cries out, all she's kept inside, kept from everyone, for so long, Phoebe can't help but wonder, "Why here? Why now? This old dry-cleaning shop? This near perfect stranger?"

"That's right. That's right. No need to explain. We don't need words here, do we? Not us gals. Useless." Flo pulls away from Phoebe far enough to look at her face. "Maybe you need to sit a minute?" She looks over at the molded plastic chair near the front door. It is pink, like Flo's slacks, but faded and dulled with dirt. Phoebe shakes her head and tears continue to pour from her eyes.

Flo puts her arms back around Phoebe and talks on to soothe them both. "I've had my share, that's for sure" she says with shakes of her head. "Ask anyone. They'll tell you. 'Flo's had her share.'"

Phoebe believes Flo, believes she has had her share. Of what it doesn't matter. She collects herself enough to speak, a smothered voice into Flo's shoulder, a shoulder that smells, comfortingly, of cool peppermint. "It's not really the Mrs. or Miss bit. I mean, what difference does that make," Phoebe begins. "It's more—"

"You don't need to tell me, darlin'. Things is never what people think. It's like my sciatica. Makes my legs hurt—oh, lord do they hurt—sometimes all the way down to my ankles. But the doctor insists the pain is coming from my back. Can you imagine?" Flo shakes her curls. "Every time I go in to see him, he asks the same dumb ass question, 'How's the back, Flo?' when it's my damn legs that hurt." Flo returns to rubbing Phoebe's back. "These doctors! Idiots, most of them. Haven't a clue about what's really the problem. Or care for that matter."

Phoebe thinks about Dr. Gail in particular and lifts her head from Flo's shoulder hoping to gather herself back to herself. But it's no use. She has more crying to do. Flo softly sings, "That's all right...that's all right," over and over, giving Phoebe time. Finally, Phoebe wriggles out of Flo's embrace but holds onto the woman's plump forearms. "You're right. They haven't a clue."

The two stare into each other's eyes. Phoebe's crying is slowly coming to a close. Red blotches, mixing with her freckles, have made of Phoebe's face a rash of small wildfires or desert roses. The two smile. Phoebe squeezes Flo's arms then lets go in order to grab a tissue from her purse. As she does, a car passes by outside, its windows open, and the two hear the last chorus of an old Beatles' song spill through the door, loud and clear: "*Love is all you need*" They laugh in unison but afterwards, Phoebe clenches her teeth, squeezes her eyes tight and tilts her head back to keep tears from spilling anew.

"More?"

"No. I'm good now. Really." Phoebe blows her nose and speaks at the same time so she's hardly intelligible. "You must think I'm crazy."

"Stop that. Crazy is folk that never cry."

Phoebe puts her right hand across her heart. "From your lips."

Flo taps her forefinger to her temple. "Flo knows what she knows" She turns and grabs Phoebe's dress hanging from a tall rod beside the counter. "Take your dress and get yourself to work."

Phoebe fishes in her purse and pulls out her wallet.

"Put that away, darlin'. This one's on me and that's for sure."

"Seriously?"

"Fact of the matter is, if I'd stuck to policy, this dress of yours would be long gone. Donated. Policy's 60 days and we're way beyond that. I set it aside. Heaven knows why but I set it aside. Hid it really. Buried it with stuff awaiting alterations. And then this morning I said to myself, 'Flo, just call. Give her one last chance.'"

Phoebe takes the garment from Flo, turns toward the door, then turns back around.

"What is it, darlin'?"

"I'm thinking you should just donate it." Phoebe hands the dress back to Flo.

"You sure?"

"Absolutely."

"Truth be told, I've got a granddaughter—slip of a thing like you. Well, nearly as slim. Just got asked to the junior prom."

"She'll like it?"

"Be over the moon. Anyways, I'm thinkin' you've outgrown it." She sees Phoebe look down toward her tummy and rushes on, "I'm not talkin' about your figure darlin'. I just see you wearin'—hell, I don't know—somethin' brighter. Like my pink pants here." Flo slaps her flank. Phoebe can't help but laugh trying to imagine herself in hot pink pedal pushers. "Don't you go laughin' at Flo." Flo laughs, too, but then speaks more seriously. "You standin' here with your feet nearly in first position says you're a dancer. Or pregnant. Am I right?" She stops a moment and looks hard at Phoebe. "You shakin' your head yes or no?"

Phoebe answers with a smile.

"I see it all the time with gals come in here. Sometimes before they know it themselves. Feet out is the body makin' room."

Phoebe is half out the door when she hesitates and turns.

"You can stop by any time, you know."

Phoebe nods.

On the short drive to work, and all through the day, the phrase, "The comfort of strangers" rings in Phoebe's head, like a bell marking the hours from a church tower. Dr. Gail and all the others were always pressing her to cry—staring at her, waiting, waiting, waiting for her to release them from something. It made Phoebe want to scream. And then to walk into the dry-cleaners—dust balls dancing in the corners, odor of chemicals hanging in the air, fingerprint covered counter, old Singer sewing machine with a rack of clothes stuck with pins to the left—and finally let go. Of all places and with Flo, of all people.

In the middle of lunch hour, waiting for an order to come up, Phoebe says out loud, "The world is so fucked up. And so amazing." Henry hears her, turns toward the counter and replies. "You're crazy, you know that?"

"You're wrong big guy, you're wrong."

Phoebe imagines that if she were ever to stop at Towne Cleaners again, and ask for Flo, she would get a quizzical look. "Flo? We've never had a Flo here." But she would never stop there again.

THIRTY-ONE

George and Eddie sit side by side at the far end of an undulating bar in a converted mill, now an upscale watering hole in Cos Cob. Most of the bar crowd is congregated at a distance, closer to the front where patrons enjoy a dazzling view out the floor-to-ceiling window of the cascading waterfall that once powered a mill. Eddie chose this spot when George called to say, "Let's meet for a drink. I've got something important I want to share with you."

"Worth's," Eddie had said without missing a beat. "I know the bartender. Go there all the time. Great spot."

"So I've heard," George said. "Worth's it is. Thursday around 6 work?"

"Done," Eddie replied. He hung up the phone and stared out the window for a moment. He could make out, just barely, the vroom of a small jet on ascent from Westchester County Airport. His house in Greenwich is not far from the flight path. *Lear,* he thought to himself. *Big hitter heading to some rendezvous.* Oh, how Eddie wants to be in that league! But he is pleased enough for the moment, nearly puffing out his chest. His little brother has asked to see him, and him alone. *What the hell is up? Divorcing Harriet? Nah. Moving to another law firm? Unlikely. Starting his own firm? Well, I guess that's a possibility. Maybe George wants to scale down, have more control. Yeah, I bet that's it.*

Eddie wondered only briefly and then puffed out his chest in earnest concluding, *I bet George just wants to spend some quality time, alone with me.* It is that thought that puts a zing in his stout legs as he walks to Worth's to keep their date three days later.

Eddie spotted his much taller, leaner brother immediately, standing near the revolving door up front. "Follow me, Georgio" he said, beaming, and he led George away from his favorite perch up front to seats where they could still be seen but not heard. Now that they're seated, he puts his hand on his brother's back and cocks his head at the bartender. "I'll have my usual Silas, and my brother, George here will have…?" Eddie moves his hand to his brother's shoulder and gives it a shake. "What is it you're drinking these days, Bro?"

"Tequila and tonic. My new favorite."

"Damn, George. Tequila? Really? Second surprise of the night."

"What was the first?"

"Well, whatever it is you called me for."

"Oh, that—"

Silas steps in. "You have a preferred brand?"

Before he can answer his brother jumps in. "Give him that Hollywood brand, Silas."

"Casamigos?

"That's the one." He turns to George. "Good?"

"Fine."

They sip their drinks. George is in no hurry to start the conversation that prompted this rare one-on-one. He could have rehearsed for weeks and still failed to come up with a proper script to explain his plans to Eddie. Eddie for god's sake. Of all people.

People often joke that Eddie is full of hot air. But that doesn't mean he can imagine floating above the earth. On the contrary. George well knows that as far as Eddie is concerned, earth is where it all happens—money is made, receptionists, nurses and lovers succumb to his charms. His holes-in-one bring on cheers. His expensive European vacations fuel endless tall tales. His kids' report cards demand congratulations. Bartenders know "his usual." Even the fact that he can afford to send his wife for Botox injections and girls-only spa vacations—the details of which he shares with any audience eager to listen—feeds his conviction that life on earth, and his life in particular, is very good indeed. If you can afford it. And he can. To him, there is no contest. It is trysts, new cars every year, fine food and wine—earthly delights—that make life worth living. He often wonders why his successful brother is such a spendthrift and really rather a stick in the mud.

George takes another sip of his too strong drink, and wonders, *How on earth do I make Eddie understand? Maybe I should just make up some other excuse for the meeting.* He starts with, "Are you guys going to join us on Nantucket over Columbus Day? Might be the last chance. Not sure if we'll close the house after that."

"Can't swing it." Eddie sucks on an ice cube from his drink and talks, "Eddie juniors got a football game that weekend and Dana's got soccer practice. Non-negotiable. Gotta be home." Eddie pops a pretzel in his mouth, "Whatever happened to families being able to take holidays together on school holidays?"

"Yeah, well, that's long been a thing of the past. We're in the same predicament. Ben's got a game, too. But Harriet and Lila can get away." George squeezes more lime into his drink. "We've got to work that out. Ben's a good kid but we don't want him home alone for a long weekend."

"You certainly don't!" Eddie laughs. "Word will spread. 'Party! Party! Ben's parents are away!'"

"That's all we need." George grimaces playfully then shakes his head. "I really don't worry about that. You know Ben. He's solid. Trustworthy. But you're right about the other kids. They seem to just know when parents are away. A sixth sense. But I want Ben to have company—not come home to an empty house. They run those boys ragged at practice."

Eddie has polished off all the nuts and pretzels. He shoves the empty bowl over to the lip of the bar and calls out, "Silas!" who nods and puts his pointer finger up to indicate "Give me a minute."

Eddie is nibbling, nibbling, nibbling because he is impatient. This rare solo date with his brother provides a certain pleasure, but, nevertheless, he wants the marrow. He takes another handful of fodder from the replenished bowl, crunches it, and says, "So, Bro, out with it. I'm getting hungry."

George takes a sip of his drink. He would never purposely put someone in suspense. But how to start? He fishes a single cashew out of the snack dish and moves it around the bar like a fish swimming in the sea. "I've barely told a soul what I'm up to, Eddie. Shared my idea with Harriet barely a week ago."

"Ha! And me second? I'm flattered." Eddie pops the cashew George has been fiddling with in his mouth. "So, shoot already."

George took a slug of his drink. "I've done some research, met with a few folks in the field. Well, actually, there aren't that many people in the field. Anyway, I've gone and made an enormous investment..."

"Investment in what?" Eddie is alternating sips of his drinks with handfuls of nuts.

"A prototype. I'd thought to use the barn to work on it, retrofit some parts. But I don't think that'll be enough space. I'm going to need something more like an airplane hangar. Maybe something out at Westchester County."

"Jesus, you're a lawyer. Words, bro, words—spell it the fuck out."

George realizes he hasn't said the word, the unimaginable word, "dirigible," or even the tamer one, "airship."

Eddie blasts on. "You talking about some newfangled bike, maybe? Must be a real motherfucker to need an airplane hanger." Eddie flags down Silas. "Refills, bro, we're dying of thirst here."

"A dirigible—an airship. I'm getting a prototype from some engineers out on the West Coast."

"A what?"

"Dirigible."

Eddie grips his drink with greater and greater force. If it weren't a glass as stout as he is, it might have exploded into pieces. "What the fuck? A Goodyear blimp? You're kidding, right?"

"Not a blimp, Eddie. An airship."

Silas deposits fresh drinks in front of the brothers and takes the snack bowl away. While Eddie guzzles George continues—detail by detail—sharing technical specs—the aerodynamics, the materials, how the gas cells will be configured—hardnosed facts to forestall or even prevent sharing the epiphany that launched his dream. As he talks, he watches his brother's face, an ocean of colliding expressions, with the occasional blast of foam in the form of the tiniest specks of saliva on his brother's lips. He ends with, "My goal is to fly the thing. Where, I'm not sure. But sail through the clouds I will."

Eddie has been holding back, incredulous—how could he not be? Hearing this final sentence, he throws back what remains of his Manhattan. It comes out in little spits as he raises his voice, face flushed, "But you don't even like to fly, George. You avoid it like the plague."

George nods. Even winces. Outside of Harriet, his brother is the first family member or friend with whom he is sharing his dream. Why? Because once Eddie's on board, and he will come on board, George knows Eddie will have his back, no matter what. If anyone dares to say, "Your brother is nuts," Eddie will stand up and challenge that person to a duel. Or maybe just launch into a fisticuffs.

For all his bumptious ways, and unimaginative appetites, Eddie has a heart like a half-deflated balloon: soft, malleable. He loves George and is even in awe of him, though it is only others who see that awe every time the two are together.

When the two brothers were in grade school Eddie overheard his parents talking about the results of an assessment test every student had to take. After his father said the word "genius" Eddie crept closer to the door, pressed his ear right up against it. He guessed it was George's test results they were discussing—George had always been preternaturally focused and had a photographic memory. He was head-and-shoulders above any of his classmates in every subject. Nevertheless, Eddie hung on to a shred of hope; he longed to be "the genius," the one singled out. But he heard his mother sigh and say, "Well, we've always known he was different. But a genius? Well, of course we know it's true. But do you think George knows it himself? I hope it won't be a burden."

Surprisingly, George's distinction only made Eddie love his brother more. The way he saw it, having a genius for a brother cast a glow over him as well. He liked to be in that glow whenever he could, as here, now: it is a glow even brighter, more resonant, than the whiskey-colored light turning the zinc bar at which he and George sit, side by side on high mahogany stools with green leather seats, to gold. Eddie is so keyed up he lowers his feet to the metal rungs near the base of the stool and spins around, this way and that. "Hell, George, the reason you never go to Europe is you'd have to swim to get there."

George realizes that his brother's feet don't reach the floor as his does. It fills him with love, love for a brother who he knows must have felt himself come up short all along, and quite literally. He watches his brother spin around by using his loafered feet on the rungs of the stool to propel himself. George stops him spinning by grasping his older brother by the shoulder,

"You're right, Eddie, I have hated flying. But—." George ponders whether to try to share the emotion that precipitated his plan, and how. He predicts he will fail but starts, "Have you ever had a vision, not of yourself, exactly, but of the world—a vision of something wildly different, a perspective wholly new, from what you've known…" With every word, George realizes how impossible it is to articulate what he is reaching for. Every word is a step onto loose gravel at the edge of a cliff.

As for Eddie, he doesn't want to disappoint his younger brother by saying something that confirms he doesn't understand. But he has to say something to keep the conversation going, a technique he practices daily in his work as a pharmaceutical rep. "Keep 'em talking or keep on talking until you make a sale." He responds with, "Yeah, I know what you mean." He stabs the cherry in his empty Manhattan, sticks it in his cheek, chews, and talks. "Sometimes when I am on long drives, cruising along I-84, I think to myself: 'You could just keep driving, Eddie—just go and go and go and stop somewhere in the middle of nowhere, a place you've never been to." Eddie stops, swallows the cherry, and laughs before adding, "As long as it has a five-star hotel! Not that that isn't easy when your territory is Fairfield and Westchester counties. There are no middle-of-nowhere's in these parts."

Staring into the mirror behind Silas, George sees half of his own face, and half of his brother's, on either side of him. All together, they are an oval Venn diagram: Eddie and George do not overlap. George is quiet, thinking. Bellow again comes to mind: "And when your heart is full, keep your mouth shut also."

He watches Eddie stir the lone ice cube in his drink with his forefinger before he asks, "You are kidding about the blimp, George, right? That I know. I mean, isn't that what the Hindenburg was? The fireball?" Eddie looks around for the snack bowl and makes a face.

George is getting hungry, too. "Why don't we get the bar menu. We can just stay here and eat, right?"

"Yeah, of course." He motions to Silas, "Menus, Bro." Then he turns around and puts his hand on his brother's shoulder again. "I see you've got an itch. But, Jesus, why not just go for a Lamborghini, a Ferrari, or some other gorgeous Italian. Hubba hubba." Silas slides menus in front of them. Eddie picks his up then puts it down. "What about a Bugatti, George. Yeah, that's the ticket. A Bugatti. Why not? Hell, your bikes are nicer than your car. Much better. A Bugatti would cure you."

"Cure me. Lord, maybe you're right, Eddie." For the first time George comes up against the idea that he is a pathetic sap. He tries to laugh. "Ha. Yes, yes, you may be right." Now all he can think is that maybe this whole idea is just some perverse version of a mid-life crisis. How pathetic am I? His heart sinks at the thought. George believes his vision is singular but the characterization "mid-life crisis" threatens to ground him.

Eddie hasn't stopped talking. George tries to listen. "Have you ever been to Heritage Motor Cars on the Avenue? Some of the most beautiful bodies you have ever seen." Eddie is on a roll. "You can take any one of those babies out for a test drive—even a fucking Bugatti Chiron if they happen to have one on the floor."

George stops listening. He is thinking about the other George. The one he saw in the mirror and walking the tree line. The one staring out the window at his office. He silently invites him to come closer and with that invitation feels himself overtaken from inside, as if someone just his size is entering through a tiny opening in the soles of his feet, slowly stretching up and out, to his fingertips, his toes, filling his thighs, calves, stomach, lungs, heart—every nook and cranny—to bursting. The fit is perfect. He feels as if he were once hollow but now is replete. Simultaneously, he has the sensation that his blood is rising up into his head all at once in near ecstasy—thrumming in his ears, making it impossible to hear anything but his own heartbeat which is as palpable as a thick tongue.

Do you know that feeling? It is happening to George now. He sees that his brother is still speaking, raising his eyebrows in a question. But George is so absorbed in what is taking place inside his own body he can't make out the words. He smiles and answers not Eddie's question but his own. "No. Not a mid-life crisis. Not crisis at all. An affluence." He stops, looks into his own eyes across the way in the bar mirror. Or is it the other George? Who is shadow? Who is light?

He repeats the word again, louder now, "An affluence."

Eddie knows the word affluent, of course, but is smart enough to know this is not what his brother is talking about. For once he keeps his mouth shut, allows the glow of George's otherness burnish the love he feels for his younger sibling. And in this rare quiet moment with his brother, George glows in the gold light of the bar, thrills at the trilling of his blood.

<h1 style="text-align:center">THIRTY-TWO</h1>

The nights when Magnus doesn't stay over, and they are few, Phoebe places pillows around herself to simulate the comfort she feels when his sturdy arms encircle her, just above her tummy and below her breasts, his knees tucked right behind hers. But it doesn't work. She doesn't feel safe. It's a feeling she will have to resign herself to when Magnus moves back to Norway. It's only thanks to sheer exhaustion that Phoebe eventually falls asleep and, right before daybreak, dreams a dream she's had, in one form or another, since childhood.

She is running and begins to beat her arms, very hard and very fast, until that heavenly moment when she lifts right off the ground. At first, she's barely an inch up. But by using every bit of her strength, and beating her arms harder and harder, she catches the wind like a kite and, finally, floats, her arms just steering, her fingertips grazing the clouds. Everything below—houses, cars, bikes, stores, streets, her school, even the lake with all of its many fingers—becomes smaller and smaller until they are simply pattern. It feels akin to the moment that comes (and it can only happen once in your life) when you're learning to ride a bike—that rush of joy when the person running alongside you lets go. The moment when no one is holding you up, but you are pedaling, alone, in perfect balance, seemingly aloft.

Still in the dream, a bouquet of cosmos floats in front of Phoebe and she tries to grab them. Reaching, reaching, reaching.

Big thud: body. Smaller thuds: elbows then hands. Phoebe's awake—and how—amidst a riotous tangle of bed sheets and pillows on the wood floor next to her bed. Good lord, I have beaten myself out of sleep, out of bed, in my furious attempt to fly.

Her chest heaves, hungry for oxygen. Wishing she were still high up above this earth, she stretches her limbs out in every direction across the floor and stares first at the ceiling and then down the wall to the small work of art hanging to the right of her bed. It is a print of Albrecht Durer's watercolor of a young hare, probably the only object that has been with her since childhood, no matter where she has moved. When she was young, she was fascinated by the perfectly rendered fur and whiskers—one soft, the other stiff as broom bristles. Often, she would put her fingers on the glass and try to touch both.

Now she focuses on the hare's black eyes. Without her glasses hare is not hare. Instead, the animal's long ears are wings not spread wide but upright; its paws with their long, sharp, black nails are talons. Hare is enormous bird diving for prey that too late hears the soft whistle of air through wings, feels itself helpless in the grip of something inevitable.

Yes, she misses Magnus. Phoebe turns onto her stomach, her pregnancy a soft cushion. A spider with fine legs—a series on sharp "n's" on either side of its body—moves sideways out from under her bed. "Just doing its thing," Phoebe thinks, and lets it be. The nausea arrives. She makes it to the bathroom just in time but doesn't begrudge the sickness. On the contrary.

THIRTY-THREE

"Where are you guys?" It is Samantha, who has called George's cell. "Haven't heard 'boo' in weeks?"

George is incapable of a lie: "Hey, Sam. We got home a couple days after Labor Day. Would've called but barely settled and now Harriet's off with the kids—took them to see her parents for a couple nights before we have to get Ben and Karen off to school. I stayed home. Papers to sign at the firm."

"Is this perfect or what? Greg's away, too. With his mom for a night." She waits briefly for an answer. George is silent. Samantha continues, "I'm coming over. You promised. Remember?" She speaks again, now without any question in her voice, "The barn. Be there in fifteen."

Why argue? Sam's call, the fact that they are both free? Both alone? Hell, it was inevitable. He has work gloves on and, as he peels them off, the other George appears. Together they slide the great barn door open and wait, elbow to elbow, in a reverie. It isn't long before they spot Samantha walking across the field that separates house from barn towards them.

Now Samantha stands in the center of the barn, stamping grass off the soles of her espadrilles and looking up at the raw arching beams. George slides the barn door closed. Light from four dormer windows in the pitched roof and other, double hung ones set high front and back illuminates silver dust floating through the air to some invisible music. George is trying to make out the tune; he doesn't hear Samantha ask, "What was this used for, anyway? Too nice for animals."

"Sorry, what?"

"This place—what was it for?"

"Oh, we bought it from built wooden boats—sailboats, masts, and all. But I guess he put up the masts after he rolled the boats outside."

Samantha walks towards a far corner. There's a worktable that spans an entire wall over which a pegboard holds tools of every stripe. The outline of each is drawn in black underneath. Needle-nose pliers are atop the table and two rows up, three over on the board is their bird-beak silhouette. "How clever you are, George." Sam picks up the pliers and replaces them on their peg. "There!"

On the adjacent wall, bicycles, helmets, rubber inner tubes, bike clothes, a pump and long strands of glistening chains hang from hooks. Another bike is upside down on a metal stand. Samantha spins the wheel of this one and puts her finger on the chain. It turns black with grease. She looks for a cloth to wipe it clean. George's shadow starts walking towards her, but George steps in front, gets to Samantha first. "I like you too much to fall in love with you, Sam." He's quite sure words have been put in his mouth.

"What did you say?" Samantha lifts her eyes to face George and he has no choice but to repeat himself as she stares him down.

"I said, 'I like you too much to fall in love with you.'" This second time he's certain he speaks for himself.

"Well, that's quite a mouthful!" Samantha looks around, "Is it okay if I take a seat somewhere?" George extends his arm, pointing to a long bench with a cane seat and back. Samantha plunks herself down thigh to thigh with George's doppelgänger who is waiting there, wearing a soft smile. "I need a cloth or something." Sam holds up her forefinger and smiles. "Couldn't keep my hands to myself."

George grabs a rag out of a bin near the door and sits down, snug into the outline of his smiling twin. If possession is taking place, he's the one that is going to take it. Sam takes the rag but before wiping her finger clean, makes a dark fingerprint on George's face. He draws back. "What's that for?"

"To remember me by." Samantha replies and then roughly rubs her finger with the white cloth, leaving a series of black and gray smudges. No one breaks the silence. No one feels awkward.

Samantha might have taken offence at George's words, stormed off; but it would have been disingenuous. Instead, she hands George back the cloth and in so doing grabs hold of his hand and laughs, a really deep-throated laugh, nearly to tears. "You are something, George Paxton." She turns and gives him a quick kiss on top of where she marked his cheek. "And so right to have said what you did. Because you know what? I adore my husband, maybe I am even in love with him. Still."

"You are a strange one, Sam"

"Strange, or maybe not. I wanted proof of something. I have that now. But I suppose it was a lousy way to go about getting it."

George looks puzzled. "I am not sure…"

"Oh, hell, George, I half wanted something to happen. What, why, heaven knows. Just because I'm a psychologist doesn't mean I have a clue about my own motivations!" Samantha shakes her head. "No. That's not true. I wanted—not what you were thinking, maybe—but to come close, close enough to know that I am—always have been—right."

"About yourself?"

"Me? Maybe that, too."

It didn't matter to George. Sam mattered to him for a different reason. He was relieved when she sat back, circled her arms around his chest, and bestowed another quick kiss. "And hey, we have each other as an insurance policy…you know, if we ever find ourselves alone in our dotage and want company. You're my guy and I'm your gal."

In reply, George just ran a hand up through her short hair, paused then ruffled it.

On a table next to the bench one of George's books on airships lay open, words on one side, a large photo on the other. Samantha pulls it into her lap, "What in heaven's name is this? A blimp? Is that what they call them?"

George sighs, takes the book from her. "That's what most people would say. Too silly a name for these incredible machines. Airship is the right term. Anyway, this is one of the K-series. Used during World War II as patrols over the Pacific." He turns to another page, marked with a blue sticky note, and reads aloud. "Of the 89,000 ships escorted by airships during World War II, not one was lost to enemy action."

"Who knew!"

"Who knew, indeed. Men on these ships would spot enemy subs and radio their positions to allied ships in the vicinity." He pulls another book from the table and taps the author's name on the cover. "I met this man on Nantucket—amazing old guy. He was involved in the whole initiative. He's going to help me."

"Help you?"

"I've left the firm, Sam. I'm making plans to fly one of these ships of the air."

"The hell you are!" Sam says this but believes him all the same. She shakes her head gently, incredulous and smiling. He takes her hand and squeezes it warmly. "I knew you'd get it."

"What came first?" Samantha pages through another book, stopping at pages with photos.

"Meaning?"

"Did you meet the blimp man and then become obsessed or did the obsession come first?"

"You're something, Sam. The latter. Most definitely. The rest was pure serendipity. Or maybe synchronicity. Or maybe just inevitable."

"Like the end of your marriage..."

George is startled. "What's one got to do with..."

"Get real, George." Samantha stares at him as she says this and he doesn't look away, doesn't blink. It feels as if something inside of him wants to escape but he holds firm.

"I didn't ask for this to happen—the obsession, I mean."

"No? But of course you did. You've always been asking for it."

"A way to end my marriage? That's not really..."

"No, no. I mean, yes, that is inevitable now but that's not what I mean. I mean always asking for something bigger. Something more. Something—." Sam stops speaking. She is struggling to think of the right word.

"Something what? And please don't say 'mid-life crisis,' like Eddie did."

"You told him? That you wanted to fly a blimp—"

"Airship."

"Blimp. Airship. Whatever."

"There's a difference."

"OK, sorry. It's just Eddie. Of all people."

"He's blood. My brother—"

"Right. You had to tell him. Got it."

"And most especially before he got wind of it from someone else. That would be the end. Maybe even turn him against me."

"You're right."

"Met him at Worth's the night after we got home."

"Just can't imagine him ever understanding, not in a million years."

"Enough that he's on my side."

"Even if he never gets it, never gets that you, that you are...." Again Samantha stops. She is searching, still, for the right word. George waits. He wants her to find that word, to hear her speak it out loud. And in that space, his twin moves back out of the shadows and steps into George fully, completely. Samantha shivers.

"What, Sam, what?" When she looks at him, he sees that she knows, sees that he is becoming. Becoming. What does it matter if she can't find the word? Neither can he. He kisses her again, differently, nearly with force. On the lips. So different. They both know it, both know there is no word for this, either.

Samantha will always remember that kiss precisely because it left her not speechless, but wordless. George was speaking a language she intuited but which was beyond her ken—prehistoric cave paintings evaporating as she tried to bring the lantern close. She loved George for wanting to share the gift and would forever feel a yearning not for the man but for what he was able to become. She went so far as to understand that it was not something he could simply pass on to another, through a kiss or any other means.

No, indeed.

The word was inside George, a gift, yes, but a burden, too. He prayed he could live up to it.

Samantha left, wistful, knowing that she would never fly herself, or ever again come as close as she just had.

THIRTY-FOUR

One last time. For good. That's what Phoebe tells herself as she phones Ruth, her best friend from high school. She really does want to tell someone the whole story—in her own words, as Dr. Gail had begged. But more, with her heart wide open. And she wants to do it before she feels the baby move. The first flutter kick. *Her* baby. She believes it will give her peace. And Ruth is probably the only person to whom she can tell the whole story. Even if her stepparents were still alive, Ruth would be the one. Sure, their lives had taken different paths, oh so different. But they can always take up where they've left off—no matter how much time has passed, no matter how wide the gulf in their situations.

Ruth lives in Atlanta where her husband is a renowned interventional cardiologist at a university hospital. Need I say more? She has every creature comfort and two young children who seem to be flourishing in school. But her life doesn't just look good from the outside; it really is good. She was art director at a prestigious design firm for many years. Now that she's married, and the children are young with busy school lives, she works just as hard at a children's museum and an arthouse theater, ostensibly as a "volunteer," but perhaps even harder than she ever worked at her "real" job. Ruth is always full steam. No matter what needs to be done, she does it and does it with great flair—from designing logos or heading up fundraising campaigns to signage, exhibitions, event planning. She is also exceptionally kind. Her husband, her children, her many friends, and most especially Phoebe, adore her.

Phoebe, as we know, is a waitress; supposedly, initially, to support her work as a choreographer and dancer with a local and always-struggling dance troupe. But her job at the restaurant—a beloved gathering place for the friendliest and best people she knows—provides her with more satisfaction (and heaps more financial security) than her poorly attended dance performances. So, when people ask, she no longer says, "I'm a dancer and a choreographer. Oh, and I help out at Just Good Food on the side." Instead, for nearly a year now she's taken

taken to smiling and just saying, "I'm a waitress at Just Good Food." A 42-year-old waitress. Well, that will have to be enough for now.

But how does it happen? How does it happen that two young women, one slim and artistic—a dancer—with long red hair, freckles galore and a smile charmingly broad and crooked, the other dark-haired, dark-complexioned, green-eyed, with a figure always riding the fine line between voluptuous and a bit heavy, end up living such different lives? When they went about as teens they drew stares because they were so strikingly opposite—Phoebe so white, Ruth nearly blue black. And they were always laughing. They were in the same seventh grade class. That's where they met. After that, the school did its best to assign them to different class sections to avoid the inevitable combustion. It was as if the two were elements like hydrogen and oxygen. When ignited not by heat or flame but simply by meeting each other's glance, an explosive release of energy, namely uncontrolled laughter, would result.

Whenever they were in the same room everyone else would be in a high state of expectancy, if not anxiety, wondering when that combustion would take place. One time an usher at the local movie theater had to escort them out because their he-haws were upsetting the other moviegoers. When they got out into the sunlight on the street they had to bend over and hold their tummies as they wiped the tears of laughter from their cheeks.

In their senior year, Phoebe was plucked from the local ballet troupe in which she danced to be one of the more prominent cygnets in a Christmas performance of *Swan Lake* in Atlanta. It was a huge honor. Ruth came to the opening, of course, and had a seat dead center and right up front. That was a terrible mistake. At one dramatic point, when Phoebe was supposed to be holding a pose to one side of the prima ballerina playing Odette, she and Ruth locked eyes. That was all it took. The fact that they were at the ballet, a performance that demanded quiet, made an explosion all the more inevitable and inversely proportional out-of-control.

Ruth's shoulders shaking with barely contained giggles in her seat was one thing. Phoebe succumbing to laughter on stage was another. Bathed in the stage lights, her pink feathers quivered with tiny convulsions for all to see. It was disastrous. After the performance, the audience still clapping, the ballet master roundly reprimanded Phoebe in front of the entire cast. He would have fired her, too, if a replacement had been possible on short notice.

The girls' behavior was applauded by their peers, chalked up to immaturity and even tolerated by grownups when they were in seventh grade. But, by this time the girls were seniors, heading off to college. Word spread about what had happened at the *Swan Lake* performance and at school the following week even Phoebe and Ruth's classmates looked at them askance and whispered, "Those two are insane."

Is it little wonder, then, that Phoebe is calling Ruth? The irrepressible inevitability of their laughter is also the measure of their love for each other. You cannot be unselfconsciously silly with another human being unless you can be completely yourself. Phoebe knew she could share with Ruth the story as Dr. Gail dreamed of hearing it.

"Ruth?"

"Phoebe. Oh my God, Phoebe! I was wondering where you'd been. I should have picked up the phone. *Mea culpa! Mea culpa!* Can we make a date? Soon? I am so sorry I haven't been in touch. I just put the big fundraiser for the children's museum to bed. No excuse, I know. I know. Lord, I miss you, girl!

"That's why I called. Do you want to drive down here or would you rather I come up to Atlanta?"

"I'll come there. I'm ready to get-outta-Dodge. I can arrange something for the kids after school so I don't have to rush. Maybe Wednesday?" Ruth stops. She is looking at the blackboard in her kitchen, which is covered with dates and notes. "No, that's no good. Thursday. Would Thursday work for you?"

"Perfect, yeah. That's great. I'll just work breakfast. Dolores can do lunch for me. So free by 11 or so. Meet at the restaurant?"

"That's fine. But I want to spend some time at your place, too. We can take a long walk from there. Maybe even go for a swim."

"A long walk would be good. Lots to talk about."

"As always. All good, mostly good, I hope."

"I'm working on that. It'll just be great to talk to you. I haven't really had anyone."

"Had anyone? What does that mean?" Ruth pauses but there is no response from Phoebe, so she continues. "Bad me. You're ok, right?"

"Am. And stop saying 'sorry.' Now's the perfect time, really, Ruth."

"I'm getting a call. So, quarter to eleven or so on Thursday. Can't wait. Love you."

Phoebe says, "Love you," back. But Ruth has already rung off to take her other call. No matter.

THIRTY-FIVE

As planned, Ruth arrives at Just Good Food while Phoebe is finishing her shift. After giving one another a quick hug, Ruth sits down with a cup of coffee. Watching her old friend weave amongst the small tables, she knows immediately that Phoebe is "with child." Oh, she is still lean as a bean pole, but she is leaning backwards the tiniest bit as she walks and the girl who has never had even a hint of a tummy now does, a little pooch, right in front. She catches Phoebe's eye and uses face and hands to express, "Oh, my God!" Phoebe gives her a *Mona Lisa* smile in return.

The moment Phoebe finishes work and the two step outside Ruth grabs Phoebe by the arm. "What's with the little blip?"

"Blip?"

"Little beer belly on your boy body." She stares at Phoebe's stomach and continues. "Wish we weren't in separate cars as man oh man do I have questions. I thought you and Alex were kaput, so, tell me it's the chef. He is one gorgeous man. And always got his eye on you, I might add."

"Henry? No way. Gives me the heebie-jeebies."

"Maybe because you're actually attracted?"

"Not."

Ruth makes a face. "You're impossible. I'll follow you. But quick. I want answers!"

She follows Phoebe back to her place—the tiny, ugly tract home Phoebe bought for a song and transformed into a sweet cottage through sheer imagination and hard work. The moment they are out of their cars, Ruth bursts out. "So..." Phoebe stops her. "Let's put our things inside and walk. I want to walk and talk."

"As I said: infuriating." Ruth rolls her eyes and drops into a chair to change into sneakers.

"Ready?"

"Ready."

The pair start off and fall into an exaggerated swinging of their arms and gulping of air. Ruth speaks first: "I should visit more often."

"Yes, you should."

"To see you, of course, but it is just nice to be in such open space. Trees. Fields." Ruth points. "Hay bales?"

"This is the country, after all."

Her impatience clear, Ruth says, voice rising, "So? So? Speak, girl!"

"The guy who did it was eating an orange."

Phoebe starts in the middle or at least a little way into the story because she is recalling, again, this vivid detail. One of many stored in a bottom drawer in the darkest, back corner of the least used cupboard.

"Whoa, whoa, whoa. Phoebe, my God. I am just trying to take in the fact that you are pregnant. You are pregnant, right?"

Phoebe nods and Ruth continues. "Anyway, what do you mean, 'the guy who did it' as if he doesn't have a name." Ruth stops swinging her arms. "And 'eating an orange.' What the f- does that mean?"

"Sorry. I was just remembering that. Again."

"OK. Well, back up, back up. Good lord. Do you want to sit down for this, Phoebe? I mean *I* feel out of breath."

"No. I really want to walk. Let's keep walking."

Ruth crosses her hands over her upper chest to steady herself. There is a long slow incline in the road ahead and she's breathless. "I forgot how hilly it is out here. Is your fat old friend going to make it?"

"You? Look at me!" Phoebe looks down at the nearly imperceptible bump that's just begun to shape-shift her slim frame.

"How far along are you anyway? We spoke just before the 4th, didn't we? That's what? Month and a half ago."

"11 weeks or so—about to go into my 3rd month."

"So, you already knew…"

"Well, it had just happened."

"It?"

"I called you that same week. But really because I wanted to say, 'Bon Voyage.' You were packing up to go to your niece's wedding, remember?"

"But you'd wanted to talk?" Ruth's shoulders drop, her head, too. "I jumped off the phone that day. I remember. There was so much to take care of…"

"It's fine, Ruth, really, I wasn't ready at that point. I didn't know how it would all turn out. Not then. Not yet."

"I'm so damn self-involved sometimes. If I'd known it was urgent…"

"I just wanted to hear your voice, my dear. Really."

"We were only gone a week. You could have called when I got back."

"It was still too soon. I needed time to think. And then, when I was sure, you might have wanted to talk me out of it. I wanted to be beyond all that." It is Phoebe's turn to lay her palm atop her abdomen. "I am certainly beyond all that now. And beyond sure."

"That's all that matters, kiddo. And Alex? You said, 'the guy' but it is Alex isn't it?" Ruth slows and looks over at Phoebe who is expressionless. "Orange or no orange." Phoebe winces. "Tell me you didn't do some *in vitro* thing? No, you said, 'the guy.' So, Alex, right? Unless I've really missed a lot in 4 months."

Phoebe is just staring straight ahead. A sphynx.

"Oh, my god. I was right. It's the chef? Tell me it's the chef?

"God, no—"

"Anyway, he's supportive, right?" Ruth finally stops and looks at Phoebe who is focusing on her feet and shaking her head "No."

"No what?" Ruth asks.

"No to everything, Ruthie."

"We're going to be 42 this year. How did we get so old? I know people have babies at this age but isn't it sort of…"

Phoebe interrupts. "I took the test for Down's. They tested me for everything, actually. All sorts of icky things. All's well as far as that goes."

"OK. Well. It's just that I was so much younger when I had the kids. And I have Harold. Support from every direction. You're damn right I would have tried to talk you out of this. But maybe you and Alex or some guy I don't know about yet, want this. You'll get married?"

Phoebe can't bear any more of this. "Stop, Ruth, just stop."

"Stop?"

"Walking. Talking for a moment."

"Ok, ok. I'll shut up."

"It was a stranger—a not so perfect stranger."

Ruth is out of breath and speaks in nearly a whisper. "You? You had—what's that phrase—a 'hook-up'?"

There is no reason to be harsh with Ruth. But Phoebe can't answer that question. Not right off. They walk on. Phoebe picks up a branch by the side of the road, removes the little twigs and walks on using it as a walking stick and, also to tap out the word she speaks next.

"I was raped, Ruthie. There is no 'we.' This is my baby. Just mine. All mine."

They are at the top of the hill now. They stop and look not at the houses that line one side of the road but at the open field with tall grass and graceful trees on the other. The sky is blue and fat cumulus clouds make it more so.

Ruth starts talking just to catch not her literal breath but something harder to quiet. "Looking only this way…" Ruth lifts her chin to point west. "… we could be anywhere. Out in Colorado or in Provence or Greece or maybe Australia." Then she takes Phoebe's hand, squeezes it hard. She can't quite bring herself to look Phoebe in the eye. "I am so happy to be out here in the country. With you. I—"

"Are you?"

"Phoebe, my god. I honestly don't know what to say first. 'I'm so sorry?' 'How the hell are you coping?'"

Ruth turns now to look at Phoebe, squarely, "And of course I feel guilty I didn't pay more attention when you called. You must have been frightened out of your friggin' mind. Maybe still are."

Phoebe begins to walk again, now on a downhill track. It is steep. A small, oval pond blinks in the distance. They walk more quickly, their shoulders thrown back to keep their balance, their eyes trained on that blue eye. Ruth, who, after the birth of each child, moved very comfortably and decidedly from voluptuous to full-figured—and who is even more beautiful as a result—, moves like a gentle beast. Even so, you wouldn't mess with her: ferocious strength lies underneath, hinted at when she narrows her eyes and looks at the world askance. She walks ahead of Phoebe and from the back Phoebe watches how gracefully her weight shifts from one hip—a haunch really—to the other.

Ruth turns to Phoebe and her black face burnishes beautifully blue in the strong sunlight. "I keep interrupting, girl. Forgive me. Start from the start. I came to listen."

"OK. So, a couple years ago I found this sandy strip on one side of the lake—perfect spot to get in the water for my swims. Back and forth, back and forth."

"Wish I had your discipline…"

"More my need for it. Anyway, except for weekend water-skiers, and some fishermen, I never see a soul. I park on the road in front of a slab where there used to be a house—the property's for sale. From there it's just a short walk to the point where I take off."

"Maybe you can show me. Warm enough for a skinny dip?" Ruth says. Phoebe is silent. "What am I thinking? Of course, if that's where…I'm sure you don't go there anymore."

"Didn't. But I've started up again. We can drive over. Anyway, one afternoon at the very beginning of July…"

"That's just before we left for Greece…"

"Yes. So, while I'm swimming that day I look up and see this guy standing on the shore right where I always leave my towel and glasses. I was only about halfway through my laps, and I cursed thinking the gig was up—that whoever it was, was going to ruin my routine. Tell me I was trespassing. That he'd bought the property or something."

A truck comes up the hill and accelerates as it passes the women. In its wake Ruth and Phoebe put their hands down along their thighs to keep their skirts from flying up.

"Asshole!" Ruth screams at the driver then she turns to Phoebe and pats her shoulder. "Couldn't help myself. Sorry. Go on—"

"You talk like that around the kids?"

"Never. Perfect lady at home." Ruth scans the road for more traffic before moving alongside Phoebe. "Go on."

"I came out of the lake, ready to apologize for parking my car, for leaving my stuff and…" Phoebe stops walking for a moment. Ruth doesn't want to speak or interrupt. She simply waits. They both take sips of water from the bottles they brought along. "When I got close enough, I started apologizing, asked if he'd bought the property. It was a guy. Probably around our age. No, a bit younger."

"You got a good look?"

"Well, you know I'm as good as blind without my glasses. He was wearing a cowboy hat which made it hard to see his face, and a tool belt with all sorts of tools hanging from it."

"Like a repair guy?" Ruth wondered.

"That's what the police thought. It was a clue at any rate. Anyway, as I was apologizing I was also thinking, like you said, 'Oh, maybe he's a workman. Not the person who bought the property. Maybe a surveyor or someone hired by the new owners.' He was in the way so I couldn't grab my towel. Or my glasses." Phoebe is putting her feet down, one in front of the other, and tapping her makeshift walking stick, in tempo with each word she speaks. "He was eating an orange. I think now that he was taking a break—had just driven down this old road with no houses out of curiosity, walked down to the lake, watched me swimming. Stood there in the weedy grass, eating his orange."

Ruth feels her toes hitting the ends of her sneakers as they continue downhill. It is a pressure she doesn't like.

"He didn't answer. He just grabbed me. I had on a two-piece suit. Bikini. Stupid. I've got one like boarders wear. You know, with sleeves and short legs. Wish I'd worn that. Would have made it more difficult."

"'More difficult'? Oh, God, Phoebe. Of course you've told this all before, right? To the police or someone?"

"God, yes. Over and over. But to tell you is different." Phoebe briefly grabs her friend's arm and squeezes it. "It was after one of those crazy thunderstorms—power out, trees down. Crews from other counties come clean up sometimes. That's what the police said, anyway. Why it was harder to nail anyone; why they decided it wasn't anyone local."

"'It?' Oh, Phoebe. Phoebe."

"I screwed up, too. Afterwards. With the evidence or whatever."

"Nonsense."

"He was big, or at least tall. And strong. I was still holding my goggles and cap sort of tangled in one hand. They were slippery. And I was dripping wet. In a two-piece! When I hit him the first time it was with that hand and the blow just slid off him and I dropped my goggles and cap. For some stupid reason I turned to them pick up. Crazy. Habit. That's when he put his hand over my mouth from behind. His hand smelled like oranges. Then he put his other arm around my stomach and pulled me into him. I bit his hand. That tasted like oranges, too."

Ruth stops walking and turns to Phoebe. Phoebe stops, too. But she keeps her eyes on the pond ahead, the open eye that is closer and bigger now. Staring. Cold.

"He never made a sound. I guess he undid his fly, still holding me. I couldn't move. I was screaming into his hand. Then he pulled down my bathing suit bottom and pushed me down on the ground. I really couldn't scream when he was on top of me. He was heavy and his tool belt—whatever was in that damn thing—was cutting into me. All those metal tools. That hurt so much—all these things cutting into my lower back and my thighs—that I barely felt the rest."

"Phoebe..."

"Yep. 'It.' All so fast. So fast."

They are walking again. Ruth doesn't dare speak. She has to let Phoebe tell this. Finish.

"People always say 'I was frozen with fright.' That isn't how it was Ruth. My mind felt very sharp. If you were frozen you wouldn't feel anything. But I felt pain. Animal fear. It was as if some powerful beast had overtaken me." Phoebe realizes she has stopped breathing, just as she had that day. "I had to force myself to breathe afterwards. I was just glad when he got up and those metal things weren't digging into me. I had so many bruises and small cuts afterwards."

Ruth keeps quiet. But she puts her hand on Phoebe's arm, which Phoebe reaches around and squeezes again.

"After he stood up, he didn't run away. That surprised me. Still does. I lay there and watched. He picked his cowboy hat up from the grass, slowly, and slapped it against his leg. I didn't dare move. Everything before had been so fast. So it seemed as if he were leaving in slow motion. I was thinking, screaming inside, 'Go! Go! Get out of here.' Eventually I heard his truck start up. A rumble. I could feel it on the ground, so it had to have been a pretty big truck. The police assume it was a utility truck. But who knows. Anything would have seemed loud because it was so quiet otherwise."

As if on cue another truck barrels up the road and Ruth takes in a breath, prepared to curse again but Phoebe stops her. "Let me finish."

"Yes, yes. Sorry."

"I closed my eyes until I couldn't hear anything. And when I opened them, I turned my head so I was facing the lake. I looked out at the water for a moment and then focused more closely. On the ground right beside me was the orange peel—a beautiful curve of orange skin with the soft white fleshy hollow gnawed clean. That's what he'd left of it."

THIRTY-SIX

"My brother's going to join us over Columbus Day. He called while we were in the car." Harriet was standing at the sink, back to her husband. In fact, the two had hardly faced one another since their return home from Nantucket.

"Henry?"

"Of course, Henry." Harriet had two brothers but only Henry was single and close enough to travel solo for a long weekend. Still, there was no reason for her to be sharp, but she was sharp. "Said he's barely taken a day off since he started working at that café down in Georgia. He's hoping to gather some cranberries, maybe even rose hips if they're any left. I told him blueberry season is way done."

George crossed the kitchen to stand beside his wife who was dumping ice and water from the cooler she and the kids used for drinks and snacks on the drive home from her parents. As soon as she put it down, he took it up, shook out the last drips of water, and began to dry it. "More the merrier—especially as we won't have Ben and Karen. Lila will love going foraging with him. George turned to his wife and continued, in a playful tone, "Just hope he's not so in need of a break he won't want to cook for us!"

Harriet's reply was not playful. She grabbed a corner of the kitchen towel in George's hands to dry her own and said, "Yeah, heaven forbid you have to eat what I cook!"

"Why would you say that?" George put down cooler and towel to cup his hand on Harriet's shoulder and try, gently, to turn her to face him. But she stood firm. "When do we ever not cook together? I only meant we all—you included, you most especially—love it when your brother cooks. He *is* a trained chef after all."

Harriet walked away from George and only when she had put several feet between them did she turn to her husband. "Frankly, I'm sort of surprised he's coming. It's not as if he and I are that close. We barely even speak on the phone."

"Well, I'm glad he's making the effort. He's fun company. Driving up? Flying?"

"Didn't say but he'd be stupid to drive all that way just for a weekend. Really stupid."

So. That was it. George knew it in a flash. Harriet must have overheard him tell Lila, "I'll throw it in the car and we can leave it on Nantucket for the winter" when she'd asked about bringing her new boogie board to the island over Columbus Day.

"Call me stupid then because, yes, I am planning to drive—at least one way." George walked over to the kitchen island, pulled out a stool and sat across from where his wife stood. "And not just because I love the ferry." He tried but failed to sound lighthearted.

"Whatever."

"You and Lila will still fly, of course. I'll leave a day or two before, get the house open, groceries..."

"Fine." Harriet cut in before George continued.

"Then I'm there to pick all you guys up. Anyway, I want to leave a car on the island. I'm thinking I'll go back and forth as I begin work on my project. I like having Ernst for advice. Encouragement. Anyway, it's something—one thing—I want to talk about." George pulled out the stool next to him. "Sit a moment?"

"I'm fine standing." Harriet crossed her arms over her chest.

Tomorrow, Harriet would be back to her usual work schedule, gone by 8, home between 5 and 6. George was free of that, free of the law firm. Over the coming weekend Ben and Karen would leave for boarding school. Having their two eldest away from home for the first time would upset the balance of their home. But, hell, it was upset already.

Harriet took George out of this reverie. She slapped her hands down on the kitchen island. "I refuse to move." She had flown right over any emotional mine fields right to afterwards, to the practical. It didn't seem a leap to either of them.

"No need. We've got two places. You've never loved Nantucket. I appreciate that you have spent part of your summer vacation there every year."

George was thinking of the children, thinking they would have their same homes, their same parents, and the familiar pattern of their summers—a month with one parent, then the other—simply extended throughout the year. He was thinking ahead. Not that far ahead. To after the split. To now.

"Fine."

George responded without thinking, a sentence that was an even further leap forward. "Why don't I just bunk in the barn for now. Not that you'll see much of me. I'm starting flight school over at Westchester Airport in a few days..."

Harriet made a sound, half laugh, half snort. George went on.

"Accelerated ground and in-the-air training. Over eight hours a day. Course is total immersion."

The walls of the kitchen didn't sway. Lightening didn't strike. The tiny red arm on the oven clock advanced to the right with a click and the refrigerator thrummed its comforting tune.

"Barn's always been your space anyway."

"Exactly. We can sort out the long-term after."

Harriet repeated that word, "Fine" once more. Neither had said the word "divorce." It was understood.

They were both silent until Harriet shook her head.

"What?" Harriet shook her head again and again.

"What?"

"You know the only thing that really bugs me?"

George shrugged his shoulders.

"Knowing I will have to see Samantha smiling like the cat that swallowed the bird."

"Canary. Ate. Cat that ate the canary." As soon as he said this, George felt an ass. Bird, canary, what did it matter? He was ashamed of himself.

"You're such an ass, George."

"She won't do that. She wouldn't want..."

"Don't bother, George. Not now."

He saw no point in arguing when they really never had. "You're right. And sorry about the canary bit."

Harriet finally perched on the stool next to George, but not before pulling it several inches further away from him. She stared straight ahead, elbows on the counter, palms cupping her chin. Even after George said her name, as a question, "Harriet?" she kept staring off towards the hallway.

"Harriet, can you look at me a moment?"

She turned her head only briefly. "I hardly know what that means, George. Look at you? Why bother, when, frankly, I can't see you anymore." She paused. "I mean I don't see you anymore, haven't for a couple months." She pretended to call out as for a lost cat. "George—? George—? Where are you, George?"

"Well, I am here."

"Really? Really?" She said this with anger and as she did she reached over and pincered George's arm several times, tiny pecks.

George didn't begrudge his wife the attack. He waited until she was finished. "I don't know how to describe it, Harriet. Maybe I'm not the George you've thought of as your husband. This other self..."

Harriet broke in. "Don't bother."

"Bother?"

"With words. Any more words. It's fine. I don't know—honestly don't care—what's become of you. Clearly the kids can still see you."

George lifted both hands, palms up, in supplication. As he did, he looked out the window and saw his doppelgänger, walking in a small circle, hands with fingers intertwined behind his back. It was an attitude of contemplation, perhaps some impatience. George felt this was too much, a show of hubris that did not sit well.

"Haven't got the words anyway."

"And you a man of words." Harriet nearly spit it out.

George winced and opened his mouth to speak but Harriet stopped him, saying loudly "It's fine," and then more softly, "All fine—fine, fine, fine." She stood but turned before she left the room. "It's as if you believe you are the only character in this novel of yours, George. But guess what? I'm a main character, too." And with that, Harriet left the room.

This small speech and repetition of the word "fine," pained George, greatly. It reduced all the years before—all their years as a couple, as a family—to nothing more than "fine." It could be worse. No doubt that is what enabled them both to be calm, well, relatively so.

He was a fool. Of course she was a main character. Maybe one day he would look back and see her that way. And maybe she would do the same for him.

He looked out the window and the other George stopped walking, stared back, nodded, and smiled that enigmatic smile, reminding him that there could be something more than simply "fine." But George was not in the mood. He couldn't inhabit that other self at the moment.

THIRTY-SEVEN

Describe every damn detail of the dirigible George eventually flies? Need we? More important to know all the hours George spent studying both on the ground and, eventually, up in the air, instructor by his side, in order to fulfill all the requirements for his pilot's license and instrument rating. And he followed that with the special training for airships. There were day flights and night flights. The few hours he was free he skedaddled home, met Lila after school, and sat while she had dinner, especially if Harriet were working late. Try as he might, though, he was not all there, and his daughter knew it.

"Earth to dad, earth to dad," she said one night.

George laughed and said, "Good call, my little whirligig, good call. You see I am up in the clouds even as I sit here." He laid his palm on the table and made a whoosh sound as he made his hand take off like a plane, twirl and land on his daughter's head.

"Can I go up with you one day?"

"For sure. For now, finish your veggies and I'll help you with your homework. Then I've got a night flight, so I'll have to leave when Mom gets home. But I'll be back later. Be here for breakfast and to take you to your bus in the morn."

"Bus schmus"

"What kind of talk is that?"

"What I want to know is if you're still coming with us to Nantucket for Columbus Day."

"Are you kidding? Me? Miss going there with you guys?"

"Phew."

"Already scheduled some time in the sky there so I can get my instrument rating." George gathered up Lila's plate and glass and took them over to the sink. "Don't tell Mom, but I'm hoping for some heavy weather or fog. Conditions to really put me to the test."

"If there's fog can't you use a telescope to see the astronomers?"

"Not in a plane. Not a telescope."

"Binoculars?"

"I'll show you one day. Planes have pretty high-tech instruments these days and I'm learning to trust those instruments."

"Instead of your very own eyes?"

It was a question George felt got at the heart of so much, right to the heart of this whole shift in his life. Letting go of what he thought he knew in favor of letting himself be guided by some higher power (Lord, he couldn't even believe he used those two words) even if that higher power took as prosaic a form as a terrain awareness and warning system.

"Dessert? I know we've got some of those fruitsicles in the freezer."

"Coconut one. Yes, please!"

George unwrapped a frozen pop, handed it to his daughter and sat back down at the counter beside her.

"Thing is, you can't trust your own eyes when you're in heavy fog and you can't see stars, let alone the horizon." George put his arm around his daughter's shoulder. "I'm learning that there's times your eyes tell you one thing and your ears another."

"Yikes. If you can't trust your own eyes or your own ears, what do you do?

George was pensive and didn't answer right away so Lila repeated her question in between taking little bites of her coconut popsicle.

"So, whata ya do, Dad? Whata ya do?

"You do what I'm doing, kiddo. You learn to trust in instruments and gauges—things outside yourself." George paused. "Which is sort of like trusting something deep inside yourself, too."

Lila shook her head and finished off her fruitsicle. "That makes no sense at all."

THIRTY-EIGHT

It's lunchtime when Ruth and Phoebe get back to Phoebe's house, a mere concrete rectangle if you look closely. But Phoebe has disguised those ugly bones with a wild garden and window boxes, which overflow with orange and yellow nasturtiums. And she laid a path of huge, irregular stones, inter-planted with moss and thyme that wends its way from the street to the front door which she painstakingly stripped and sanded to reveal real wood. They go inside. There's one, modestly-sized open room: a square with the kitchen in one corner, dining area just beyond, and living room making up the rectangle left over. Ruth immediately collapses at the big, pine farmer's table that serves as Phoebe's work and dining surface. Phoebe slides a pile of books, papers and her laptop to one side with one fell swoop of her arm. Ruth takes off her shoes and begins rubbing her toes.

"I had Mr. Handsome set aside two pieces of quiche for us. I'll make a salad to go. Good?" Phoebe is sliding open drawers and grabs silverware, which she dumps on the table for Ruth to set out.

"Are you kidding?" says Ruth. "Sounds great. What can I do?" Phoebe looks at her friend; sees how settled, how comfy, she looks. "You're here. That's more than enough. Just sit. Talk to me."

Phoebe measures out coffee, pulls take-out containers and lettuce from the fridge, grabs tomatoes and lemons from a basket on the counter, a huge bottle of olive oil from the cabinet over the sink. The containers go in the microwave. She punches a few buttons and hits "Start." Her back is to her friend until she turns to make the salad.

There are six chairs around the table, each one different—five are wooden and high-backed with rush seats. The sixth is an antique metal chair with heart-shaped scrolls forming its back. All are painted a different shade of blue. Likewise, the shelves in the kitchen are open and filled with mugs, plates, pitchers, all blue.

"Turquoise?" Phoebe is reaching up into those shelves.

"Not that one. The one that's sort of sea foam. Please."

"You got it. And I didn't even ask. Would you rather have a glass of wine or something else?"

"No. Coffee's perfect. Sugar, too. And half-and-half if you've got it. Please." Ruth smiles but focuses elsewhere, out the window. In a bit of a reverie. "I keep thinking of '*Leda and the Swan*'—the Yeats poem..."

"Leda?"

"The myth..."

"You lost me."

Phoebe brings Ruth's mug and her own black-and-blue one to the table along with cream, sugar. Then she turns to fetch their plates.

"I'll email it to you," Ruth says. "It's the tale of when Zeus takes the form of a swan and rapes Leda—which sets all sorts of momentous events in motion. '*A sudden blow: the great wings beating still...*'"

"'*A sudden blow*'..."

"Yes, and it goes on, '*Above the staggering girl...*'"

Phoebe crosses the kitchen again, this time carrying two plates with a slice of quiche on each. "You quoting poetry. Impressive!" She sets the plates on the table and asks Ruth,

"Spinach or ham and cheese?"

"Let's share." Ruth takes her knife and cuts the pieces into two.

Phoebe turns to grab the salad. Over her shoulder she says, "A huge swan? That's disgusting. I can't think about it. I don't like birds, except when they are far, far away, up in the sky. The idea of being in close contact. Having enormous, dirty wings wrapping, flapping around me. Touching me..." Phoebe shivers, "Can't think about it."

"Dirty? I don't think of swans as dirty. Anyway, it's the suddenness, the brutality, that reminded me."

"And her staggering..." Phoebe finally sits down but doesn't start eating immediately. "I staggered, too. When he had me in his grip."

Ruth eats quickly, is nearly half done in a heartbeat. She stops for a sip of coffee. "God, I wish you'd called me, Phoebe. I would have raced right down." Phoebe doesn't answer right away.

"Yeah, should've. Maybe. But I felt so ashamed."

Ruth stops sipping her coffee and stares at her friend. "Ashamed?" She raises her voice. "But that's ridiculous, you..."

Phoebe interrupts. "I know. I know. But that's how I felt, Ruthie. Scared. Dirty." Phoebe pauses before repeating. "And, yes, ashamed."

Ruth puts her head in her hands. "When you knew he was gone, did you go to the hospital first?"

Phoebe shakes her head.

"Police?"

Again, Phoebe shakes her head "No."

Ruth waits.

"I went back into the lake." Phoebe looks out the window. A hummingbird flies in and hovers over her flowers. It's wings, too, are "beating still" as it draws nectar from the flowers with its long beak.

"What?"

"Stupid, I guess, as it messed everything up. The swabs or whatever they usually do right after." She pauses because Ruth takes up then puts her mug down with a bit of a bang. "Sorry. Sort of gross, I know. DNA or whatever tests they would have done. My gynecologist, the police, my therapist—no one could understand *why* I did that."

"Went back into the water."

"Yeah."

"Well, I guess it is sort of weird." Ruth says this flatly and doesn't see Phoebe wince.

"But that's what I did. I finished my laps. The counting calmed me." Phoebe is trying to help her friend get it. "And I thought I could wash it all away."

"Then you went to the police?"

"I didn't, Ruth, I waited a few days. And I went to my own doctor, first. Then the police. They all freaked out about my swimming after. But what do they expect?" Ruth starts to speak but Phoebe talks over her, in a voice mimicking someone else speaking: "'You are telling us you *swam*? Right after? How could you do that?'" And then she continues in her own voice. "They either asked me out loud or were thinking it. I know. Whatever. For me, it was the only thing to do right then. The only way to feel clean, to calm myself. To breathe. To force myself to breathe. Because I felt like I couldn't breathe."

Phoebe waits. Hopes Ruth will understand. Needs her to understand what the others didn't. But Ruth just asks, "Any coffee left?" Phoebe gets up, shakes the thermos. "A tad," she says to the kitchen window.

She returns to the table and refills Ruth's cup. Ruth takes a gulp. "So. You were a bad girl. A very bad girl." Ruth says this with an exaggerated voice as if she is speaking to a naughty child. Phoebe looks at her, expressionless, as Ruth continues. "Yep. In every way. You destroyed the evidence they wanted or needed or whatever. Maybe they even thought you did it on purpose?"

Phoebe feels a shard of hope. "Exactly. They made me feel guilty about swimming. It's like they thought 'Oh, it couldn't have been *that* horrible if she could jump back in the lake and swim right after.' They even asked if I had seen the guy before, or if I knew him. I think they thought I destroyed the evidence on purpose. Especially when I refused to take the morning-after pill or later, consider abortion. And when I couldn't identify the guy, no matter how many photos they showed me, or even in their stupid line-up, I know they were thinking I just wouldn't identify him. No matter what. On purpose. For whatever reason."

"All so sudden, and then he had you face down."

"And no glasses."

"But you could still swim." Phoebe looks up, in equal parts fearful, hopeful. But Ruth throws her arms out and almost screams, 'I can still swim, damn you!'"

"Though at that moment, it was nothing like defiance. I just wanted to wash it all away." Phoebe takes a sip of coffee but coughs and drops of the drink bead and bleed onto the pine table. "The water stung though. I had cuts, big and little, from the tools, his nails."

"Phoebe, I...I would have fallen apart. Honestly. But not you, kiddo. Not you."

"So, you get it? Get why I..."

"As best I can, Phoebe, I do."

With the tip of her knife Phoebe plays with the coffee she's spilled, making a drawing of a little dancer with wings, leaping, her arms raised to an imaginary sky.

THIRTY-NINE

Now imagine a small, hi-tech craft—a ship of the air—that George will not so much assemble as tailor from the prototype to be shipped to him from Ernst's nephew, Dieter. Like it's ocean-going cousins it will feature state-of-the-art navigation systems like GPS, weather sonar and the like. But we are getting ahead of ourselves.

George knew after studying the specs Dieter forwarded that his barn in Connecticut would never accommodate even the compact ship he had his heart set on. What to do? He marveled, again, at the near absurdity of finding himself wondering how to garage a dirigible. A dirigible! Good lord. Nevertheless, that was the question on his mind the Friday of Columbus Day weekend as he took a rough old back road through Tom Nevers Head, then across the sandy stretch that hugged the cliff above the shoreline, on his way to meet Harriet and Lila's flight. He was so caught up in his ruminations—"If not the barn, where?"— he might easily have missed it, an old metal-roofed Quonset hut of a hangar—damn huge and shaped like the back of an armadillo—quite a way off from the rest of the airport. There was even the cracked, grass-riddled remains of an old runway adjacent. To stop and take a closer look immediately was impossible: he wanted to be on the tarmac waving when Lila and Harriet landed. But after the pair had arrived, after grabbing his wife's suitcase from the conveyor belt, he stopped one of the ground crew. "Question."

"Yeah?"

"I spotted a hangar—half a mile or so from here. Dirt road access. Do you know what that's all about?"

"Oh, that. Metal structure, right?"

"Exactly."

"Think it's left over from when the army base was here. They housed blimps you know. Reconnaissance. You can ask Biggs, the operations guy. He'll know."

"Nobody using it now?"

"Heck no. But it's airport property, not conservation land."

"Biggs around now?"

"Off island. But he's back tomorrow."

The next morning, he headed back across Tom Nevers Head but this time made the sharp right and bumped the dirt road right up to the old hangar. Before he left Lila had run out of the cottage, coat over her striped Dr. Denton-type pajamas calling out, "Dad! Wait! Where are you going?"

"On a mission, Whirligig. You up for that?"

She nodded her head "yes."

"Had breakfast yet?"

"Nope."

"Me neither. You be my wingman and we'll get breakfast at the airport after." George had already walked around and opened the door for his daughter. He put out his hand to shake hers. "Deal?"

She shook his hand hard saying "Deal" back as she hopped in the car. George wondered whether he ought to send her back into the house for proper clothes but deemed that at 7 years old what she was wearing was proper enough.

In fact, the abandoned hangar was perfect, even larger than he'd guessed and less run down as well. He tested several outlets with his cell phone charger and there was power. Who would've thought? There was even an office with a small, green metal desk, a matching file cabinet, several windows with rusty cranks to open the louvres, a bathroom, surprisingly clean, and a room with a Formica counter—a firework pattern of gold and avocado—that clearly had once served as a small kitchenette. George turned on the sink faucet which spit rusty water again and again before it coughed and then ran clear. The toilet gasped when he hit the handle but proceeded to flush. Dandy. The barrel-shaped roof was metal, the floor concrete.

"Why are we here, Dad?" Lila was not impatient, as some children might be; she had found a scroll of papers and unrolled them, putting small stones she grabbed from outside to hold down the corners. They were maps of the land and waters surrounding the island and she seemed to be trying, with her tiny forefinger, to touch a spot she recognized.

"You know how I tinker with my bikes?"

"Yes."

"Well, I have this idea of tinkering with something much bigger, more complex, something…"

"Something so you can see more than 'the eye can see'?" Lila quoted what Ernst had said about Maria Mitchell.

"You amaze me."

Lila cared not for praise. She stared up at the roof. "This place is totally cool."

"Agreed. Let's go get breakfast."

"Pancakes."

"As you wish, m'lady," George bowed to his daughter.

On their way into the airport restaurant George spotted the guy he'd spoken to the day before. He nodded at George and crooked his thumb over his shoulder. "Biggs is in the office."

"You want to pick a table and I'll be right there?"

"Can we sit at the counter?" Lila asked. George poked his head around the corner into the café, saw a string of empty stools. "Sure—-let's pick our seats." Once he had Lila settled with a menu to peruse, he went over to meet Biggs, who suited his moniker in height and girth—no name tag needed.

"Steven told me about you," Biggs boomed. He took a gulp of coffee before he went on. "What in God's name would you want that old hangar for?"

George provided as few details as possible, and Biggs seemed more eager to lease the place than to press for why's and wherefores. After a short back and forth about terms, George made a generous offer to lease the run-down hangar, landing strip and the several acres that surrounded them.

"I can let you know mid-week, Mr…?"

"Paxton. George Paxton."

"Mr. Paxton."

"George."

"OK, George." Biggs smiled. "We meet Wednesday mornings and I'd be damn surprised if the board weren't damn happy to grant you a lease. As far as we're concerned, it'll mean damn less grass to cut. You give me a call Thursday morn and we'll settle it." Briggs took another gulp of coffee and handed George his card. "Good as done."

And so it had happened, and with incredible serendipity, that George was able to secure just the space he needed to assemble and garage his dirigible.

<h1 style="text-align:center">FORTY</h1>

"I assume you aren't coming home with us." Harriet spoke to George's back. He was reading, feet up on an ottoman, the enormous picture window looking out over the moors in front of him. He craned his head around to look at his wife, one eyed, as she continued. "I guess 'hope' is a better word—I hope that's your plan. Quick, clean cut." She pretended to hold a knife and drew it through the air this way and that, speaking rapidly, "Whoosh, whoosh, whoosh."

George turned his head back around, watched birds snatching berries off bushes for a moment, then slowly stood. His book fell to the floor and he left it there, awkwardly splayed. As he took a few steps towards his wife he put a hand to his lower back as if it were stiff, as if he were a very old man. "Yes," he answered, "I think my staying on here is the best plan. We can figure out Thanksgiving and Christmas...," George paused before continuing with a vague wave of the hand, "...and all the rest, later."

"Like getting your stuff. Every last bit of it. Out of Connecticut. For good. Nothing here I care about save for my clothes. Maybe a couple of the lightship baskets the kids made. And one or two of the hooked rugs."

Lila, stretched out on her tummy behind the couch coloring, and invisible to her parents, squeezed the yellow crayon she held in her fingers with all her might and waited. Waited for this conversation to be over. Waited for her mother to leave the room. Now her father said, "Same for me as far as Connecticut goes. Clothes, bike stuff. My cast iron pans. Books, of course. And a few of my parents' pieces if that's ok."

"Take what's yours, George." Harriet started for the door, then turned. "I ran Henry out to the airport early. He's gotta work

162

tonight. Told him about us on the way there. Not that he was surprised. He said to say 'goodbye.'"

George just nodded. Harriet continued. "Our plane's at 4, you know. Run me and Lila to the airport around 3:15, ok?"

George let fly an arm repeating Harriet's word, "Whoosh—" as a long exhalation, which carried her out of the room. She slid the packet doors together behind her with a sharp snap.

Perfect silence. George felt the knot in his stomach begin to untangle. He sat back down and stared out the window. An orange-beaked oystercatcher—fattening itself in preparation for migration south—stopped grazing and flew straight at him. George jumped up, his hands palms out to signal "Stop," fearing the bird would smash into the window and die kamikaze-like. It stopped short and perched a moment, sideways on the sill, its bright yellow iris—a bull's eye ringed with red—mesmerizing.

Lila lay silent, still gripping her yellow crayon. She hadn't a plan only some inchoate, irrepressible impulse, like the need to sneeze. The yellow crayon fell onto her drawing pad with a soft bump-bump and she let out the big breath she had been holding for some time. An enormous sound in the otherwise silent room. The oystercatcher flew off. A shadow fell across George's face, and he spoke his daughter's name softly, as a question, as if he were in pain. "Lila?"

Silence. He repeated himself in the same tone. "Lila?"

This time she answered. "I'm staying." She emphasized the "I'm."

George saw no reason to contradict her. Not now. He would figure out a way. He watched as she slid herself out from behind the couch and across the worn wood floor on her elbows. When she reached the side of the chair in which he sat, she rolled over onto her back and looked up at him, her green eyes calm and hard to stare down.

Sheer impulse again, she laughed. George couldn't help but join in. When they paused, he cautioned. "But you might have to go home with Mom for now and then come back for good after Christmas, my little Whirligig."

"That's not so long," she said. "It will go so fast." She lifted her arms and made them dance in the air singing out. "Whoosh, whoosh, whoosh!"

Several hours later, after waving goodbye to Lila and Harriet, George drove over to Stump Pond, where he risked scratches and tick bites to walk through scrub oak and tall grass in search of the hidden forest. Most thought it a myth. But George had found it once before. It was one summer during college when, riding back into town after a long day at the beach, and drunk with the motion of huge breakers, he'd cast his bike aside and stumbled headlong through the moors. These same moors. But which direction? He hadn't a clue. All he remembered was the sense that he had entered a fairy tale, a seductive fiction. Stopping to ponder he spotted his doppelgänger, several hundred feet away. With a cupped wave of his hand that now familiar other-self motioned, "This way!" George sprinted to catch up. His doppelgänger broke from a walk to a jog into a run, a dark and then a light figure, weaving this way and that before disappearing into—yes, there they were—a deep crowd of pines at the cusp of flooded bog.

George entered the hidden forest.

He felt as if he were swimming, bathed first by cool then by warm currents where the sun managed to penetrate the dense warp and woof of knotted trunks, knobby branches and muzzy evergreen limbs. The burnt red pine needles underfoot were damp and slippery as if flooding rains had recently ebbed. Moving too quickly, his blood pulsing to a rhythmic beat in his ears, George nearly fell, catching himself awkwardly on one hand. Rather than stand up, there, on that sweet pungent floor, he again lay back, eyes closed, opening and closing his arms and legs in slow arcs just as he had all those months ago.

Over his head between his arms, and down between his legs, soft piles of damp pine needles gathered, forming two perfect ovoid mounds. The scent of pine sap rose in waves, both soporific and aphrodisiac. Blood crashed rhythmically in his ears anew and George felt himself dizzy, pulled under as if by an undertow. To keep himself from drowning he opened his eyes, but the shards of blue sky visible overhead were like cracked mirrors. Only by turning over and burying his face in needles, hands into the soil, was he able to take a breath. He filled his lungs with air.

Was this the heart of the hidden forest?

Soon it would be dusk, but he wanted to push deeper. He stood, leaving the tangle of needles to fall away from him as they may. Up ahead was an enormous beech tree, fat arms low to the ground and many more—slender, smooth—reaching up and out at higher and higher intervals. A beech. It shone like silver. Several such trees, centuries old, graced the Paxtons' Connecticut yard. Here such trees were even more of an anomaly than the pines.

George laid his palms on the trunk, smooth as porcelain save where it was tattooed with hearts large and small, most crudely cut, a few more artfully carved with sharper knives. Whoosh, whoosh, whoosh. There were hearts with arrows entering one side and exiting the other. Many had initials etched in their centers. One, an empty heart, looked freshly cut. George looked around but his doppelgänger was nowhere to be seen.

He wondered which of the lovers who'd etched these symbols still walked the earth, still loved? He ran his fingers, sticky with pine sap, along the outlines of hearts and arrows and into the Erics, the Sheilas, the R's, the T's, the Emmas and the Rogers, the A's, the S's, the Toms, and the Danas. A few scars were healed over with translucent skin—slippery, vulnerable. It repelled and pained him to touch these wheals and think of the tree straining to heal them. They were not bloodless. He circled the tree, looking up and down, wondering if he might find his own name or initials, perhaps connected to another by a "+"—the name or initials of some past or yet to be known love. But, no.

The past is a foreign country, he thought to himself. "Likewise, the future." He said it aloud, to the pines, to the beech, and then changed the phrase to suit him. "The future is an unknown country."

He fingered the Swiss Army knife attached to the key chain in his pocket, found the long indentation along its top edge and opened the blade with his thumb. Over and over he ran a finger along the knife's sharp edge until finally, mindlessly, he cut himself. He looked at the blood beading on his finger and brought it to his mouth to suck it away. The taste of it was so rough, so real. The taste. That taste. As if he had sucked on an ancient, rusty key. What was that taste? That memory? He imagined an old padlock and felt the blow of a hammer against his temple, the spot where a tiny artery now throbbed.

Yes, the blade was sharp enough. It would do. Even so he left the one blank heart on the tree as it was—anonymous.

FORTY-ONE

"Remember when we made tiny cuts in our wrists and pressed them together to mix our blood?"

Having finished lunch, Ruth moves from table to couch and immediately collapses, kicking off her sneakers as she does. "Good lord, Phoebe, yes—freshman year."

"No, sophomore year. We both had singles."

"We were so drunk."

"True. Even so."

"So what?"

"I don't know. I think it's cool we did that. Made a pact. The whole blood sister thing."

"Honestly, I'd forgotten all about it."

"Not me, look—" Having handed Ruth a glass of water, Phoebe folds her sleeve back, turns her arm wrist up, and points to a scar, shaped like a bird print on the snow-white inside of her wrist.

"Good grief, Phoebe. That's from way back then?"

"A permanent tattoo."

Ruth brushes this comment away with a wave of her manicured hand. "Amazing we didn't both get tetanus." She grabs one of the couch pillows and arranges it under her head. "What'd we use as a knife anyway?"

"Think we borrowed someone's Swiss Army."

"Crude."

"You no doubt used the knife tool and I probably sawed at myself with the end of the wine opener. Hence the scar."

"One of our many stupid acts."

"Don't say that. I like remembering our little pagan ceremony."

"Phoebe, you are a bit nuts."

Phoebe lifts a large vase of sunflowers, a few blooms rather droopy, and moves it over to the sink. "Supposed to be. I'm pregnant." Phoebe folds her shirt back down over the scar and says, "Nuts or not, no matter how you cut it we're blood sisters, babe. Part of you is in me. And vice a versa."

When Ruth makes a face, Phoebe adds a bit more playfully, "Sorta? Kind of?"

"Why are we dwelling on this?"

"Just...the blood knows."

"Knows what?"

"Everything important."

Ruth is completely stretched out on Phoebe's sofa now, feet dangling off the rolled arm opposite her head. Watching Phoebe pull dripping sunflowers out of their vase, she props herself up on an elbow and ask, "What did he look like?"

"Who?"

"Him—the guy who raped you."

Phoebe stares at her friend a moment. "Don't say that. I don't use that word. Don't think about that. About him." Phoebe turns away, dumps the old water from the vase into the sink, winces at the rotten smell, and puts the faucet on full blast blurring her words, "This baby is mine. Just mine." Stem by stem she pulls sunflowers from the sink, chucking those that are soft and smelly into the trash before recutting the half dozen that remain erect. "It's not as if he were repulsive or anything. Well, looking, I mean. He was just a guy. Youngish. Lean. Like a million other guys you might pass on the street. Normal."

Ruth lifts her head off the sofa pillow. "Normal?"

"I mean normal-looking—whatever that means. And me with no glasses. And barely a moment before he had me face down in the grass. The dirt." Phoebe sticks one sunflower after another into the vase. "I do know that when I came out of the lake, albeit blurry-eyed, there was nothing in his face or his eyes to scare me. I actually thought, 'Oh, if this guy's bought the house maybe he'll let me come and use his beach.' That's what I thought. That's really what I thought. He looked nice enough. You have to understand how fast it all happened. Slam bam."

Ruth gets up from the couch, grabs a tray from the kitchen, stacks up what remains of their lunch things from the table and returns to the kitchen. "Dishwasher?"

"That would be me. Just drop everything in the sink. I'll do them later." She points to the top of the refrigerator. "Grab that tin with the stripes on it. I made oatmeal cookies."

Ruth pries the lid off the tin, murmurs, "Yum..." and takes them to the table where she sits. "He never said anything?"

"Just 'Sorry.'"

"'Sorry?'"

"He walked away, very slowly. And as he did he said 'Sorry.' And then a few seconds later, 'I'm sorry'—louder—as if he wanted to make sure I'd heard him." Phoebe brings the vase to the table. Even with fresh water, fresh cuts, their necks and faces face downwards.

"So odd." Ruth has already started eating a cookie.

"I've thought about it a lot. Don't know quite what to do with—with the apology. He did what he did. Like the bird in the poem."

"Swan," says Ruth.

Phoebe tries to turn one of the sunflowers face up before she picks out a cookie but doesn't eat but continues, "Swans are birds, Ruthie. Anyway, I keep thinking that if I hadn't swum at that exact time in that exact bathing suit at that exact place, I wouldn't be having this baby."

"Or if he hadn't turned down that dead-end road at that exact time." Ruth pauses for a bite of cookie and then says with vehemence. "And, yeah, if he hadn't been a disgusting animal!" Ruth chews and talks. "Or if you hadn't stopped swimming—if you hadn't come out of the lake."

"If I hadn't stopped?" Phoebe has a cookie up to her mouth but just holds it there, suspended. "Oh, man. I hadn't thought of that. But you're right. Maybe." Phoebe still holds the cookie in mid-air, uses it to punctuate her words. "If I'd just kept doing my laps? Hadn't gotten out of the water? Maybe. But then—."

"I'm not trying to make you feel like you did anything wrong. God knows none of this is your fault."

"If I hadn't gotten out..." Phoebe stares at Ruth.

"You were being...conscientious or polite or whatever. You..."

Phoebe lays the cookie back on the plate and snaps it in half. "I'm surprised the police didn't hit me with that. She puts on a pretend voice, low, critical. "'Why'd you get out of the lake to talk to the guy if he were really a stranger, huh? You sure you didn't know him?'" She goes back to her own voice. "Is that where you're going, too, Ruth?"

"God, no, Phoebe, I wasn't suggesting that. At all. You were just being yourself. Open. Nice."

"Maybe it's one more another reason why I went back into the lake afterwards."

"You lost me."

"I wanted to try to stitch back together the hole that had been ripped open, the hole in the air, the hole in my life. The hole in me. I must have thought...." Phoebe pauses, searches for what she wants to say. "Must have felt that finishing my laps would be like gathering up the sides of something and pulling it back together, so I could pretend it all never happened."

Ruth cuts her off. "Well, that would have required an abortion. At the very least."

"Don't say that, Ruth."

"Sorry, sweetie. Really. Sorry."

"That's where I get so muddled. You saying I could have avoided everything by staying in the water before it happened, or by terminating the pregnancy after, is not right. Not right at all. It's not the same. Could never be the same."

"I never said it was. Not at all. For heaven's sake. I would never think that."

"Well, either way, no baby for Phoebe."

"Oh, come on, Phoebe, it didn't have to be that. You could have met someone, really been with someone, and gotten pregnant. Or done *in vitro*. Something. Anything. It didn't have to be some anonymous creep eating an orange."

"You think? Really? Who, Ruth, who? When was I going to meet this someone? I'm 42 for God's sake. You have two children. I was going to grow old and never have a child. I truly believe that. I'm glad I didn't speak to you sooner. I know you would have urged me to get an abortion. Right? And I might have listened to you. It's not as if you have strong feelings about that. Some religious conviction or whatever."

Ruth looks up from her coffee cup, face flushed. She speaks softly. "You promised never to tell anyone."

"And I haven't. Won't. I'll go to my grave, lips sealed, but..."

The color is still in Ruth's cheeks. The table between them is still the same table but the distance between Phoebe and Ruth has grown.

"Anyway, that was different. I knew the guy."

"Not that well, though, right? And I don't remember. Did you ever tell him? That you were pregnant? That you were going to get an abortion?"

"Are you kidding? No way. I didn't know him that well." Ruth is defensive now. "And he was sort of a jerk. But he wasn't a rapist. He ended up marrying that girl from Cincinnati who was in all the theater productions, remember?" Ruth eats a second cookie furiously; crumbs fall from her lips as she continues. "It's not like we were even an item. It was just sort of a fluke. Me on the rebound or whatever you want to call it. And both of us drunk."

Phoebe is quiet. Ruth continues. "Anyway, of course I wasn't going to have a baby. That baby. Then."

They are both quiet. Ruth doesn't want to think about her past. She wants to talk about what happened, is happening, to Phoebe now. That's why she's here, right? "So, he said he was sorry."

"Does that make any difference?"

"About the fact that he raped you? About the terror you must have felt? Still feel? No. Of course not. But I can see how hearing that and thinking about it afterwards—now—is confusing. Makes you feel, oh, I don't know—."

"That he wasn't completely indifferent?"

"Something. I don't know. It doesn't erase the fact of what he did. Criminal. He's a criminal. Repulsive." Ruth brushes all the crumbs she's created to the floor with a sweep of her arm. "Sorry. Don't know why I did that. I'll sweep it up later." Phoebe waves this away and Ruth continues, "But to go back, you are right. I admit it. I probably would have—I'm sure I would have— urged you to take the morning-after pill, get an abortion—make it all go away—once you knew for sure."

'Make it all go away' hangs in the air. Ruth's face reddens. Phoebe, hands clasped around her belly, breaks what is a long silence: "How does it end?"

"How does what end?"

"The poem about the swan."

"The Yeats? With a question."

"Which is—?"

"I'll have to look it up."

Phoebe stares at her.

"You want to know now?"

"Yes."

Ruth stops eating cookies. She pulls out her phone and taps on the keyboard. She starts using her forefinger to scroll down but has to stop and wipe her fingers as cookie crumbs mess up the screen. She reads aloud. *"Did she put on his knowledge with his power...Before the indifferent beak could let her drop?"*

"'The indifferent beak'..."

"You want to hear the whole thing?"

"Sure."

Ruth recites the whole poem. Phoebe asks her to read the last two lines again. Ruth speaks them slowly. *"Did she put on his knowledge with his power...Before the indifferent beak could let her drop?"*

"Eating an orange. Talk about indifference. That was before he attacked me. And after? The poem says, 'put on.' Why 'put on'? Why not 'take on.' How do you 'put on' power?"

"You tell me, Phoebe. Because it seems you did—have." With that, Ruth looks at the clock over the sink, is shocked or at least pretends to be shocked, mumbles the usual bit about "time flying" and needing to get home. She puts on her shoes, gathers up her things, looks at the mess of crumbs she brushed to the floor and steps around them.

Phoebe walks her out to her car. Ruth gives Phoebe a kiss and a promise to be in touch before backing out and driving away.

Sitting alone on her front stoop, Phoebe realizes that she and Ruth didn't share one laugh. Nothing could be more out of character. But that doesn't upset her. Not in the least. Ruth realizes the same thing. At the same moment. She pushes a button to roll down the windows. She needs more air. But open windows only bring the whirr of speeding cars and hot, humid, suffocating pressure. She closes them, turns up the air conditioning. Is she crying? Could be. Could be. Driving north and east her handsome face is cast in shadow the whole way home.

Phoebe begins to dead head the nasturtiums in her window boxes. The late day sun, sliding slowly down the sky lights up her face and turns her long red hair to gold. Some alchemy has taken place.

FORTY-TWO

Thanks to Ernst's nephew, Dieter—who shared his company's proprietary software and passwords—George logged hundreds of hours "taking-off," "flying" and "landing" an airship via computer simulator all from the comfort of his living room in 'Sconset. He'd bought an enormous external monitor for this and in-between that same monitor glowed with page after page of regulations, technical details and meteorologic particulars he was determined to master. Many was the time Lila said "Dad?" and then, "Dad!...Dad!...Dad!" with increasing urgency, even if she were standing at his elbow, in an attempt to get his attention so happily absorbed he was in mastering every nuance of flying such a craft— everything from the technical aspects and weather systems to take-offs and landings.

A few days before delivery of one of his firm's semi-rigid ships, Dieter flew to Nantucket from California. The two had forged a strong bond over the course of their many Zoom calls and Dieter insisted on being on Nantucket in person to go over every detail and be on board with George for initial test flights.

Though Dieter would be staying with Ernst and Johanna, George offered to fetch him at the airport, give him a quick tour of the hangar and field, then take him to dinner. In fact, he insisted. Yes, Johanna and Ernst no longer drove at dusk or night so he was helping them out. But his motive was selfish as well. He was eager to meet Dieter and have him to himself for a few hours—so much to talk about.

Waiting for Dieter's connecting flight from Boston to arrive, George realized he hadn't the foggiest notion what the man looked like. He imagined someone in the mold of Dieter's Aunt Johanna, only younger—someone exceptionally tall, exceptionally slim—and it was such a man he looked for as passengers walked down the metal stairs onto the tarmac. College-age kids with backpacks leapt off first followed by an elderly couple with a small dog, moving slowly, gripping the handrail. Next down the stairs was a woman with a fat ponytail and two skinny kids in tow. Then came a couple of guys in business suits, engrossed in conversation. (George couldn't imagine Dieter wearing a suit especially on a long flight from California).

Finally, as if he were waiting for annoying press to pack up their cameras and leave, a man in his 40s, appeared on the top step of the stairs, looked left, right, then straight ahead at George, smiled, waved. He seemed implausibly small, implausibly slight on that top step. His short brown hair stood upright in the stiff breeze, as did the man. Could this be Dieter? He was nothing like George imagined. But as he walked ever closer, hand extended, eyes fixed on George, smile growing broader with each step, George adjusted his impression: diminutive and slight became wiry and powerful. The muscles and sinews in his extended arm rose like seismic eruptions when he took George's hand and gave it a series of vigorous shakes. Most of all it was his gaze that made anyone or anything else in the vicinity fade into insignificance: it brought to mind something George had read about Picasso, the artist with the *mirada fuerte.*

"George," Dieter said, for yes it was Dieter. "You're just as Johanna described you. So good of you to meet me."

What was George to say in reply? Dieter couldn't be more than 5 foot 3 or 4. He wondered how many times others meeting him for the first time—the COO of Aerostatics, Ltd—must have signaled their surprise at his physical stature in less than subtle ways. George's first impulse was to put his hand down onto Dieter's shoulder. But he feared it might make Dieter feel shorter to do so. Besides, he felt himself paralyzed by the warm intensity of Dieter's attention, as if the energy of this man wrapped round him. What did they call it in the Star Wars movies? A force field? He said, "Welcome. So great of you to make the trip, Dieter—take the time. Let's grab your bag and get the hell out of here."

And so began what would be what would become several visits, this first lasting almost a week—generous given the demands of Dieter's business in California. The two liked each other immediately, were primed for mutual admiration thanks to what Ernst and Johanna had said of each to the other. Once they'd snatched Dieter's suitcase off the conveyor belt inside the terminal, George took him to his favorite Nantucket haunt, The Brotherhood of Thieves. As they pulled out their chairs to sit, George blurted out, "How the heck did you ever get involved with airships in this day and age?"

Dieter laughed, "Fine. Me first. Then you."

The two sat and George answered, "Deal."

Dieter unwrapped his silverware and put the big green napkin in his lap. "In some ways, I guess it was inevitable. In others, completely fantastic."

"I can relate," George said.

"But no question it is all thanks to Uncle Ernst. Such a cool guy."

"Totally cool. Impressive."

"He and Aunt Johanna lived near my family when I was growing up. We always had Sunday dinners together. I was completely in awe of him—so tall, so smart. Modest. Dignified. I'm still in awe."

"I'm with you."

The waiter appeared and asked if they wanted to order drinks. George asked his companion, "You like beer?"

"Do," Dieter said.

"Pale? Stout?"

"I'm easy."

George turned to the waiter, "Any of the Cisco IPAs left?" The waiter shook his head. "No surprise. Bring us two Whale's Tales, if you would, then, thanks." Then he nodded at Dieter, "Go on—."

"I'd grown up hearing my dad talk about what Uncle Ernst had done in the war. Words that washed over me. But during cocktail hour, before one Sunday supper, Uncle Ernst pulled me aside and showed me a photo of a dirigible, one he'd taken himself. Classic black-and-white shot. I took the photo in my hands and something about the shape of the dirigible and the size of it, just got to me, in an almost physical way."

"They are so *other*, aren't they? Like some H.G. Wells creation."

"I don't know if I can really articulate what I felt at that moment. It's as if I were imprinted with that shape. Couldn't shake it. From the moment I set eyes on one, well, it filled my dreams." Dieter paused seeing that George, quite unconsciously, was nodding repeatedly. "My waking moments as well."

While the novelty of his epiphany was what had given George the energy to get this far, now, as the complex details of actually getting off the ground accumulated George was immensely thankful to be in touch, to be helped, by someone who shared his passion. He looked at Dieter and saw that he was watching him much as his doppelgänger did: intently, amusedly. He broke the happy tension. "You were obsessed?"

"Oh, damn, totally! While my friends were all watching *Star Trek* and *Star Wars*, I was building models of the Hindenburg and the Shenandoah. Those outer space movies and TV shows were make believe. Airships were real."

The waiter put two beers on the table. George raised his glass. Dieter did the same and George's "Cheers" and Dieter's *"Prost!"* rang out together. They smiled across the table at one another and Dieter continued.

"Even though I was intimidated by Uncle Ernst, my curiosity got the better of me. I wanted to spend all my free time sitting at his feet, as they say."

"You'll see him in the morning. They retire early—sure you know that. Johanna said she'd just leave the front door unlocked."

"Know the drill. And you know that Johanna invited, no, demanded, that we all have dinner together—as many nights as we like."

George picked up the menu of specials. "Speaking of dinner, let's get that out of the way. You like scallops?"

"Haven't really had them much."

"The ones here—Nantucket Bays—are small, sweet. And it's season. So..."

"Sounds perfect."

George called the waiter over, ordered for them both, then turned back to Dieter, "On with your story. How'd you get from there to here?"

"I was a complete egghead as a kid. Math whiz. All that." When he paused he saw that George was nodding again to everything he said. He continued. "After Dieter showed me that photo of a dirigible, I spent every second of my free time reading books about them—eventually very technical stuff—and then, as I said, I would quiz Uncle Ernst relentlessly when our families were together. 'What was it like flying over the ocean? How many enemy ships did you spot? What happened if it got stormy?' My parents would say, 'Dieter! Give your uncle a break for heaven's sake.'"

"I'm sure he didn't mind."

"No, no, he loved it. Loved how excited I was about something that had absorbed so much of his life. He'd been bitten by the bug as a kid, too, so he got it."

"And your parents?"

"Oh, they were fine with it for a while. They still have a book I filled with drawings of airships with tiny people on the ground, interiors, exteriors. Crazy detail. But at some point, I think they found my fixation a bit scary. They worked to steer me away— bought me a fancy computer, and that really took me into a whole other universe."

"Away from the floating world."

"For sure. Dirigibles faded into the background."

The waiter brought salads and the two began eating as Dieter continued. "And I was busy with school—lots of math and science and programming. Then lots of engineering and physics in college."

Dieter stopped to eat some bites of salad and George said, "Ha— same as me. Egghead part for sure. I think it sort of scared my parents. Thought I'd end up a loner. Too bookish. I majored in engineering, too, and yeah, did a lot of physics. Then I made a hairpin turn and went to law school."

"As I said, you're up next."

"Agreed."

"Anyway, I went on to Cal Tech for grad school. That's where I met my business partner."

"Stephen? The CEO?"

"Exactly. One night at Cal, I was out with a bunch of people from my program. Lots of beer consumed. You know. Grad students." Dinner arrived, and Dieter paused to comment, "Oh, this looks great, George. Perfect choice," before continuing with his tale. "We were all playing pool and at some point, somebody started talking about relief efforts going on after a big disaster. Can't recall what it was—tsunami, famine, earthquake. Anyway, this guy Stephen was pontificating about airships. "Unbelievable range and capacity! And these fuckers can land without a runway! Best way to bring in food, medical supplies, even small structures after a disaster!'"

"Kerplunk," George threw in.

"Exactly, straight down—middle of a desert, anywhere. They're big enough to carry tanks for god's sake! Stephen was right but most of the group were rolling their eyes."

George shook his head. "It is like science fiction to imagine them getting off the ground." He reached for his beer, took a last swallow, and asked Dieter, "Want another? I'm going to."

"Yes." Dieter held up his empty mug. "This from the island too?"

"Good, right?"

"Great. Maybe I'll ship some home." He kept his glass lifted and the waiter, a short distance away, nodded, lifted two fingers, and both George and Dieter nodded back,

Dieter continued. "Anyway, Stephen was hit with the usual hot air and Hindenburg jokes. Me? At his first mention of dirigibles it was like I was 8 years old again. My childhood obsession came back to life. And in that moment so did I. Came back to life, I mean. Full circle. Everything made sense."

George couldn't speak. He saw Dieter stare off towards a dark corner in the low beamed space in which they dined. George turned to look that way too, and seconds later his other self took shape, smiling broadly. He was smiling back when Dieter resumed. "The moment Uncle Ernst showed me the photo of the dirigible an inchoate yearning, maybe I would even call it a premonition was born—though I wouldn't have known how to talk about it as such at the time."

George saw now that he had been a marble on a spinning roulette wheel, going round and round and round until, at long last, he dropped into a slot, the right slot, and the spinning stopped. He turned once more, nodded at his other self and then at Dieter, who took up his story again.

"I had...it was just...this unshakeable knowing, knowledge, that those pregnant beasts of the air would...that they were in me." Dieter shook his head, laughed, and paused before finishing this part of his story with, "Oh, God I am sounding all whoo-hoo. And me a scientist."

"Not everyone finds their perfect fit."

"The whole idea of combining the challenge of re-imagining—completely modernizing—lighter-than-air craft with the mission of helping people. Well, that was it. Ka-bang. Done and done."

"The law was a calling for me, no question. And I was good at it. But that word you used is perfect—inchoate. Happened to me only recently but that's it—to have your stomach turn over with a notion you can't put into words." George looked over at Dieter who just smiled and raised his glass, this time to meet George's with a clink. It was George's turn to laugh. He did and said, "Damn. Not many people I can talk to about this. Most people are going to think I'm descending into dementia when word spreads I've ditched my partnership at the firm for this—I don't know what to call it—flight of fancy."

Dieter didn't answer. Their refills arrived and the two sat sipping and eating for a bit. In silence. George wondered if he had gone off-course, even offended Dieter, so he added, into thin air. "I'm talking about myself of course." He could see Dieter was thinking about how to respond but didn't expect the response he got.

"No flight of fancy, George. There's a reason you are here. Why I am here. Even if we don't know exactly what that reason is right now. Was it a complete fluke I met Stephen that night playing pool? Don't think so. I'd seen him around. We were in some classes together. But I didn't really know him. But after the pool night, we started getting together regularly. For hours—often till nearly dawn and every weekend—creating detailed plans for building viable airships and detailed analysis on how they could best be put to use."

Dieter paused to drink his beer before saying, "Humanitarian applications where other modes of transport were impossible."

"Places without airports or long runways."

"Exactly." Dieter finished eating and pushed his plate to the side. "I chucked my original PhD thesis and Stephen and I decided on a paper together as co-authors—*Value Ranges for Differentials between Internal and External...*"

"Another round for you two?" Their waiter interrupted from the bar and the pair nodded without even looking up as Dieter continued. "Anyway, for Stephen, building a modern airship was an engineering problem to solve and I was happy to plunge into those details myself, into the concrete. Our thesis became our business plan, robust enough to show investors. Hell, the idea of 21st century airships was so novel—and to be honest, so strangely sexy—we had VC people fighting to invest. Lots of hard work plus folks putting their money where their mouths are means we've got viable craft that have flown missions and achieved some real successes."

"You are making a difference."

"I hope so. I think so. Anyway, it wasn't a fluke I met Stephen. Same here."

"Meaning?"

"We're both students of physics, George. We don't believe in flukes."

"Right you are. Just colliding particles."

"I need to hear your full story, but give me a break, George. I've only known you what, a couple hours? You are not nuts, not by a long shot. Believe me, I've met my share. You had a long, successful legal career. I'm sure you've helped hundreds of people. Just a different arena. When Ernst told me about meeting you in the library on Nantucket, he made it sound as if nothing more natural could have occurred. Coincidence? I don't think so. Neither does he."

"I'm going to choose to agree."

"We get Silicon Valley guys with so much money they don't know where to spend it next. A couple have bought small craft from us, just to add to their fleets—cars, boats, jets. They like being able to one-up others by saying, 'Oh, and I have a personal airship.'"

"And here I am..."

"Stop with that. They're completely different. Trust me. Those folk are great for Stephen and me. They demand all sorts of customizations and pay a pretty penny for them. It helps fund our humanitarian mission. This is different. You are different."

"Because?"

"Honestly? I don't know, George. We'll see when you get up there. You are a man of words and there's a story to be written. And, at the rate we're growing, we're going to have to move from hired guns to in-house legal counsel."

George didn't answer but he smiled, and Dieter went on. "Just floating ideas, Bro, just floating ideas."

George raised his glass a third time. "To the brotherhood."

FORTY-THREE

"Hey, sista," Phoebe is standing outside her house, cell phone to her ear.

"Phoebe—hi." Ruth sounds breathless.

"Quick question."

"Sure. Shoot. Quick though. I'm herding my little kittens so we can meet mom and dad for brunch."

"Are you going to be weird about this?

"This...?"

"This as in me. As in my baby?"

"You really have to ask? No—God, no. She'll...he'll...be yours. That's all that matters." Phoebe can hear Ruth's feet on her gravel drive.

"It's just that you're the only one, well, only real person, friend, co-worker who knows." She stops, wonders if it even occurs to Ruth that on the other side, Phoebe is the only one who ever knew about Ruth's college abortion. She can hear a dog barking and then Ruth's husband, Howard, shout, "You coming, honey?"

"Late, per usual. Call you later?" Phoebe hears a door shut and the kids, in unison, shout, "Mommy! Mommy! Come on!" But Phoebe needs more confirmation before Ruth signs off. The two haven't spoken since Ruth visited. She wishes she could cut her wrist anew, and Ruth's, too—rub their wrists together to seal their secrets. She knows the driveway is long enough for them to talk a bit longer.

"Did you tell him?"

"Him who?"

"Your husband. Howard!"

"No. Promise. I mean I did tell him you're having a baby. He's going to know that when he sees you. He assumes Alex is the dad. He just said, 'Ah ha. Well, I'm happy for her. So, when's the wedding?' That's it." Ruth shouts "You guys get in the car. I'm coming!" then speaks more quietly into her cell to Phoebe. "We'll figure it out when the time comes. Some story."

Phoebe hears the car start. Ruth continues, in a whisper, "What are you going to tell everyone—the crew at work—anyway?"

"Immaculate conception."

Silence.

"Kidding. *In Vitro*. That's what I told Magnus. I slept with him that same week. Night."

"Ruth!" Howard is shouting at his wife and Ruth shouts back, "Right there..." then says to Phoebe, "Magnus? The old Norwegian dude?"

"Yes." She waits a beat. "Actually, he and I have been spending most of our eves together."

"This is too much. I can't do this now."

"Sorry."

"Really—this is more—"

"More what?"

"God knows, Phoebe. I mean, I guess you'll have a test after the baby's born?"

"Why on earth would it matter?"

"So, you know—know if it's Magnus' or—" Ruth has raised her voice.

"Going away party for him in a bit. Then I'm going to swim after. I'm going to be sad—very—to see him go. Anyway. It doesn't matter."

"Jesus, Phoebe. Not the lake, I hope. Gives me the heebie-jeebies. Go to the 'Y' where there's a guard, other people around..."

Phoebe hears Howard ask, "What gives you the 'heebie-jeebies?'" The car door shuts.

Thanks to the noise of the car starting, Phoebe's not sure if Ruth hears her reply—"Lake's fine. Lightning never strikes the same place twice, right?

It's juvenile and superstitious. Even so, Phoebe wishes she had a knife handy to cut her wrist, maybe both, squeeze out some blood on one side and then the other. Rub them together. Unsure of one sister, become her own.

FORTY-FOUR

A lone firefly flashes a few feet above the lawn and then blinks out. Phoebe waits for the next. But no. It seems it was just the one, signaling to her. Signaling what?

She continues to wait. In the dark. In vain. Where are the conflagrations she used to witness as a child?

She remembers one late August evening—it was her tenth birthday—when her foster parents took her to dinner at The Willow Inn, long closed now. It sat alongside the undulating river that springs from the northeast side of the lake, up high on a foundation made of huge slabs of chiseled stone. To reach the front door you had to climb half a dozen steps made of that same stone, like tombstones laid flat. Some of the dining tables were arranged alongside a long span of floor-to-ceiling windows that looked out onto the river. But Phoebe and her parents were seated two rows away from those prized tables. Her stepdad would never have thought, would never dare, to ask for a view.

They were in the middle of dinner when there was a collective intake of breath. Phoebe felt it in the pit of her stomach. It came from the diners seated right next to the windows. Many of them were already standing up, napkins sliding off their laps. Others were turning in their chairs, exhaling, saying, "Oh! Look—!" or "Can you believe it?" Waiters and waitresses paused, mid-service, holding bottles of wine or coffee pots suspended over crystal glasses or porcelain cups. Busboys came to a standstill balancing trays laden with dishes on their shoulders.

Phoebe leapt out of her seat. She had to see what they were seeing. No one minded the slim, young girl slipping between and amongst them. She stood with her arms up, fingers splayed and nose pressing against the glass.

Hovering over the river was what seemed to be hundreds, maybe thousands, of lightning bugs, glowing on off, on off. Phoebe wasn't aware of anyone around her. If there were sounds, she didn't hear them. She took a deep, deep breath and unconsciously held it, just as she does now in late autumn before jumping into the cold lake. It felt as if the walls of the dining room were sucked in, too.

Who knows how much time passed before she felt her stepmother's hand on her shoulder. She was gently shaking it as she whispered to Phoebe. "I said come back to your seat, Phoebe. Now. Your dinner's getting cold." In a louder voice, smiling at the diners sitting nearby, she added, "Let these nice people enjoy their meals." Phoebe knew her stepmother was embarrassed.

But Phoebe turned back to the window—she couldn't not—a rare breach of disobedience. There were fewer flashes of light now but she had to keep watch until the blurry glow of the last firefly dissolved. Until river and tree line and sky were the same darkness.

Walking back to the table to join her stepparents, she saw that the world inside—the other diners, the servers, the busboys—had resumed its normal motion even while she had not, even while she had kept apart from it, trying to hold on.

It was the most beautiful moment of her life. Or so she thought then.

And now here she is—just a few miles but a myriad of years away from that childhood evening—about to give up and turn back indoors when one more lightning bug appears. And then another. And another. Not thousands, but right here in her own front yard, close to her, there are suddenly hundreds. That's when she feels it. The first kick. Close to her solar plexus. A little foot seeming to dance to the bugs flashing on and off.

Phoebe is her young self and her older self. The Phoebe of now, the solitary person, yes, but also the Phoebe of way back then, the girl inside of something wholly bigger, not a single lightning bug but a whole constellation of coruscating light and dark.

In the weeks to come she will try to work it out. All of her life she has watched and waited to be "in love." Now she knows that wasn't quite right. She feels herself to be not so much someone in love but someone *of* love. There is a difference. She has become the difference, part of something outside of herself and inside, too. It makes her powerful.

This love is not something witnessed, like the fireflies of her youth. She is inside of this with her unborn child. It is as if that long-ago night has become manifest.

She is that night. She is all of the fireflies, all of the light, all of the dark. All the movement of the river and the rising and the setting of the sun and the mist and humidity and the rocks and the water coursing over them and the trees that drink from the river and drop their leaves.

FORTY-FIVE

"Ben and Karen are doing well—great, actually. Both made honor roll first term." It was the first time Harriet had phoned since leaving Nantucket after Columbus Day weekend.

"Yes, yes. They told me. Proud of them." As George spoke he was watching Lila running around in the back yard trying to catch, what? A dragonfly? A bird? Though she'd flown home with her mother, she'd begged and begged and her parents agreed she could return to live with her father on Nantucket. "Can you hold on one sec? He opened the door and shouted, "Hey you, come in here and eat some breakfast!"

"How's she doing?"

"Like her sister and brother. Well. Really well. The little community school here suits her. We made the right decision." George paused, and in a laugh said, "Well, I guess Lila gave us no choice!" Then he continued, "Anyway, the teachers are always taking their classes over to the harbor or for hikes through conservation land. Lila loves all that outdoor stuff." George paused, opened the door, and called out once more. "Lila! Now! Breakfast!"

"I won't keep you. I know you've got to get her off to school."

"You don't want to have a quick 'hi'?"

"It's fine. Just wanted to confirm that Ben and Karen will come to you for their Christmas break."

"Absolutely. And I told them they could both have a friend come the day after Christmas and stay through New Year's. Lila will love having the house full of kids. She's been skating a lot. They can all go to the rink for free skate."

"Good. Good." A pause, then. "Oh, and I signed all the papers."

"Me, too."

"So you saw. Even about Lila being full time with you."

Less said about that the better but George had to acknowledge that Harriet had not put up a fight over that. He suspected she was relieved, with the older kids off at boarding school, she would be completely free to work. He answered, "Thanks for that, Harriet. Really." He wondered briefly whether to bring up his plan to take a first voyage in his dirigible in the spring. And to bring Lila with him. But why start a fire. Instead, he continued, "Oh, and wanted to say congratulations. Karen told me about your promotion. Kudos."

"Busier than ever but I like that."

"Next thing you know you'll be CEO or…"

"Ha!" Harriet cut in. "We'll see about that. Before I start—and that's why I am confirming about Karen and Ben—I'm taking two weeks off. The Caribbean."

"Lovely."

"With a friend."

"Even better"

"Another lawyer."

She was making a point. "Ah, well be careful with that!"

"Corporate this time."

Did she want him to ask for more detail? He just wanted to finish the call. "Just let me know flight information. For Karen and Ben, I mean." Say something more, he thought. "You sound happy."

"Seems like." There was silence for a moment. "I'm sorry George…"

"You're…?"

"Sorry. Yes. We made three great kids but a mess of ourselves."

"Well, I'm sorry, too. I am…" The door opened and closed. "Quick hello with Lila? She's back inside now."

"No, no. Tell her Mom will call her later."

"You bet."

FORTY-SIX

The day of his combined birthday/good-bye party Magnus wakes early, in the dark, in Phoebe's bed. She is curled towards him, hands cupped together under her chin as if in prayer. That is simply the way she sleeps best. He should know. When they said their private goodbyes, in the middle of the night, she didn't beg, "Don't go!" nor he, "Come with me." By some miracle, what they have together is enough. Choosing to be together for a spell rather than fall helplessly in love is enough. Phoebe's breathing, as always, is soft and regular—a soundtrack that Magnus will miss. Through the half-open door, light from the bathroom nightlight falls in a straight line down the middle of the moss green blanket separating the pair: her side, his side. Magnus chooses not to disturb that barrier this morning. Enough is enough.

He remembers one of the last times (was it the very last?) that he went ice fishing with his father. It must have been less than a year before his father died. They had just set up folding chairs across from one another, a two-foot hole between them, when the ice cried out—a stunning scream a body might make in response to an attack. They knew the lake so well. This was an anomaly. But it was spring. There had been a stretch of warm days. The sun was beginning to coax the lake back into motion. Then came the loudest report of all—a locomotive-like roar and vibration that echoed over and over and over. "*Uffdah!*" Magnus' father cried as they watched the simple "O" between them turn shattered glass after gunfire.

Magnus rolls over, ever so gently, and gets out of bed. He takes a long look at sleeping Phoebe. Sometimes her breathing is so imperceptible he is tempted to hold a mirror to her lips to see if it clouds over. Could she have died in the night? But no, he sees the mound of her hip rise and fall. Ahh. He gathers up his clothes, dresses downstairs, opens and then shuts the door without a sound. Driving home before sunrise he thinks, "May as well get accustomed to this—dark in the morning, dark at night." He knows that's what will welcome him in Norway—dark save for a short window in the middle of the day. But, of course, life will be lit by beloved family and friends.

His most precious belongings—everything that accompanied he and Dorothy through their long life together (even the worn, the outdated, the chipped, the cracked)—are crossing the sea to Norway in the corner of a huge container. The rest is packed into his trunk of a suitcase and the battered leather carry-on bag he's left open for last minute things.

Magnus opens the door to his house and the sun, just up, illuminates the folding card table he borrowed from a neighbor after the movers left. On it, arranged like a game of solitaire, are his airline ticket, passport, a few bills to pay, checkbook, stationery and envelopes. His car is sold. Not wanting any additional goodbyes after the party, he's hired a car service to drive him to the airport an hour after the party ends.

He sits down on the folding lawn chair, borrowed from the same neighbor, and that chair puts him in mind, again, of that early spring day ice fishing with his father.

After the most heart-rending crack, Magnus' father whispered, "Don't move, son." And so they sat. Completely still. For several minutes. Longer even. They were always quiet when they fished but this was different. The sun shone. The silence was perfect until they felt a shiver and the lake coughed, a death rattle, sending a flood of tears from the ragged round eye Magnus and his father had cut in the ice.

"It's best we walk in opposite directions." Magnus nodded in reply and his father continued. "Gather up your things and meet me back at the shore." That is when Magnus sliced his face open, what scarred him for life. He was so focused on taking careful steps, as if by holding his breath his weight would float above the ice, he'd slipped and come down full force on the sharp-cornered metal tackle box he carried. Blood sprayed everywhere painting a livid pattern on the pale blue ice. That was it. He'd never gone ice fishing again. Anyway, his father was dead by the time the river froze solid the next autumn.

Phoebe wakes. Eyes still closed, she stretches her hand over and pats the bed this way and that. No Magnus. She opens her eyes. Light is spilling out from under the window shades. She half sits up, immediately puts her hand over her mouth, throws her legs over the side of the bed and makes it to the bathroom sink just in time. She throws up, not violently, but enough that she immediately turns on the faucet to flush the sickness away. She bends down and takes water into her mouth, too, swishes it and spits it out before splashing it—icy cold— on her face. When she straightens back up, she looks at herself in the mirror, the acid taste of sickness turning sweet in her mouth.

Magnus left his bathrobe. It is hanging from a hook behind her, the bulky shoulders slumped, the collar askew. She thinks of all the times she placed her palm, flat, on Magnus' grand chest with its tangle of strawberry blond curls, just there, between the two sides of a robe which never could quite entrap his grandeur. In time, she will wear it, thankful there's more than enough material to wrap and belt around her pregnant belly.

Across town, Magnus picks up his passport, slaps it on the table, slides his airline ticket inside and repeats aloud what his father said, all those years ago, when they retreated so carefully off the crack-ridden ice. "It's best we walk in different directions."

FORTY-SEVEN

George stands in front of a shelf of nut butters and jams while Lila, on the other side of the aisle, ponders granola. The pair had only just landed, in a big open field near a lake that was, happily, just miles from where Uncle Henry lives. George sent a text immediately, hoping they could share a meal, hoping Henry might suggest a place for them to stay for a few days. Henry had written right back, asking for their exact location before sending a cab to ferry them into town. Soon, they would check into the bed and breakfast he'd suggested. But first, George wanted to grab a few staples—almond butter chief among them—in hopes they would set sail again soon.

It was not what George had planned on for his maiden voyage: shifting winds in advance of some squalls had gently, but rather insistently, pushed the dirigible off course. It was a hiccup, easily and safely managed, but it was enough of a hiccup that George vowed not to bring Lila on any further jaunts. She could return to her mother for a spell while he continued his quest for…? *Yes, for what, George*? he asked himself. The comments of friends and family rang in his ears: *"What on earth are you thinking?"*

All this ran through his head as he reached for a jar of almond butter and paused, jar in hand, until he realized someone was speaking.

"Love that stuff. I live on it." George turns toward the voice, which has a sweet, drawl to it, and finds there is a woman standing quite close to him. She is wearing a drab waxy raincoat, much too big for her. Raindrops still clinging to it appear nearly iridescent.

George and the woman look straight at each other for a moment, a moment a good beat or two longer than what we all know, instinctively, is the normal, the polite amount of time to lock eyes with a stranger.

George takes in the green eyes, the tiny bump or scar on the cheek—a punctuation mark at the top of the dimple that appears as the woman smiles, turns and reaches her arm up to grab the jar adjacent to the one George still grips saying, "Crunchy." George hears such tender music in that voice as the woman pulls the jar down and finishes with, "Gotta be the crunchy."

George has never known a red head so never seen an arm like this, slender, white and awash with copper freckles. Is he staring now? Probably. The freckles are like snowflakes, each a different shape. A turquoise bracelet, leather and studded with tiny silver stars, circles the top of the woman's wrist, the clasp on top. It is all he can do not to grab hold of that bracelet and turn it slowly around, around her wrist which is wide with a prominent bone on the outside—a bit out of proportion— as are her hands, which are large and square with pronounced knuckles.

Never in his career, hell, never in his life, has George been at a loss for words. Clients came and sat across the desk from him at the law firm year after year and he immediately knew whether it was best to chit-chat about the weather or to touch on some more personal detail shared in pre-conference emails in advance of a meeting. Or whether his clients were the no-nonsense, let's-just-get-to-it types. But at this moment, he freezes. He finds he rather likes this feeling. Maybe he mumbles something like, "Crunchy. Yes, indeed."

In years to come he will remember this first, brief encounter and wonder if it were his body or his soul that were most affected. If you were to have asked him, right then, the moment she walked away, "What did that woman talking to you look like?" he would only have been able to say, "I think she had on a raincoat. And there was a pen or a pencil stuck through her hair, right above her ear."

But if called in to ID her in a police line-up, even hours or days later, he has always been certain he would have known without any doubt whatsoever which out of a hundred redheads—hell, out of a hundred women—she was.

<h1 style="text-align:center">FORTY-EIGHT</h1>

Half an hour later—nearly enough time for him to regain some equilibrium—a second random encounter (or was it inevitable?) enables George to study the woman and further lock her in his brain.

"Where should we have lunch, Whirligig?" George says to Lila when they exit the grocery. "We'll eat—and then settle into the B&B your Uncle Henry suggested."

Lila scans the street and, as he guessed she would, points towards a small, freestanding building with a deeply pitched roof and a bright red door over which hangs a wooden sign, carved to look like a long arm. The hand on that arm points towards the door. On it is painted, in purposely but artfully ragged letters: Just Good Food.

"That one. The one the finger's pointing to."

"You nailed it. That's where Henry is chef."

"Really? Chef?"

George takes Lila's hand and they set off across the street.

Wooden floors. Wooden tables. And bouquets of real flowers—ranunculus. Green and white checkered tablecloths made of that shiny material that wipes clean. And red cloth napkins. Cloth! He smiles. Then he sees her. The red head. Her back is to them and her hair is in a long braid. She has on jeans and the back of her apron is knotted tightly at the small of her back. The pen stuck in her hair catches the light and shines briefly. Her arm is reaching up to take plates down from the counter where Henry and his crew take the orders. He watches as that turquoise bracelet slides down toward her elbow. That freckled arm. She turns with the plates in her hands, and he sees, now that she isn't buried in the huge raincoat, that she is pregnant—a beautiful, incongruous mound that makes her lean backwards ever so slightly as she walks. Her legs, her strides, are long. Graceful.

She is balancing two plates, concentrating, focusing on her destination which is a table with two middle-aged women right next to the booth into which he and Lila slide. The women both look up and

194

smile when the waitress puts omelets in front of them. Obviously one woman knows the redhead well as she takes her by the wrist, *that* wrist, and pulls her closer to the table. He catches the introduction. "Jane, this is our beloved Phoebe."

"George? Lila!" George was so intent on this woman—Phoebe—he didn't even see Henry come out of the kitchen and up to their booth. "You found us—perfect—just in time for lunch."

George started to stand. "Henry. Good to see you, man."

"Sit, George. Sorry about the damn rain but happy to see you both."

Lila has slid out of the booth to throw her arms around her uncle's legs and hug them. "We are having such an adventure, Uncle Henry."

"I'll bet."

George puts his hand on Henry's shoulder. "Any chance you can take the night off so we can have dinner together?"

"Sure. Come here. Seven-ish? Mondays are slow. I've got a helper."

Lila has slid back onto the banquette. "Not now?"

"Too busy sweetie. We'll catch up over dinner. Oh, and I already called for you—right over there—the blue clapboard house. Sweet little place for you two to stay."

George nods. "Great. And dinner at seven's perfect. Sorry we didn't have much time to talk when you were on the island with us."

"Hell, George. No apologies. Lila kept me busy picking berries and riding bikes, didn't you, kiddo?" Henry rustles Lila's hair and she smiles.

"Well, I was distracted."

"Understood. No worries, Henry. My sister's doing fine. Per usual. It's all for the best, right? Back to the kitchen for me. Later! Our lovely Phoebe can take care of you."

Phoebe, still standing at the adjacent table, turns when she hears her name. Walking away, Henry says over his shoulder, "My niece and brother...er, soon-to-be-ex-brother-in-law, George, Phoebe." Phoebe pulls a small pad from her apron pocket, slides the pen from atop her ear, and steps in close to the booth. George puts down his menu, takes Lila's, too, and hands them to her.

Phoebe is drawing a large "G" on her order pad. "Ha. It's you. Mister almond butter." Phoebe points her pen at George. "Henry visited you one weekend, right? Up north?"

"Good memory."

"Were a small team here." Phoebe raises her eyes from her order pad to look George in the eye. "Everybody here knows each other's business." Phoebe pauses, looks at George. She likes what she sees, the face feels familiar. Right. But she addresses Lila. "What tickles your fancy, young lady?"

"Turkey wrap," Lila says and, after getting a smile from her father, adds, "Please."

Phoebe turns her gaze back to George, who asks, "How about the Greek salad. Good choice?"

"Great choice. And to drink?"

"Have chocolate milk?" Phoebe nods "Yes." "So, one of those and an iced coffee...?" He stops and looks at Phoebe who again nods "Yes."

"OK, then. Iced coffee for me. Cream and sugar."

Like a fool, but also because it seems the only, the most straightforward thing she has ever done, Phoebe remains standing there for one second, two seconds, three seconds. Longer than normal. Longer by far. *Say something, you idiot*, she thinks to herself, *or at least go—go put in their order*. Four seconds, five seconds.

George breaks the happy weight of the awkward pause in the action by pretending to hit a drum with drumsticks, and even says, "Ta da!" Never has he done anything so awkward, so adolescent. He'd forgotten what it felt like to blush.

Thankfully, Phoebe had already skipped away to put in their order after which she returns to the table where Alice and Jane sit.

"Can I?" says Alice. And without waiting for an answer she cups her hand over Phoebe's belly. Phoebe doesn't pull away. Quite the contrary. She puts her hand over Alice's, holds it there.

"Of course, Alice. Maybe you'll catch a kick."

Her friend, Jane, says, "How far along are you?"

"Almost eight months."

"And still working?" Jane shakes her head in disbelief. "Ooof. On your feet like this."

"She's still swimming, too, aren't you, Phoebe?" Alice speaks the question as a statement.

"Nothing stops me swimming." Phoebe looks off, away. "Nothing."

As she says this she hears the little bell on the front door of the restaurant jingle and looks that way. A woman with two toddlers, comes in, and behind them a tall, lean young man with black hair, black eyes. A man like any other with his nice little family. "It's him," Phoebe thinks to herself, "My God, it's him."

Why does she know for sure now when he was in the police lineup just months ago? Because he *was* in the line-up. She knows it. Now. But she didn't then. Maybe the glass between them was too thick. If there is such a thing as a sixth sense, maybe the glass occluded it. Or maybe she was just too overwhelmed that day. Everyone was watching her so closely, just waiting for her to react. All she knows for certain is that this is him: the guy who was eating the orange.

The back of her throat feels as if it is closing right up. She can't swallow. She staggers back, ever so slightly. Enough so that Alice's palm falls away from Phoebe's tummy. "Phoebe? You all right?"

Phoebe doesn't answer immediately because she is silently mouthing. *Please don't sit in my section. Please don't sit in my section. Please don't sit in my section.* She is willing it as she answers Alice. "Yeah, fine—thanks. Fine. Just a tad woozy." She turns and watches the man's little boy swing near to one of her tables, holding a little plastic airplane aloft before he lands the toy on a table by the window, imitating the noise of a jet as he does. It's one of Dolores' tables. Thank the lord. Thank the lord. The toddler's parents and sister follow, sliding into the booth.

As Phoebe heads toward the back door, she passes Dolores. "Cover me for a few, can you?"

"Sure, sweetie." Dolores has kids; she knows the sudden shifts borne of pregnancy.

It's sunny out. The blue dumpster just to the left of the door shines like a sapphire. Leaning against it, Phoebe inhales the horrid rotting smells that pour from its lips, open to an "Ah—" because it is over full. Tomorrow is pick-up. She tries to press the tough plastic top down, seal the lips, but gives up. But the effort and the familiar scent bring her back to earth, enough so she turns, reties her apron, and heads back inside, crossing the room to her section without looking side to side.

FORTY-NINE

"Can I bother you for one more thing?" It is George, in the booth right beside her. He is saving Phoebe. Even if he doesn't know it. She turns around completely and he continues. "Lila wonders if we can add French fries to our order. She saw some go by on their way to another table, in one of those little paper cones—."

"Of course. Henry's *frites*. They're the best. The best. I live on them." Phoebe wants to smile but she can't. She is in turmoil. Sick. George sees fear in her eyes and wonders if he's been too familiar. Simultaneously, he wants to stand up from the table and scream. He wants to touch this woman.

For God's sake, George, get a hold of yourself. You are in a glorified diner in the middle of nowhere. Get a grip! This woman is pregnant. In a few hours or days you will leave this middle-of-nowhere diner in this middle-of-nowhere town and set sail for the next middle-of-nowhere spot. Why on earth did Henry bring his talent here anyway?

Phoebe walks back to the kitchen to put in the order for French fries and waits there, absently rubbing the scar at the side of her mouth, knowing it will only take a minute or two. As she waits she can't help but look over at him—the guy—sitting with his family. He is cutting his daughter's food into little pieces for her. When he finishes, he hands her the fork with a smile, turns and cups his son's shoulder with his big, tan hand. His wife reaches across and cups her much smaller, whiter hand over his. She is plump and pretty but her mouth is a saw. Sweet she cannot be.

It is then that she watches the guy look her way. But he is looking beyond her. He's looking at Henry. Smiling at Henry, head tilted. A wry smile. She turns around in time to see Henry, nod and smile back. When she turns again the guy is still looking at Henry, and he nods, too, before his focus narrows. He sees her. She watches his face as he takes in her long braid of red hair. Her freckles. Those singular details nail her. She knows it. He stops his scan at her stomach and color comes into his face. His smile vanishes, replaced by a grimace. He looks away quickly. Phoebe's heart turns into a fist and slams her chest.

"Your fries, Mademoiselle." Phoebe snaps her head around to the window into Henry's kitchen as if away from a movie screen. As she grabs the fries Henry stares over her shoulder. Over at the table by the front window.

"You know him?"

"Him who?" Henry lifts the cone of fries in their metal cage Phoebe has set back down under the warming light and hands them to her. She doesn't take them.

"That guy with the little kids and the wife or whatever. At Dolores' table."

"Why?"

"Why? What do you mean, why? Because you were staring at him."

"Wasn't. Never seen him in here before."

"That's not what I asked you."

Henry still has his hand on the cone of fries. "What's your problem?"

Phoebe reaches up to grab the cone, but Henry holds on long enough to cause a tug of war that sends the fries scattering across the high stainless-steel counter.

"Goddam, Phoebe, what's your problem."

"Your problem I'd say. They're for your niece. Do 'em over."

A fresh cone of fries in hand, Phoebe puts on a smile and heads back to George and Lila's table.

In his unconscious nervous state George knocks his knife and spoon right off the table just as she arrives. What on earth? Had he really been reaching for Phoebe's wrist and stopped himself? The cutlery bounces on the floor. Even before it comes to rest both George and Phoebe dive down to fetch it, their foreheads knocking against each other as they do. They come up for air flustered, sort of gasping for air, soft red splotches on both of their foreheads.

Lila looks from her father over to the waitress and back to her father again. Without even thinking, she raises her hand up and down in front of her father's face: "Earth to Dad. Earth to Dad."

FIFTY

Phoebe lies on her back in bed and stares at the ceiling. It's what's they call a popcorn ceiling, white and bumpy—like snow that's fallen and blown about over tiny sticks and stones. They were popular in the 50s but now everyone hates them, scrapes them off or covers them with drywall or beadboard. Everyone but Phoebe that is. She can't afford to redo it. But she wouldn't even if she could. Maybe because her ceiling looks as if before it dried completely, it was walked or even danced upon by birds with three-pronged feet leaving a pattern akin to stars. The footprints of birds dancing on snow. That is one thought Phoebe thinks as she tries to sleep. It must be 2 a.m. by now. She looks at the clock. Close. It's actually 2:43. Four wakeful hours and counting. She touches the sore spot where she conked heads with the man at the restaurant. Henry's brother-in-law. Former brother-in-law: George. When she showered before bed she saw the rose-shaped, rose-colored mark in bloom on her pale forehead.

By sticking to her same work schedule, by going back to her long daily swims, by never altering one habit, Phoebe has kept it together. Kept herself together over the course of the eight months since it happened. She'd even begun to feel calm. But today, she felt the sharp stab of fear. It is fear that is keeping her up. Not fear of ever encountering the guy again. She withstood that blow. Earlier today in fact. And she's not afraid of childbirth. Even at 42. Even though her obstetrician pointed out all the possible complications.

He also remarked on how "lucky" Phoebe was to have gotten pregnant. That was before she shared the circumstances. "Pretty tough to conceive when you're over 40, Ms. Macauley. Less than a 5% chance. So. Rather amazing." Phoebe was in the exam room when the obstetrician said this. Sitting on the crisp white paper the nurse had rolled down the center of the padded table with metal stirrups at the end. "Tough to conceive." Phoebe rolled the word "conceive" over and over in her head and sentences came to mind. Sentences such as "It's nearly impossible to conceive that I am having a baby."

On into the night Phoebe tries to get at the heart of what is filling her with such anxiety. What is keeping her awake. Not fear of giving birth. Not of being a single mother. So, of what? Of what? She tries to puzzle it out. It takes half the night—longer, even—during which ferocious storms move in, hover, and then move away at least for the moment. It is nearly dawn. The thunder, which began by shaking the walls and moved through accompanied by lightning and fierce downpours is now a low growl in the distance. Then it is completely quiet, and Phoebe is completely calm. She has figured it out.

Light is coming in through the shutters painting pale pink stripes across Phoebe's freckled face, the white inside of her forearm, her right foot which extends out from under the white comforter. Her eyes light up into a half smile and then a half frown. She acknowledges that the answer she thought she was seeking was in fact what she even more tenaciously, ferociously was fighting to keep at bay. All through the dark hours. It is not what was done to her that scares her. Nor even having to see the guy again. It's accepting that what she has always dreamed of is coming near. Is within reach. Everything she never conceived could happen is happening. First and foremost, a child. Her child.

In a few days, she will dream his birth. "He" because that is what she will dream—of a son. A son who will nearly tear her apart is biding his time, getting ready to burst upon this world. But not yet, not yet. A son with a full head of crazy red hair, just like hers. One she will call...what? Her father's father was a George. It has always seemed a complete name to her. One that couldn't be turned into a nickname easily. Well, there's time to think about that. In her dream her son is born not in a hospital but right on the earth, literally. On the grass. She looks the name up on Wikipedia, and it says: "George: One who works the land." It all fits. All fits with her dream of having a son. She is going to have a son. Born on the land.

That birth doesn't scare her. No, indeed. But the idea that her dream of having a child may be coming true, is coming true, does. She puts her hands on her stomach. Nary a movement. Frightening, too, are the brief encounters she had with that nice man with the daughter. Not the guy, the man. First, they stood side by side in the grocery aisle. A mere nothingness, right? And then she stood in front of him. Took the lunch order. Turkey. Greek salad. French Fries. They spoke to one another. Yes, indeed. Not many words. Not a conversation in any real sense of the word. And yet, enough. Enough to give rise to this fear. Fear rising like the need to sneeze. Over and over she wonders: Could those few words, could sharing the same air with that man for those few moments be enough? And if they weren't enough, there was the fact that they crashed their heads together. It was farcical, fantastic: a *coup de foudre.*

And sandwiched in between these two encounters she saw *him*. The guy. When she'd gone into the parking lot out back, she could have called the police. Had him picked up. Or was it too late for that? She didn't know how these things worked. The law. Anyway, they had no evidence. Though they could do a blood test soon, she supposed. A paternity test. But she didn't want that. She liked to think that blood didn't just move down through generations in some purely scientific, biological way. She wanted to believe that it moved sideways sometimes, even uphill, through the air, across oceans, plains, rivers, mountains, estuaries, fields—flooded salt flats and sand soft deserts— to find its true vessel. Years from now Phoebe's son will say to her, "They sent me to the right mom." Imagine that he could feel that? Say that. Say the something that will forever put all her fears to rest.

Oh, what nonsense. Lack of sleep has made her loopy. Or maybe not. There are so many ways to give ourselves peace of mind. More important than ever with a child growing inside. Is that what this is all about? Pregnancy hormones?

Phoebe gets out of bed and makes her way downstairs and into the kitchen. The same sun shining on her in bed is bursting through the downstairs shutters creating bars of light, like staves, across the bare wood floor. Birds outside sing the notes.

Phoebe sits at her pine table recalling the day before. She guesses that when the guy came into the restaurant and saw her, he must have been torn. He had his wife and his young children with him. How would he have explained it if he'd stood up quite suddenly, right before their food came, and said, "We have to go. Now." Instead, he took his chances. God, yes, he took his chances! Maybe he believed that his apology had been enough. He didn't eat a bite. A huge plate of food was placed in front of him, and he never lifted his fork. She saw that. Saw Dolores bring him a takeaway box and the wife pack it up for him.

Did he bring his family back to her town on purpose? Was a return to "the scene of the crime" something he couldn't resist? He was not a regular. In the 7 years she had worked at Just Good Food, she had never seen him walk in the door. She asked the rest of the waitstaff. All of them shook their heads, "No. Never laid eyes on him before. Or the wife. Why?" Phoebe didn't answer. Only Henry seemed to recognize him. She knew he knew him. But he wouldn't say so.

You may not believe it, but Phoebe hadn't wanted to pour boiling hot coffee in the guy's lap. Nor did she want to say something awful, something that would change his life forever. She didn't want to walk up to his wife, point to her swelling belly, and scream, "This! This! This is your husband's doing." She didn't want to scream that because she doesn't believe it. Go ahead. Call her loony if you will. Say she has fabricated this theory to shield herself from the terrible reality. Believe like Dr. Z that the reckoning is still to come. Believe what you will.

As for Phoebe, she really does believe there is something thicker than blood. Or that by some miracle blood finds its own way, its own best vessel. The welcoming holds of which take in the precious cargo, secure it, and set sail. After all, she should know. Phoebe was taken in by foster parents who were too old to adopt a baby. They told her they were called to her, and then they fought for her, convinced the agency that no parents could be better. And they loved her all the more for all the years they had wished for a child. Now they were dead. How she missed them! Any records leading back to her birth parents were lost. And anyway, Phoebe wasn't as curious as some might be. She never doubted that the parents who took her in and adopted were blood.

Without burning him with coffee or screaming at his wife, Phoebe knows that the guy's life (or maybe this once she says to herself, or even out loud, "my rapist's life") is changed forever. Unalterably. Just as hers is. Changed most the minute he said, "Sorry." Or perhaps right before—the moment his power bled out of him and into her. Yes. How can seeing her and seeing her pregnant not have sucked whatever life her rapist (she says it again) has left right out of him. Left her rapist (a final time, rapist! rapist, rapist!) with no way to ever lift his spirits or be fully grounded again. Anyone seeing him when he saw her would have said, "The blood drained right from his face." He will forever be unmoored. But she really doesn't wish that on him either.

Sitting on one of her six blue chairs—the metal one whose back is shaped like a heart—Phoebe laces her fingers around her belly and shuts her eyes for several long moments. She's arrived at the opening of a cave. She peers in and first sees only deep velvety black. But as her eyes adjust, black turns to indigo then iridescent Prussian blue. And she can make out dazzling crystalline stalagmites rising out of the floor and pale saffron stalactites dripping from the ceiling. She can't help but be drawn in.

Long, long ago she was born and now she is going backwards, back to the place where she began in order to—to what? To start fresh? To swim out again?

FIFTY-ONE

The storms that came and went overnight are at war again and it seems as if they have no intention of letting up. One rolls off and the sun briefly flashes on the puddles, turning them into mirrors, only to be followed by the gray backs of new clouds, surfacing on the horizon, breaching up into the sky. There's even talk of a hurricane on its way.

"We're grounded again, Lila." George turns, puts his cellphone down and smiles. Lila smiles, too. She is sitting on one of the twin beds in her pajamas making a necklace—threading little stainless-steel bolts and washers onto copper wire. "That's good," she says.

"Why good?"

"We like it here, right?"

George was nodding "Yes," when his cell phone rang. It was Harriet, her voice loud—loud enough to carry all the way into the room.

"Are you fucking kidding me?" were the first words out of her mouth.

George quickly interrupted, "Hold on—please—and lower your voice." He turned to Lila and said, "Hey, kiddo, why don't you jump in the shower and get dressed?" Lila made a face but obeyed and Henry returned to the call. "Lila was sitting right here next to me, Harriet, and I didn't want..."

He barely got the words out and Harriet shouted back, "Henry called and told me what happened!" She stopped to catch her breath before continuing, louder still, "You had my daughter with you in that... that thing and crash landed?"

George kept his voice calm and even, "Didn't crash, Harriet, not by a long shot. But I hear you. Not to worry." And *sotto voce*, even though he could hear the shower running full blast, he added, "I'd already decided I should send Lila to stay with you when I fly again."

"I mean, what were you thinking, George? What on earth were you thinking?"

No one ever says, "What on earth were you thinking?" to be kind. It's a chastisement—something you say with edge to your voice, to a friend, a sibling, your co-worker, your partner or, in this case, the man you're divorcing. "You did *what*? Why?" The hell with that, George thinks. And he goes on thinking, as if in answer to everyone who's questioned his decision—hell, his sanity—when they've gotten wind he was quitting the firm and determined to fly in an airship: *I'm not doing what I'm doing to purposely shock anyone. There's no "I'll show you…" in all of this. No "I'll show you what I'm capable of, who I really am!"*

"No, no, no," he wants to say to them: "It's quite the opposite. I don't want to show anyone anything. I simply want someone to stand back and be astonished in a good way. Someone to notice and speak a quiet, "Wow" or just shake their head and smile wildly. I certainly don't want to hear, "Of course" as in "Of course it makes perfect sense that you are flying away in a dirigible." To say "of course" is not a compliment; it's a dagger. Better someone just fucking acknowledge that I am off any course they ever imagined I could be on. "Of course" is a little death. I know. Because, of course, I have been dying, slowly dying for years.

George stops mid-reverie when he sees that his silent watcher, his doppelgänger, is standing in a dark corner of the room. He addresses him: "Yes, yes, I see you there, with your half smile. And I have to thank you—thank you for kicking 'of course' to the side of the road. Thank you for making roadkill of 'of course'—stinking bloody roadkill."

"Dad?" Lila steps out of the bathroom, bathrobe on, a toothbrush hanging from her mouth, "Were you just talking to Mom?"

"Just now?" George wonders what Lila heard.

"'Stinking…bloody…roadkill'" she says and giggles.

"Did I say that out loud, Lila? Wow, that's funny. It's a line from a movie I dreamed about last night," he lies, and for good reason. "What can I say? Your Dad's a nutty guy!" George sticks out his tongue and wags his head like a funny cartoon character then stops and says, "You finish with your teeth and get dressed. My turn to jump in the shower."

Showering, dressing, George thinks about the waitress, Phoebe. Maybe it's her braid which weaves thoughts of her into his memory of that summer before his senior year—so long ago—when, working on Nantucket he met that older woman. She had a braid, too; but her's was short, sleek and blonde. She was the hostess at the Harbor House restaurant and lived in a small room in the attic of the hotel. Didn't exactly date, he remembers, but we slept together almost every night. Haven't a clue how that happened, but, jeez, I do remember the racking cough I had from too many damp days, no sun, long hours working outside. I would go into a furlong of coughs in the middle of the night and she would just hold me tighter. Don't recall there was much talk between us, but what talk we had focused on big things: constellations and high tides, Graham Greene novels and faith, Rauschenberg collages and John Cage music. We would meet-up late—after her shift ended—climb the stairs to her room and curl up in her single bed, sometimes her on the outside, sometimes me.

All my buddies—who were working the summer as chambermaids, waiters, busboys or as gardeners like me—would be going out in a group to drink, to dance. "You comin' or hangin' with your old lady?" they'd ask. That's what she was to them, the "old lady." I never questioned what she wanted; never occurred to me. And strange as the relationship was, it didn't seem strange to me.

Looking back now, George wonders if that woman was seeing the person he would become, what is it now, nearly three decades later? The night before he flew back home to drive up to college the two met, as usual, but that night, before they climbed the stairs, she whispered, "I'm taking you on a walk. Hold my hand and close your eyes—tight." Right after you set out, she caught you peeking, sighed and said, "There's no point in this if you don't trust me." You'd nodded "yes" and walked beside her—over pavement and stone and sand and her hand was firm and moist and maybe once or twice or three times she curled a finger into your palm, not to be sexual but to say, "You see. I am here, watching out for you. So just shut up. Be the blind one." It was not a case of love although looking back George realizes that it *was* love, knows that he must have sensed that she saw if not what he was right then, what he might become.

Never trusted anyone so completely since, George thinks. Not even close. Until. Well, we shall see. That woman—Phoebe—makes it seem possible. Honestly don't know if she is as striking as she struck me. Clearly her parts are at odds: that bony body, those too big hands awash with orange freckles, that aquiline nose, wide eyes, crooked smile. But, damn, all together it has shut me up and opened me up in one fell swoop. Phoebe: she's what made me remember that older woman. I would go over to her place at the hotel by bike. If you ride a bike fast enough the pavement blurs, turns to a rich charcoal that flows like water under your feet. Thoughts can do that, too. But asphalt is not water. Fall and you'll be burned, flesh embedded with dirt and tiny stones they'll scrub with something akin to a Brillo pad when you go, bloodied from ankles to thighs, wrists to above your elbows, to the emergency room where the tired intern will say, "Only way to get these wounds clean is to scrub them," and he starts in with a bristle brush, winces and says, "Sorry" when he hears you gasp. That happened to George—the fall, the brutal scrubbing, the new skin—pink and tender— revealed when the scabs fell away.

"Dad, I need pancakes. Now! Please?" Lila has opened the door to the hallway and is standing half in the room, half out, tapping her right foot, her right arm akimbo on her little hip.

"Aren't we demanding," George says before he grabs the keys, meets her at the door, musses her hair, and replies, "Let's go, then. I've never been so hungry in my life."

FIFTY-TWO

Phoebe comes into Just Good Food through the back door and pokes her head in the kitchen. No one there. She hangs her swim bag and sweater on a hook then moves on, tying the strings of her apron behind her she walks into the restaurant, first pulling them tight around her mounded tummy and then trying it higher, up over the mound before settling for having it smack around the baby growing inside.

Chef Henry is sharing a booth with the man—that man, that man!—and his daughter. George. He's made a Jacob's Ladder which he is stretching from the table top up. As Phoebe walks closer, she sees that the girl—Lila, wasn't it?—is concentrating with all her might, holding the pointer fingers and thumbs on both her hands up in an L-shape. Henry transfers the ladder loops of string onto her fingers. The girl's father—George, Phoebe, his name is George, is smiling. She arrives at the table to hear him say, "You've got it, Lila, you've got it." Lila giggles, turns the linking rectangles vertical, stretches it from the table towards the ceiling, and replies, "We could use this to get up and down from the ship."

"Stairway to heaven, looks like," Phoebe says. Henry and the man, in unison, say, "Exactly" and Henry stands. "Back to the kitchen for me. George, Lila, I'll leave you in Phoebe's good hands once again."

Lila is staring at Phoebe's forehead. "Is that from yesterday?"

Phoebe touches the spot she tried to cover with makeup. "'Fraid so. But not to worry. Doesn't hurt. Not at all."

George reflexively lifts his hand to touch his own forehead. "Nor mine."

FIFTY-THREE

The alerts began as a trickle like a slow drip in an upstairs bath easy to ignore, until one morning the ceiling gives way and the chandelier falls——a mess of glass mixing with an ever-widening pool, complete with tiny waves, water-falling off the rounded sides of the dining room table onto the aged Oriental carpet beneath.

What was a mere tropical wave on August 30—a trifle, a honeymoon couple smooching in a hammock—had, a day later, become Category 3 Hurricane Isobel. She stretched this way and that, rubbing up and purring against one current after another with greater and lesser intensity before leaping forward.

Newscasters reporting from Southwest Florida delighted in showing clips of empty Costco and Home Depot shelves, and shop and homeowners using sandbags and boards to shore up their properties. They were right to prepare. Kaboom, on September 6th Isobel pounced, a feral Category 5 hurricane, claws very much out, riding winds that peaked at 180 miles per hour. She leapt across Cuba, briefly licked her paws, and then curled around the Caribbean before making landfall on Marco Island on September 10. Isobel most certainly did not come in on little cat's feet.

The day after Labor Day one of Phoebe's customers at the restaurant said he'd heard on the radio that once she was bored with Florida, Isobel might run right up through the middle of Georgia. "Seriously?" she said, holding the coffee pot in mid-air. "Pour, my dear," he said. Phoebe filled the man's mug as he continued, "Totally serious. Fickle girl, that Isobel—on the prowl and heading our way."

"Nonsense," Phoebe replied, "We don't get those sorts of storms here."

But it wasn't nonsense.

The Governor of Georgia began declaring states of emergency beginning that very afternoon, first in counties along the coast and eventually including every county in the entire state. A mere tropical storm. Mere? Ha! Isobel pawed her way into Georgia Sunday night and clawed forward Monday—September 11th of all days—dropping over seven inches of rain. All the while the wind gusted from 50 up to 75 miles per hour.

Phoebe woke in the wee hours of Monday to find the ancient alarm clock next to her bed flashing "2:02." The power must have already gone out and on again. She lay there and listened to the rain for a few minutes before rolling her pregnant body out of bed. She wanted to get to the restaurant where there was a generator. She even put together a little sack with toothbrush and such thinking if worse came to worse, she could curl up and spend the night in a booth rather than return to a dark house.

In town, in their charming but far from shipshape bed and breakfast, George and Lila had been woken up not once but three times by a poorly designed emergency light that flashed like an ambulance beacon every time the power flickered off then on. When he lifted himself up on his elbows and looked over at the twin bed a night table away, Lila looked back, serious for her, and said, "Good grief! What a night!" Such an adult thing to say. It made George laugh. He swung his legs onto the floor and gave his daughter's head of curls a tousle. "Let's get breakfast, kiddo. Now. While we can."

Lila ran to the window, pulled back the heavy curtain and shouted, "Sign is lit, Dad."

"OK, then. We're in luck. Clothes! Raincoat!"

Lila was standing at the door when George came out of the bathroom, tucking his shirt into his jeans. In her haste to get to breakfast, or perhaps oblivious or devil-may-care, Lila had paired plaid shorts with a striped shirt, her yellow duck boots and a baseball hat. Her mass of curls stuck out the sides as if an eggbeater had been used atop her head.

"You are a sight, Whirligig." George bent down and kissed the top of her head.

"I wanted you to be able to see me."

"We're you planning to disappear?"

"No but you know."

"Know what?"

"How you tell people I'm the bright spot in your life?"

"Today more than ever. Let's move our buns."

George opened the door to Just Good Food and stamped his sneakers. He should have been smart and worn boots like Lila. His feet were already wet. Lila rushed past him, breathless, grinning. When she came to a stop, she shook herself and water flew off her, a few drops hitting customers sitting close by.

"You're getting people wet, sweetie. Go find a booth."

"Will Daddy."

George was looking around thinking, "Where is she?" when Phoebe stuck her head through the window to the kitchen, "I'm filling in best I can. No Henry. Must be dealing with a leak or some such."

"Bummer."

"Nobody's even heard from him."

George walked over to the window. There was no glass. It was open. Even so, it seemed a distance far too vast. He stretched out his arm and she took his hand and shook it saying, "George" and he responded, with a slight bow and another handshake: "Miss Phoebe." It was a strangely formal greeting except they didn't let go even after continuing to shake each other's hand. But it had to stop. Phoebe had work to do. She squeezed George's hand and said, "I'm kind of loving this storm."

She thought she'd spoken softly. But an elderly man sitting nearby heard her, turned around and said, "Love it? Really? This keeps up and we're all going to be without power for God knows how long."

Phoebe called out. "You're right. You're right. All this excitement in the skies is fun until it's not."

"Exactly," the old man said. "See how you like it when you're in the dark day after day." The man turned back around and had a bite of his breakfast sandwich before ending with, "Or if your water breaks and you can't get to the hospital!"

Phoebe made a face, "OK, OK—point taken!" George leaned toward her, squeezed her hand, dropped it and cocked his head back towards Lila. "We're going to sit and eat something while the stove's working. Wish you could join us."

"Gotta hold the fort here."

"For how long?"

"No clue. 'Till Henry comes in. Don't mind. It's kind of cozy in here."

"Good to know you feel that way about small, enclosed spaces." George began to walk away then turned. "I'll keep trying Henry. Did you try a text?"

"Called and texted. N/A."

"He'll appear."

FIFTY-FOUR

The storm hit Henry's house particularly hard, waking him, as it had Phoebe, well before dawn. When he padded down into the kitchen Ragout was standing, hang dog, by the side door. Despite the squalls, Henry let him out. Poor pup had to go out some time to do his business. And Henry was distracted. Over the pounding rain he could hear water dripping close by, a higher pitch. He went round to the living room and saw a dark patch on the light pine floor; rain finding its way in through a skylight just above. Ragout is a big boy, Henry thought. If he gets tired of the battering rain, he can take refuge in his doghouse.

Henry grabbed his tool belt and set to work tightening the crank on the skylight until it wouldn't budge. Then he dried all around the casing and squeezed a new strip of caulking along every seam. Feeble as the proverbial finger in the dyke, he thought to himself. He'd never heard such wind or rain. Ping after ping battered the house—the force and sound of a thousand nails being hammered.

It was worth making sure all the windows were shut, the locks that still functioned secure. Henry did this. Then he made a pot of coffee thinking it might be the last hot thing he had before the power went out or he got over to the restaurant. Cream, sugar—stirring it at the table Henry thought about all those trees running alongside the power lines. Damn Georgia Power. Of course, they never trimmed them. He wondered if that guy he'd hooked up with had already been called in to work. Whether he might see him again at the restaurant—hopefully without his family this time. With that, the red light behind the plastic rectangle on his coffeemaker went off. He looked up to note the time on the stove but, of course, the panel was black. "Hell hath no fury...."

That phrase was no sooner out of his mouth than he heard Ragout screaming over the din. Not barking, screaming. He ran outside—no coat or even shoes—and saw that an enormous, sweet gum tree had fallen onto the roof of the doghouse. Credit to Magnus, the structure was intact. Why, then, the screams? Henry ran towards his pet who was tangled in something. A vine? He didn't think; he simply grabbed ahold of Ragout to unwind the cord and free him. Then he, too, screamed, loud once, twice and then made gasping sounds. But there was no one to hear. No one to see man and dog violently shiver and sizzle to stillness, the power line exhaling clouds of smoke. The grass was too wet to catch on fire.

By the time the sun peeked back out, on Wednesday the 13th, more than a million and a half Georgians were without power. Just as Henry had predicted, trees had toppled forwards and back, in some cases held just off the ground by the power lines making them look very much like a row of drunks trying their best to stay upright.

A woman working on one of the power company crews found Henry and Ragout, in an odd sort of hug, drying in the sun. She saw red welts. Burns on Henry's hands and around his stomach where live cable had burned away shirt and skin. A man and a dog. She didn't immediately call out to the rest of the crew. It was such a mesmerizing still life. She had seen one at an art museum when she was a schoolgirl: a pewter plate on which lay a plump peach, a cluster of grapes, creamy yellow cheese and a knife, its blade with the highlight thrown from a candle painted just so. That is a still life, too.

The sun came out from behind a cloud. The man wore an earring in one ear; it shone. The dog's collar did, too. She bent down and read the tag, "Ragout." She said it out loud, improperly: "Rag Out." The man had no name, for now.

She stood back up, pulled a cigarette from her breast pocket, lit it, and took slow drags. She was in no hurry. No hurry at all. Nothing was going to get fixed today, least of all the power.

FIFTY-FIVE

The storm raged on, but Just Good Food never lost power no doubt because it shared the same electrical grid as the hospital. A small miracle. It became a gathering place for locals to nurse endless cups of coffee, shake their heads, charge their phones, rail at the wind and rain and compare horror stories of downed trees and flooded roads.

News of Henry's death arrived via the best friend of the sister of the wife of the EMT who got the call about "a man and his dog found electrocuted." Though no one at the restaurant had been on the scene, the tale of Henry's demise was told with ever more grisly embellishments as it spread from table to table. In every case, stunned silences gave way to more headshaking, and refrains of "Oh, my Lord's," "How awful's" and "Can you imagine's?" slowly crescendoing into rants directed at the power company, not that they were to blame. In the midst of this mix of whispers and cacophony Dolores saw Phoebe, ashen-faced, drop into a chair and put her head in her hands. She crossed the room and crouched beside her. "I am so, so sorry, kiddo."

Phoebe looked up at the other waitress. "It's just that it's so—so awful. To go like that. Chef Henry. Our Henry. And his sweet dog. I mean, just imagine...."

"And for you especially." Dolores broke in. "You and the baby. What will you do?"

Phoebe didn't respond. Couldn't. She was confused by this intimation that Henry's death must be especially poignant for her. It took her a moment. "You and the baby," Dolores had said. "Terrible for you and the baby." Is that what they all think? That Henry is the father?

Dolores left to top off more coffee cups and Phoebe stood, straightened her apron and looked around the restaurant before ducking back into the kitchen. No doubt about it. She was the focus of extra attention—a sudden celebrity born of tragedy. It was obvious not because her regular customers were staring but because they were trying to avoid staring. Especially the men. One or two of the female customers Phoebe knew best came into the kitchen and offered words akin to condolence. "Times like these, keeping busy is the best." Or they shook their heads, put a hand on her shoulder and said, "For you, of all people, to be stepping in for Henry. It might be too much. Is too much." Everyone wanted to be sympathetic and respectful in their misguided belief that she and Henry had wanted to keep their relationship private.

Phoebe was dumbfounded. But she decided to simply nod and say, "Thank you. I'll be fine" or "We're going to be just fine." Why disabuse every one of their false assumptions? It meant she would forever be spared from further explanation.

George and Lila, alone at a booth in a back corner, felt the alternating pulse of hush and buzz but, being outsiders, were left out of the shared breaking news. Looking out from the opening into the kitchen, Phoebe caught George's eye, put her hand to her mouth and immediately went to speak to him. "You don't know?"

George shook his head no. "Don't know what I don't know. But hard not to feel that something's up."

Phoebe cocked her head towards Lila, who was coloring in a book. She was concentrating, head down, so Phoebe mouthed Henry's name, and shook her head with her eyes closed. George got it.

"Bad news?"

"Worse. Yes."

"What's worse than bad?" Lila looked up now.

Phoebe saw no reason not to simply say it. "Henry—your uncle—was killed in the storm, sweetie."

George stretched his arms out and Lila scrambled around the table and into his lap, pressed her head against her father's chest, and began to cry. His chin pressed to the top of his daughter's head, George whispered to Phoebe, "Thank you—. We'll talk later, ok? I'll have to call Harriet." Phoebe looked at him. "My ex. Henry's sister."

"Shall I sit here with Lila?"

"No, no. She knows now. She can hear."

Phoebe returned to the kitchen. Lila lifted her head off her father's chest and asked, "Will mom come here?"

"Imagine so."

George had known Henry since he'd first started dating Harriet—known him as Henry was finishing college and going through culinary school. Known and liked the friends he brought to Connecticut for cookouts and especially liked the bartender with whom Henry had fallen in love—and the reason he'd left New York, unable to recover when his love had taken up with another guy.

He overheard a pair of women at a table adjacent to the booth where he and Lila sat talking about it.

"Why do you think they kept it to themselves?"

"Oh, you know, working together in a tiny place like this. They probably just wanted to keep it private till after."

"After what?"

"After the baby's come, of course."

"Makes no sense. We all would have been happy for them."

"Well, that's just how it is."

"You think they'd already married?"

"How should I know, Ella? Maybe they were going to do that after."

"After? What do you mean after? Who's the father on the birth certificate then? Baby's got to have a last name."

The other woman didn't answer. Her friend tore a packet of sugar open and dumped it in her cup, stirring it vigorously. "It's all ass-backwards. Supposed to be 'First comes love, then comes marriage, then comes...'"

"You're a damn fool, Ella, and all that sugar's going to make you fat."

The storm was taking its toll on everyone.

George—the person who had known Phoebe the shortest amount of time and Henry the longest—figured he was the only one who knew better; the only one left to ponder who the father of Phoebe's baby-to-be really was.

Fifty-Six

By late the following day, the worst of the storm was over. Harriet had flown into Atlanta, rented a car and immediately drove down to fetch Lila who she hadn't seen for weeks and weeks. George supposed that seeing her youngest took some sting out of losing Henry, her only sibling, but he saw neither joy nor sorrow in Harriet's face. He reached to give her a hug of sympathy, but she drew back.

Harriet took Lila by the hand. "I'm at the only real hotel I could find—a bit of a drive from here but there's no other option I could see. No way I could bear to stay at Henry's place. I'll stay in touch by text, ok?"

"Of course."

"Lila can have dinner and stay the night with me. Don't know what sort of official things I'll have to do tomorrow so she may be better back with you during the day."

"Yes, yes." George looked at his daughter. She had her arms around her mother's legs, and she nodded repeatedly at her father.

As soon as they were gone, George walked back in the direction of the restaurant. He needn't have. Phoebe was already on her way to him, and they met halfway. George put out his hand which Phoebe took and shook. "Good heavens, that was hard this morning...shaking hands...I didn't want to let go!" Without a word they turned and headed back to the bed and breakfast that was George and Lila's home for the moment.

And there they lay down together.

Imagine whatever you think would be most satisfying and you will have it about right, as long as you imagine movement so slow, so focused you would swear, as they did afterwards, that it was all a dream. Phoebe and George made a meal of each other—helping themselves, curious, with fingers and lips, to reach for and taste whatever they saw, felt, touched, desired. At one point, Phoebe lifted her head and said, "Oy, but you are married—."

George raised himself on his elbows so he could look straight at her and said, firmly, "That's all but over. Was over years ago." He paused, "Everything is settled—there's just the court date—very soon—to put a seal upon it." He lay back and Phoebe with her pregnant tummy inched up along George to straddle him. He looked at her, "And you, you...are...pregnant!"

He put his hands on either side of her and she twisted her hips, this way then that, before easing her tummy down a bit so it touched his, "Well, that's all but over, too. And about to begin. As you can clearly see. Feel..."

So, they continued, eyes fixed on the other's. Sure, there were open questions but none more pressing nor more important than answering the question that had floated in the air from the moment they'd set eyes on one another. What would this—what they were now doing—be like? They lay back finally, eyes closed, but continued to lay themselves bare, even asking to be touched, here or there. Yes, it was all very dreamy, but serious, real, as well: the weight of Phoebe's pregnancy, George's divorce, the storm, Henry's death, could not be thrown overboard, just sink from sight. But that was good, in the end—the weight of life—all the trials and tribulations, loneliness and sorrow but also the unexpected joys, comforting routines, successes, quiet satisfactions. All of that would serve as an anchor so that they could be certain what they had found in each other was rooted in earthly concerns and would not float away.

George's cell phone rang. It was Harriet. She was overwhelmed dealing with legal questions and just simple logistics surrounding her brother's death. "Go," Phoebe said. "She needs you. Go." George nodded, got up and began dressing, grabbing pants from there, one sock from under the bed, his t-shirt where? Having put himself back together, he walked over to Phoebe and gave her a kiss. "OK, I'm off." But he turned before he went out the door to ask, "The father?" Phoebe propped herself up on one elbow, "As you said about your marriage, that's all in the past."

A few hours later George returned with some food for them to share—cheese, bread, some apples and a bottle of white wine. Phoebe was reading, drowsy. She joined him at the little table and chairs in the rented room. George opened the wine and handed her a glass, "You can have some, right?"

"This late in the game? Sure, sure."

They ate and then returned to bed. Hours later, when George was laying happily exhausted on his stomach, breathing in and out of sleep, arms akimbo, Phoebe stretched out along the length of him, made of him a perfect resting place, her stomach a ripe mound resting in the hollow of his lower back, her head between his shoulders, her arms bent at the elbows, hands cupping his shoulders, breathing life back into him. Coming half-awake he turned over. They kissed and fell asleep in that kiss. Mouth to mouth. And they woke that way, too.

FIFTY-SEVEN

Phoebe had just left to head over to Just Good Food for work—whether to man the kitchen or work the tables she knew not—when Harriet and Lila knocked at the door. Harriet burst in, shoving a small bag with Lila's things into his hands. "So, so much to take care of. I've got a broker coming to look at Henry's house and they gave me the name of someone who can clear it out, sell what's sellable..." Harriet gave Lila a hug as she said this." She paused for a breath. "And thank you, George. You coming over yesterday was a huge help."

"Of course—."

"If I can, I'll fly back late tomorrow. Maybe Lila and I can spend the morning and have lunch."

"Or more," George replied. "I'm intent on continuing my journey, Harriet. I know what we agreed but am thinking until I finish—reach the West Coast, at least that's my plan—that Lila should return home with you. I just don't..."

Lila was shaking her head and mouthing "No, Dad," when her mother broke in. "I've got back-to-back conferences at work as soon as I return, George. I'm already missing so much. It's important. You'll figure it out. I'm sorry. But, please. We agreed."

That Harriet was going to let Lila stay with George surprised him. Yes, she had her hands full with a demanding job and taking care of all the details surrounding her brother's sudden death. But that unexpected and unimaginable catastrophe seemed all the more reason for her to recoil at the idea of letting her daughter travel with him one furlong further—continue on "a voyage with a fool in a claptrap dirigible" as he had overheard her saying. Not that George had any intention of allowing that. Lila had had adventure enough. Not only had George expected Harriet to demand Lila stay with her, he'd thought it for the best himself. They'd been lucky once, but luck was not a lady he wanted to trust his daughter to. Besides, the whole point of building and sailing in the dirigible had been to ply the skies himself—to make a break, leave earth and all of its inhabitants behind for a spell—wasn't it?

Harriet left. George sighed, smiled, took Lila's hand and they jumped in their rental car and drove the few miles over to the field where the dirigible was moored. Though they bunked at the bed and breakfast through the week, they spent a good part of their days in the airship which was an adventure even when it sat moored. As if in a Jules Verne novel, looking out the large windows of its convex body was to see the world anew. As he was putting away supplies and checking the weather report for the next day—he was itching to set sail again—he heard Phoebe shouting up to him from the ground, "Reporting for duty, Captain." When George looked out the window, she dropped a large backpack at her feet and saluted. Hearing Phoebe's voice, Lila ran to the window then looked to see what her father's reaction would be.

George's dirigible was tethered to the ground by taut lines wound around stakes he'd pounded into the ground. He would have to wrestle those stakes free before he took off again, free of the earth and all its people. Or maybe not. He looked down at Phoebe and waved but didn't smile back. He had considered asking Phoebe to care for Lila as he continued his flight. At least for the next leg or so. A few weeks at most. Now he knew he was looking at the possibility of not one "stowaway" but two, well, two and a half was more like it. The lines that tethered the dirigible to the ground were taut in him, too; hell, there were reasons to be tethered.

"When are we leaving? I want to go up, up, up" Lila stood before her father, hands on hips, arms akimbo, demanding.

"Well, as a matter of fact, I think tomorrow, an auspicious day, is the day."

"What's oz-pish-us?"

"A red-letter day. A lucky day. Sort of as if it were your birthday."

"But it isn't.

"Nope. But there's going to be a full moon. Which will be beautiful."

Beauty was important, but so was an extra measure of light through the night; even the new George retained a modicum of rationality. Phoebe and Lila were beside themselves with glee. George was more reserved; it was still storm season. He didn't put complete faith in either sophisticated instrumentation or experienced weather gurus who were in agreement that the blue skies which had come on the heels of the hurricane would last and spell clear sailing ahead.

As he was loosening the mooring lines to the dirigible before setting sail the next morning, his doppelgänger appeared. Unusually serious, that other self held a moistened forefinger up to the wind and shook his head. "Speak, man, speak!" George said out loud. Not that he needed to hear what his doppelgänger had to say; he'd had his own premonition, silly, really, but disturbing nonetheless; he had woken to find his watch had stopped exactly at midnight.

His crew of beloved young daughter and, yes, already beloved and very pregnant—what was he prepared to say? "partner"? "lover"?—were in high spirits. They insisted on a group hug and selfie. "Why aren't you smiling?" Phoebe asked when she saw the result and Lila tried to tickle him into a laugh. George gave them both a hug said with an accent, "Aye, me matey's, but captaining a ship is a serious business!"

A few locals—Phoebe's co-workers and regular customers from the restaurant—gathered to wave and watch as the dirigible slowly rose from the hay field. Among them was George's doppelgänger, his palm up in salute. George saluted back. Neither smiled; they were saying farewell. Soon those on the ground were tiny, as through a telescope. It was exhilarating to gain height with nary a sound so quiet were the engines. So very quiet. And it was beautiful—a Rothko-like quilt of geometric blues, greens and yellows passing below—and the air bite-able in its blue-ness. Phoebe and Lila unwrapped lunch—thick sandwiches of tomato, ham, lettuce, Swiss cheese and mayonnaise followed by berries and oatmeal cookies studded with raisins. Lila cupped her tummy afterwards and said, "Oof. I am so full!" and Phoebe cradled hers and laughed saying, "You're full? Look at me." Then, apologizing and yawning, she stretched out on one of the cushioned window seats, "This girl has to put her feet up!" More she felt she needed to curl up; there was a wee bit of tugging in her belly, a stretching that—as the hours went on—crossed a line into discomfort that was impossible to ignore even when it receded like a tide. When that tidal rhythm quickened, Phoebe found she had to keep her knees up to her chest as the only antidote to the pain. And then, she felt a rush of water spill out of her. Her first thought was, "Oh, I've soiled the cushion!" But she knew what that escaping water meant, knew she should tell George. "I will," she told herself, "Just as soon as the next wave passes. Maybe when we next set down." Lila perched cross-legged nearby, was drawing on her iPad, humming, happy. Phoebe reached down and ran her fingers through Lila's mess of curls.

It was at just this moment that George looked over at the pair: all seemed calm, all seemed bright. And why should it not be? Their next landing spot was but a few hours away. He turned back, his eyes trained on the instruments and the sky. He thought he saw some anvil shaped clouds far off on the horizon. Thunderstorms? Not for a moment could he adequately silence the chorus of voices whispering, over and over, "What on earth are you thinking, George?"

As if in reply—a mere two hours later and just before dawn, the face of the full moon smiling still—Zeus, or whoever it is up there, was preparing to make clear who pulls the strings, perhaps to make a mockery of Doppler systems and weather forecasters.

It was in this most still and uncanny moment of "before"—like a breath held—that George again looked over at Phoebe and caught her wincing, arms wrapped around her knees which were curled into her chest. *Oh, God*, he thought. And then, without warning, a wily wind shear exhaled with violence. For one second an image of a woodcut flashed across George's mind: a print with a mythical god, puffed out cheeks, prominent in a high corner of the page, his breath—a swathe of curled, black clouds—fanning out and causing the huge trees below to bend over double, peasants to run for cover, animals to cower.

The radar on board George's airship was advanced, but not of the caliber on board some aircraft and at airports where wind shear was of particular concern for planes taking off and landing. When the shear hit, the craft was immediately destabilized. George went into battle, wrestling to keep his dirigible from rising, falling, twisting and sending first Lila and then Phoebe onto the floor. Woman and girl both grabbed onto railings nearby and looked to George. "Cushions!" George said, "Hold the cushions to your chests." Had he time for reflection George would have cursed himself. There was little he could do to help his passengers; all his efforts were trained on trying this maneuver then that in a desperate effort to keep them all safe. To no avail.

Neither Lila nor Phoebe screamed; they were in an embrace, petrified and mute, Phoebe because she was experiencing unrelenting contractions now and capable only of focusing on what was happening inside of herself while George focused on what was without. Substantial and singular on the ground, the airship became fragile and deserving of our sympathy while fighting for its life.

FIFTY-NINE

Need you hear about cables snapping, carbon fiber struts collapsing, polyurethane skin tearing? I think not. What needs saying is that the three people inside were not as panicked as one might suppose; it was as if they accepted and even perversely embraced being caught up in something so astonishing, so beyond their ken.

Cacophony. That's the word. Or no, perhaps babel is better, especially as we are in a near religious moment, as four souls (because, yes, we must include the unborn child) hover on the verge of death, verge of birth. But honestly, neither word is quite right; they are just the best we can do in an effort to characterize what we are privy to: the maelstrom happening not outside the airship's windows but deep inside each of our characters' psyches whilst they plummet down, down, down.

Inhabiting these psyches, it is, perhaps, better to use the word "kaleidoscope" to encompass the mad succession of vignettes appearing and disappearing nearly too fast for analysis. Oh, and there's a soundtrack humming along underneath whatever singular sights may be flashing inside George, Phoebe and Lila's brains—a bit bittersweet but surprisingly lyrical, beautiful, as if there is some universal vibration at the heart of it all, the heart of us all.

Those who have not paid attention to our characters as we have, might clap their hands over their ears, close their eyes, and shake their heads—turn away as from a foreign movie without subtitles—with no desire to decipher the singular action. Let them walk away. We'll stay and wave "Farewell." Because it's different for us. We accept the gift of being privy to these high stakes, penultimate moments with our characters. Gratitude to, along with Lila, imagine ourselves tightly gripping a black crayon and making spirals, fatter and fatter, closer and closer together until, on a yellowed page, we've made a solid circle: a black hole that sucks all our attention. And then, as with Lila, one beat later (time cannot be measured when certain death awaits) feel a rush as the page explodes into a heavenly hail of scintillating silver stars, christening us in light.

Next up, gratitude again, to be along with Phoebe, doubled-over with contractions one moment then pain-free the next and spinning happily out of control, in the dark, bare feet on grass, with fireflies kissing our face, legs, arms, even lips until a small child runs towards us, grabs our hand and we both—we all—collapse onto the ground dizzy but deliriously happy. The fall is both imagined and real.

Once the dizziness subsides we are, finally, grateful to be—along with George— aware, very, of his doppelgänger standing very close and more clearly, more palpably than ever before. And the doppelgänger is laughing. Laughing! For a millisecond? Longer? (There is no time in this near-death space.) All we sense, along with George, is that the doppelgänger's laugh is one not of derision but of joy—fantastic, unbounded joy. Together with George we experience *it*, not the other self but the joy itself, as a million, million voices bursting forth in harmony as the doppelgänger slips into George, into us, a perfect match. He is filled, we are filled, with something akin to love.

But like cacophony or babel or even kaleidoscope that word—love— is not big enough, nor right. Nonsense you say? Maybe. Or maybe we can share our characters' revelations as their pre-crash, interior movies play—the revelation that there is something more, something beyond love—something inchoate. Because it seems as if each of them, in their fall from heaven to earth, have happened upon an ancient text whose pages—and the words and pictures on them—disintegrate as they try to decipher what is there. But that's of no matter: better to simply be grateful for the knowledge of something beyond reach, a liminal space.

Hogwash you say? If that's how you feel, leave. Or stay a moment longer; stop questioning. Simply be still and see if you can't grasp this yourself: imagine you've been hypnotized and wake feeling as if you've been taken to a place and given a gift that you cannot pass on because you cannot put hands around it. I am telling you this is possible, possible even to be witness to what the baby is experiencing in the seconds before impact. Why not? Why—even without out putting our palms on, or our ears to, Phoebe's stomach—should we not? Why should we not intuit that this being yet-to-come is experiencing a world as uniquely harmonious as a Joan Mitchell painting or a Philip Glass piano solo? Why can't we all experience a touch of synesthesia and turn the words on this page into something heard, tasted, touched?

SIXTY

Afterwards, all three told the story in his or her own way. How could it be otherwise? Such fierce happenings are always experienced with singularity. But in each case their focus when recounting "the crash" was on their concern for each other including, always, the baby yet to be born. They surrendered, not to dying, but to living. And survive they did.

Once on the ground, and notwithstanding the disarray around them, George called out for confirmation that Lila and Phoebe were okay. "I'm fine, Daddy," Lila whispered and then half crawled to where her father crouched in the rubble. There was a scratch over her eye and the threat of a bruise on her cheek. Phoebe, who he could barely see behind a bent strut, managed a smile, wincing though it was, and held out an arm that said, "Help me." George pushed aside a flap of the airship's skin. Lila ducked and leapt out into the early sunshine. He half-carried Phoebe to a patch of long grass a few steps away from the crumpled carcass of the ship. Under her weight the cool green blades flattened, crossing this way and that, woven, nearly cradle-like he thought. Lila hit the ground and immediately began doing cartwheels. George's heart was doing the same.

He settled himself next to Phoebe, took her hand and held her eyes she rhythmically breathed in, breathed out, determined to stick to the method she'd studied over and over watching videos on YouTube. And having been present at the births of his three children, George well remembered that rhythm and joined in.

While keeping within earshot of the unfolding drama, Lila stopped doing cartwheels to explore. She discovered a small patch of leaves, rocks and grass over which a thin skin of ice flashed in the sun, brighter by the second. She stared into this ice mirror long enough to believe the reflection of clouds and sky was the real world until a bird flew overhead and its beating wings appeared to break the surface—and her concentration. She looked up, startled, then used her heel to crack the ice. It made a lovely, high-pitched sound that rang out in accompaniment to Phoebe's longest, sharpest cry so far.

Lila ran over and stood at Phoebe's feet. Phoebe wouldn't have it. She managed to raise her head, even smile, and grunted. "Take my other hand, sweetie." Immediately, Lila did just that—scooted up, close to Phoebe's head, opposite her dad.

George was timing Phoebe's contractions which were coming at shorter and shorter intervals, eventually accelerating to the point where she had only moments of rest in between. No longer could she focus on the faces to either side of her or maintain any set pattern to her breathing. All bets were off. She dropped George and Lila's hands and recoiled from the slightest touch. Her eyes were open but her focus was on her body, on something deep inside. George felt helpless. An outsider, invisible. He could do little save watch in wonder.

Phoebe's screams, now in earnest, were not frightened or even frightening, at least to George. More they were grand, sonorous wails. From a short distance, a dog barked, once, twice, like an audience member coughing during a violin solo. In comparison to the animal sounds let loose by Phoebe it was a small sound. But for a moment, George's attention was diverted. Lila had covered her ears with her hands; Phoebe's cries of abandon were too much. George wrenched away and said with some urgency, "A dog. Go see—"

"What?"

"A dog. I heard a dog barking. There must houses nearby. See if you can see anyone. Find someone."

Lila ran off and George kneeled between Phoebe's legs. One minute? A dozen? Then he saw the head, instinctively reached for the tiny shoulders, and caught the baby. He was lifting it up to place on Phoebe's breast when Lila returned, out of breath, yelling—"There's a man and a lady with a dog coming this way!" She stopped and became quiet when she saw the baby. She stared at his tiny pink seahorse of a penis and said in a whisper. "A boy."

Her father nodded. "Yes, indeed."

SIXTY-ONE

We all know something about birth. We have seen it depicted on TV and in movies. Maybe read about it in books. Been through it or been a part of it ourselves, even. This birth was no different and, thanks be, went quickly and as well as could be wished out in a field. In the end a baby was born. In this case a boy with a big round head awash in fine strawberry blond curls springing forth from random spots like an old man. But this was not just another TV show; it would make all the difference in the world to the three people who were there. Just as your birth did; just as the birth of your children did or will or would if and when.

The baby cried out and with that first scream into this world came the sound of a siren. "Oh, look!" Lila pointed toward the top of an undulating rise in the field where the spinning red light of an emergency vehicle appeared. "Those people with the dog—someone—must have seen us crash and called 911."

But there was no emergency here. No, indeed. Even so, George was happy help was on its way—medical help to confirm that Phoebe and the baby were fine.

A pair of uniformed young men sprinted over from an ambulance, its crimson lights still flashing. Close behind were two police officers, both women, jogging from their squad car. They, too, had left the emergency lights flashing. The couple with the dog, who was quiet now, arrived last and kept at a distance, in awe.

George stood up, his hand out. "Happy to see you." He addressed and shook hands with the EMTs but looked over their shoulders and nodded at the others as well. "Very happy. Even though we're good—she's good." Phoebe raised a few fingers and waved as best she could. The baby cried again. George smiled. "Hear that? Good, right?"

SIXTY-TWO

The grass where Phoebe had given birth was flattened into a circle into which the EMT crew moved. One cut the umbilical cord and swaddled the baby in a blanket while the other went to work kneading Phoebe's stomach—with quite some force. Seeing her wince in pain and reach up and grab the EMT by the wrist, George took her head in his hands and stroked her hair. "The afterbirth, my darling. You have to let him. Look up—."

At his words they both looked up and watched the clouds for a moment—the last of the storm—black thunderheads giving way to brilliant white blooms against Prussian blue. The baby cried again. Lila touched the baby's tiny fingers, lifting them one by one. Phoebe turned toward George, trying to ignore the EMT who continued to knead her stomach. She shook her head, smiling and said, with a big smile, "Ginger-colored curls!"

"Yes—a veritable hay field."

"I'm thinking Magnus."

"For?"

"A name."

Lila looked at Phoebe and then turned to her father. "Is he my brother?" And when no one answered her, she asked again, "He'll be my little brother, right?"

Seeing that the EMT crew were heading back to their van for a stretcher, the elderly couple with the dog advanced closer, gingerly, toward Phoebe and the baby, slapping their hands softly against their thighs as they did, and bidding their dog, in voices calm and sure, "Heel." Immediately, the dog did what was asked of him.

"Good boy, Hudson. Good boy."

The couple looked at the scene before them and raised a hand over their mouths to mute their bursts of laughter. They couldn't believe their eyes; they had seen the crash and expected destruction and tragedy. George again stood and shook their hands. "Was it you who called the emergency folks?"

"Yes. We saw this...this thing come down. We feared...we...what is it?"

"A dirigible—an air ship. We've been traveling in it."

The couple started to laugh again but checked themselves. They didn't want to be rude. But George invited them to let loose by laughing himself, not as they were from the awesome absurdity of what they saw in front of them but from sheer relief. He knew how easily the huge palm of the violent thunderstorm could have slammed them to earth. Easily. They all could have died. So easily. They had come so close.

Soon they were all laughing, even Phoebe. Lila thought it strange that the adults were being so silly. When he finally stopped to take a breath, George surveyed the surroundings and spotted the red roof of a farmhouse. He pointed towards it and said to the couple. "Yours?"

"The farm? Yes. For some fifty odd years now." The man smiled. "And it was in my wife's family for decades before we took over."

The EMTs returned, wrapped and lifted Phoebe and little Magnus onto the stretcher. "Hospital's just over the hills there—20, maybe 30-minute ride. You can follow."

George put out his arms, his hands up in supplication as if helpless.

The couple he'd just met spoke in unison. "Not to worry. We'll drive you and your daughter over."

"Most kind..."

"Don't be silly. Of course."

They all moved toward the vehicles. Lila was spinning with excitement. George walked alongside Phoebe and the baby and, before they were lifted into the back of the van turned to the EMTs, "Stop here one sec, would you please?" Phoebe propped herself up on her elbows and she and George turned to look back at the place where they had landed, the place where Magnus had been born.

The grass there was the sharpest of greens. All tamped down in a circle. And in the center was a patch worn away and painted with the bright blood born of the birth. It was already sinking down, turning dark and percolating, down, down, down into the earth.

Before she laid back again, Phoebe grabbed George's arm and pointed to the west, as far as the eye could see. What was that fingerprint of blue? Not sky, but earth—a lake, the ocean, or maybe a mountain?

SUSAN FORREST CASTLE

Writer, painter and photographer SUSAN FORREST CASTLE was a senior writer at Sotheby's and the Guggenheim Museum in New York City and is the author of *Richard Segalman: Black and White | Muses, Magic & Monotypes*, published by The Artist Book Foundation in 2015. Her artwork has been exhibited in several U.S. cities, in Waterford, Ireland and in Venice, Italy where she has been an artist-in-residence at the *Scuola Internazionale di Grafica di Venezia* and at *Venezia Contemporanea.* She lives in Baden-Württemberg, Germany and the United States. susanforrestcastle.com